MURDER IN THE STUDIO

A gripping British crime mystery full of twists

GRETTA MULROONEY

Detective Inspector Siv Drummond Book 5

Joffe Books, London
www.joffebooks.com

First published in Great Britain in 2023

Cover art by Dee Dee Book Covers

ISBN: 978-1-83526-121-7

PROLOGUE

Saturday morning

She slammed the car door and accelerated away. Good. Another problem dealt with. Anger could feel so cleansing. That made two clearing-the-decks sessions since yesterday, and she hadn't planned either of them. The opportunities had arisen and she'd seized them. It felt like a huge weight off her mind. She'd been stuck and now she was freeing herself. Second chances didn't come along often, and she had a right to take this one.

She was driving east, the morning sun directly in her eyes. She snapped down the visor, slowed her speed and nudged the window open. A couple of deep breaths, allowing her lungs to expand.

She'd slept poorly, but she felt invigorated. Saturdays were always busy and a full day lay ahead, with new stock to put out before she opened the shop.

When she turned into the courtyard and parked, she was surprised to see a familiar car there. The blinds were open in the shop next door to hers, and that surprised her too. Jem wasn't usually an early bird. Maybe he'd needed to cadge a lift. Jem was skilled at getting people to do his bidding.

She unlocked her shop, opened the boot of the car and carried in the boxes of stock. It was already very warm. She slipped off her jacket and hooked it around the back of a chair, calling out as she dropped her bag on to the seat. When an answering call was returned from next door, she headed into Jem's.

Minutes later, she realised that this was a bad move, a mistake. They were both tired and going over the same ground, repeating arguments, shouting at each other. She heard herself being nasty and saying hurtful, provocative things. That was how she got when she was under pressure.

She ought to stop, take control and break this up, get back to her work. They both needed time and space. Instead, she spat out more spite, uttering words that were best left unsaid.

It was her last mistake. She realised that in the instant when the blade sliced into her neck and the light went out.

CHAPTER ONE

Ali had spent a while chatting to people at the party, wandering back and forth from the enormous living room to the kitchen via the conservatory. Conversation had ranged through house prices (a British obsession and not an inspiring one, as far as Ali was concerned), the proposed new out-of-town supermarket (Ali had no objection as it was to be built on the site of an abandoned garage) and the perennial problem of street litter. When he was a constable, Ali had secured fines against several litter louts and these had afforded him great satisfaction. The woman he'd just been talking to, whose name he didn't catch, had been muttering about beach kiosks, but he hadn't understood much as the noise levels had upped with new arrivals bearing bottles of wine. She left to pick up her daughter, mouthing, *Teenagers!* Clearly she resented being treated like a taxi service.

Now he was uncomfortable, slicks of sweat oiling his skin. The old house had swallowed the sun all day and stored the summer heat. One of the problems with being overweight was that he had too many folds and crevices for perspiration to gather in. He needed air and exited through the kitchen door to

3

the back garden, a substantial area featuring a raised pond holding koi carp, a stone patio with a huge rattan table surrounded by at least a dozen chairs, several tall slate sculptures and a garden room almost as large as the ground floor of his house.

Ali lay on the grass, balancing his beer bottle on his stomach. The lawn was mown to precision. Despite the hot, dry weather, it was a glossy green, courtesy of a pop-up sprinkler system. The flower beds gleamed with white, fragrant blossoms. Ali assumed that Angus Fraser, who owned the house, employed a gardener. The grounds, borders and planted tubs would take a fair bit of maintenance. Angus was the kind of man whose wealth bought staff: cleaners, housekeepers and dog-walkers.

Ali was only a couple of low-carb beers in, but his head was pleasantly fuzzy. More guests had spilled into the garden as the night wore on, seeking relief from the heat, although it was barely any cooler outside than in, despite the late hour. There was a gathering around a bowl-shaped fountain. Laughter sounded and a woman shrieked as someone flicked water on her. A man was playing a guitar softly under a trellis heavy with climbing roses — a Spanish-sounding tune. Ali was happy, resting here with the murmur of conversation in his ears.

The moon was huge, with dark swirls and patches that must be craters — or were they seas? For a man who'd grown up in the countryside of County Derry, Ali was remarkably ill-informed about such things. His gran used to say that the fairies came out to make mischief when there was a full moon. As far as he could tell, the guests playing under this moon were all human. When he squinted to one side, he could see Angus, his host and also the owner of Nutmeg, the café where Ali's wife, Polly, worked. Angus was slim and cool in a grey silk jacket and white T-shirt and trousers. How come some men never seemed to sweat? He was chatting to a couple with their arms draped loosely around each other.

That made him miss Polly. She was away caring for her mum, who'd broken her hip. She'd been gone a week and was likely not to be back for a couple more. Ali hated being on his

4

own in the house. He was a gregarious man, never content with his own company. Growing up on a farm in a large family, there'd always been someone to chat to. So, although he disliked attending parties without Pol, he'd turned up to Angus's birthday bash because it was better than watching telly alone. And Angus Fraser was a good guy. Polly was head chef at Nutmeg, and he'd been generous about her compassionate leave.

Angus owned a number of businesses in Berminster. Hence this gorgeous detached house in the town's conservation area, with thatched roof, treacle-coloured internal beams and that olde-worlde appearance that cost a fortune to maintain. (Polly came home with Angus's tales of woodworm and dry rot. He'd told her that looking after the house was like caring for an elderly, infirm relative. There was always a bit of it that needed shoring up or a specialist's opinion. And the heating bills!) Ali was happy with his modern, well-insulated box that was still within its ten-year guarantee.

A tall shadow briefly eclipsed the moon — a gangly man in T-shirt and knee-length shorts, fair hair chopped at different lengths streaming far below his shoulders. He was swaying and holding two bottles of beer.

'Hi, I'm Jem.' He smiled sweetly. 'Mind if I j-join you?'

'Feel free.'

'Ta. Angus noticed you drink these low-carb beers, so I b-brought you one.'

Ali sat up. 'Thanks.' He surreptitiously checked his smartwatch. Polly had bought it for him because it incorporated a continuous glucose monitor that charted his blood sugar. Diabetes wasn't his friend, but the watch claimed to be. His readings were OK, so he could chance one more drink.

Jem swayed down beside him, stretching his legs out with a little groan. Ali got a whiff of what he considered an unpleasant hippie smell — patchouli or sandalwood. He'd seen the guy in the house earlier, knocking back wine and flirting with a young woman, a redhead who'd been leaning into him, playing the game.

'Angus throws a good party,' Jem observed.

'Aye, he does.'

'And he's generous with the booze. This is the first I've been to. You?'

'I've come along a few times. My wife, Polly, is the chef at Nutmeg.'

Jem rubbed his stomach. 'I've been in there, eaten her food. Delicious. Her chicken with lem-lemon and garlic is to die for!' He was speaking with the careful precision of the plastered, just the odd stumble or slur giving him away.

'Aye, it is, thanks.' Ali was missing Pol's home-cooked meals, although she'd left the freezer stocked. He could fend for himself, but his cooking was based on the kind of heavy meat-fests his mother favoured, involving spuds and pastry. And left to his own devices, he had a terrible weakness for puddings.

Jem necked his beer. 'Hope I wear as well as Angus when I'm in my late forties. I asked him if he worked out, but he said no, he doesn't have t-time. Too busy swelling his bank account, I s'pose.' Jem made a one-handed 'money' gesture.

He had a lean face, the kind that looks as if the skin has been stretched finely across the bones. Probably the annoying kind of man who could eat whatever he liked and never gain an ounce.

Ali sucked in his stomach. 'I'd say you're well off your forties yet. How d'you know Angus?'

'He rents me my shop at Lansdown Court. You been there?'

'Aye, a while back.' It was an arts and crafts centre, part of what had once been a manor house. A collection of ren-ovated stables, barns and outhouses. 'I didn't realise Angus owned Lansdown.'

'Yep, part of his empire. You might've seen my work. I make art from old new-newspapers, magazines, fabric and all sorts of stuff that people chuck away.'

'Can't say I've come across it.' In Ali's opinion, it was no kind of occupation for a grown man. 'Does that make you a living?'

'Just about. Things have been a tad lean recently.' Jem cupped his hands around his mouth and whispered, 'Don't tell Angus, but I'm be-behind on my rent.'

'Your secret is safe with me.'

The moonlight slanted across a silver chain around Jem's neck. He wore a helix stud in the shape of a skeletal hand at the outer edge of his right eyebrow. Ali imagined it snagging in a towel and ripping the skin.

Jem shuffled closer on his bum, one of his flip-flops falling off. His breath was heavy with alcohol. 'Angus told me you're a detective.'

Ali's heart sank. Was this drunk going to ask him about a parking fine, or might he be a forensics ghoul, seeking the lowdown on post-mortems? Maybe he wanted Ali's opinion of *Line of Duty*, *Luther* or *Silent Witness*. He'd be disappointed. Ali mainly watched footie and rugby. 'That's right, I'm a DS.'

Jem propped his beer between his knees, hiccupped and rubbed at the grass. 'You work in town, right?'

'That's right.'

'Is there a lot of cr-crime?'

'Enough to keep us busy.'

'That's good . . . well, no, not *good*, not as in I *want* there to be crime if . . . if you g-get my meaning.'

Ali murmured agreement. Talking to drunks was tedious. He hoped the guy would go away soon.

'I was wondering.' Jem put a finger to his lips. 'Thing is, I've been kind of uneasy about my neighbour recently. Expect it's some-something and nothing . . .'

'Oh aye?' Ali spoke discouragingly. He resented the intrusion into a relaxing evening and his brain didn't want to focus on a neighbour dispute.

'Yeah, she's been sort of, not quite . . . hard to describe . . . but now and again I've wondered what's . . .' His phone pinged. 'Sod it, that's my cab outside and they get grumpy if you keep them waiting. I'll leave it for now — st-stop making a nuisance of myself. I shouldn't be bothering you in your leisure time anyway. Very, very rude.' He admonished himself with a tap on the arm. 'Bad Jem. Nice to meet you anyway.' He fumbled for his flip-flop, getting it back on at the third attempt, and then rose and staggered sideways, waving as he left.

Ali finished his beer, saw that it was almost midnight and bade goodbye to his host.

'Hope you enjoyed it,' Angus said. 'How's Polly doing?'

'Her mum's moaning is driving her potty. She told me she'd rather cater for a crowd of diners any time.'

Angus laughed. 'Well, we'll be glad when she's back. I hear that the temporary chef is competent but lacks energy. His name's Dimitri, but the staff call him Dim between themselves.'

'I'll tell Pol, that'll make her chuckle.'

'Did Jem Calloway catch up with you? Seemed to want to ask you something.'

'He started to talk to me, but then his cab turned up.'

'Typical of Jem. He's a disorganised chap, but I'm glad he called a cab as he was drinking like a fish. Give my best to Polly.'

It was a twenty-minute walk home. The streets were still Friday-night busy, the balmy air encouraging people out to mingle. A couple of girls tottered past him, screeching and leaving a drift of cheap scents in their wake. Ali stopped and loitered outside the chip shop on the high street. There'd been canapés to eat at the party, little mouthfuls of shrimp, artichoke or mushroom. Appetite-teasers that had left him craving something filling. He'd been careful with his meals for several days and Polly wouldn't be at home, quick to note signs of deviation from the mantra handed to him at the diabetes clinic: DEP — diet, eating and physical exercise. And this walk counted as a workout. The wonderful aromas of deep frying called to him. He dived in and ordered chips with a sausage.

8

CHAPTER TWO

Siv was jolted awake by a voice just before seven. She sat up, alert. After a few seconds, she realised it was her sister Rik, talking in her sleep. She lay back in bed and reached out an arm to tweak back the curtain. Blue, cloudless sky, no breeze stirring the trees by the river. Her hand stilled and she held her breath as the talking stopped. After a couple of beats, Rik shouted, '*There's no chance!*'

Siv groaned, but was immediately cheered when she recalled the prospect this Saturday offered: Rik was moving out.

Jubilation!

Her older sister had turned up without warning from New Zealand a couple of months ago. Siv had returned to her tiny home and found her on the doorstep with a ruck-sack. Since then, Rik had been sleeping on the foam bench under the window in the living area off the kitchen. ('Room' was too generous a name for the space.) Given that Siv's converted circus wagon was just about bearable for one tidy person, the addition of Rik, who was a stranger to hang-ing up clothes, putting things in drawers and washing dirty crockery, had been a challenge. But a sister was a sister, even if she'd hardly been in touch for years and Rik had been in a bad way.

Why she was in a bad way was still a mystery. Rik wasn't a sharer, and any attempt to find out why she'd returned to this small Sussex town met with silence or a change of subject. Siv was no mean player herself when it came to resisting unwanted enquiries, so she'd backed off, assuming that Rik would explain if she ever wanted to. That was unlikely, given her clam-like tendencies.

And Siv had scant knowledge of adult Rik. Her brief, uninformative emails over the years indicated that she'd travelled extensively, ended up in Auckland and had worked with alternative therapies. Siv's theory was that Rik had headed for the other side of the world to get as far away as possible from Mutsi, their mother. Whatever had happened in Auckland, it had been bad enough to bring Rik back into their mother's orbit, something Siv could never have predicted.

Mutsi lived near town, shacked up with DCI Will Mortimer, Siv's boss. They'd called at the wagon when they'd heard that Rik was around, Mutsi looking glamorous in designer jeans and silk blouson, Mortimer shifting uncomfortably from foot to foot. They'd offered Rik a place to stay in their huge house at Clifftop — Mortimer actually owned the house, but Mutsi acted as if it were hers. 'We've plenty of room, and it would give me a chance to catch up with you properly after all this time. There's so much to talk about,' Mutsi had insisted. Siv had held her breath, astounded at her mother's ability to fool herself and portray the fond parent. Rik had laughed and told Mutsi, 'I'd rather have major surgery without anaesthetic.' You were never left in doubt with Rik. Mutsi had burst into effortful tears, dabbing at her waterproof mascara, and Mortimer had looked shocked. He was childless and had no understanding of the treacherous currents of their family dynamics. Siv and her mother had an uneasy, wary relationship, which Siv managed with a combination of arm's-length tactics and vague interchanges. Rik made no secret of her hostility.

Rik had slept for days after her arrival, rarely leaving the window bench, where she'd made a nest with cushions. When Siv came home, there was evidence of meals being consumed in the shape of the noodle and soup pots crammed in the bin. Empty pizza boxes testified to deliveries on some days. Rik spent a lot of time watching TV on her iPad, catching up with old British series. *Downton Abbey* fascinated her. One evening, when Siv returned, she'd emerged from her cushions and paused the programme she was watching.

'The ads are great. Pre-paying for your own funeral! I'd no idea it was such a thing! And all the actors are so cheerful about it — as if they'd bought a winning lottery ticket. I've just seen a woman getting ecstatic about her cremation plan.'

'Demographics. Baby boomers are growing old.'

'Right. That explains all the delight about laxatives and walk-in baths.' Rik had stretched, cracking her fingers. 'D'you reckon Mutsi has bought her funeral package? Will there be a choir and a horse-drawn hearse?'

'She'll outlive us,' Siv had replied grimly. 'Her mother lived to ninety-six and her grandmother to ninety-nine.'

'How depressing!' Then Rik had gone back to watching her posh soap.

After a while, Rik had acquired a scooter and vanished for hours. Last week, just as Siv was starting to wonder if she'd ever have her home to herself again, Rik had arrived with a bottle of akvavit, Siv's favourite tipple, and two pieces of news. The first was that she'd got a job serving on a mobile food stall.

'Upmarket burgers and fries,' she'd declared. 'The outfit's called Stellar.'

Siv knew it well; the van was decorated with stars and the slogan, *Our Food Is Out of This World*. The burgers were amazing. 'Will I get a family discount?' she asked.

'I'll slip you free ones when I can.'

Rik's second piece of news was more alarming. She'd arranged to rent a room from Siv's friend Bartel. That was Rik all over. You never knew what she was planning; she'd appear and announce a *fait accompli*.

'I didn't realise you were talking to Bartel. You've only met him once,' Siv had said, taken aback, thinking, *But he's my friend!* She'd met him during an investigation and they'd hit it off. Siv enjoyed sitting with him on the riverbank, watching him fish. She'd taken Rik to his place for supper — pork with potato dumplings and plum cake sent from Poland by Bartel's mother. There'd been a lot to drink and he'd taught them a traditional circle dance.

'He's good fun and he's got two spare rooms, so I asked. Don't ask, don't get.'

Siv had been relieved and put out at the same time. Bartel hadn't mentioned it to her. 'When did you agree this with him?'

'I phoned him today. Glass of firewater?'

Siv had called Bartel, concerned that he'd been put on the spot and was doing her a reluctant favour. (She'd moaned to him a couple of times about Rik's messiness and the sleep-talking.) He'd reassured her that although he'd been surprised by the request, all was fine and the rent would be handy.

'It's just that . . . Rik's a law unto herself,' Siv had said. 'In some ways, I barely know her now and I've no idea why she's turned up suddenly. You don't have to do this because we're friends.'

'Rik's OK, we'll rub along,' he'd declared. 'Don't worry, Madame. I liked her when she came to supper. So direct and refreshing. And a bit mysterious. We're two adults, we can work things out, like in the Beatles song.'

Siv reckoned that Rik's membership of the adulthood club might be provisional at best. 'What about Astrella?' She was Bartel's girlfriend, who worked and lived in Brighton. Siv hadn't met her, but had spotted them with their arms entwined in town.

'Back in Latvia.'

'Oh. On holiday?'

'For good. Complicated circumstances.'

'Do you miss her?'

'A little. I'll live. Plenty of pike in the river.'

He'd calmed Siv by adding in his deep, rumbling voice that the arrangement with Rik was for three months initially, to see how it panned out.

She tugged on shorts and a T-shirt, paced the few steps to the wagon door, unlocked it and stepped down barefoot on to the meadow. The rough grass was cool and dewy. She strolled down to the river, sat on the bank and dangled her feet in the water, shivering with pleasure at the cold shock. The Bere glided by beneath the climbing sun. After weeks of intense heat, it was lower than she'd ever seen it.

Siv took stock. Her husband, Ed, had been killed in a road accident in London. Months later, she'd resigned from the Met and moved back to Berminster, where she'd spent her adolescence. She'd taken a DI job in the local police and rented her wagon from Corran and Paul, who lived in a huge converted barn across the meadow. It was an isolated, quiet spot, just what she'd needed to grieve and try to stitch her life back together. Not long after she'd settled in, Mutsi had pitched up after years of intermittent contact and failed relationships in her native Finland. She'd then added insult to injury by snagging Siv's boss and moving in with him. Now Rik was here. Siv felt surrounded, resentful. Invaded. They were a fractured family and she'd been doing fine on her own.

At least she was getting her home back today. She returned to the wagon, switched on the kettle and threw a window open. She could just see the tip of Rik's head in the sleeping bag, her black spiky hair sticking up from the crown. Like a fledgling in a nest. Rik was slow to wake, always had been, resisting the pull of the day. When they were little, the deal had been that Siv foraged for breakfast and Rik ensured some lunch or supper — whichever their mother had forgotten.

Siv switched the radio on and made coffee. She put a mug on the window ledge by her sister and shook her hard.

'Wakey-wakey. Coffee there for you. Shake a leg if you want me to drop your stuff at Bartel's.'

Rik had her thumb in her mouth, her habitual sleeping posture. She muttered and made a burrowing movement. Siv went to have a shower, turning the radio volume up. When she was dressed, she found Rik sitting up, sleeping bag wrapped around her, chuckling at her iPad.

'What's so funny?'

'Mutsi's blog.'

Their mother wrote a popular blog, *60Chic*, where she dispensed wisdom on diet, clothes and lifestyle for the mature woman. Siv glanced at it occasionally, tickled by the blindingly obvious statements that inspired people. *It's so important to hydrate. We all need some me time. Positive ideas help us through the day.* Rik had become fascinated by it and checked in regularly.

'Listen to this, Mutsi's surpassing herself,' she said in her husky voice. Rik always sounded as if she were recovering from a bad cold. She adopted a breathy tone. '"Hi, I'm Crista Virtanen and I want to share my tips for navigating this complicated world with you. These are a few things I've learned along the way: expect to feel sad sometimes; there are days when it's normal for anger or uncertainty to creep in."' Rik snorted. 'Who'd have thought it? Oh, and this gem: "Grab some you time every day, no matter how busy your schedule. Those grandchildren can wait!" Mutsi's always made sure of time for herself; she has real proficiency in that area. And finally, the crowning advice: "Don't give up on sex as you get older, it boosts your physical and mental well-being. It's a way of expressing yourself, like dancing." Does Will Mortimer read this?'

'No idea. I expect so — Mutsi would insist.'

Rik fluffed her hair out, shook her head. 'Crumbs, it must send his blood pressure soaring. Maybe that's the idea. She's hoping he'll expire and leave her with the house and his money. It's a sad reflection on us that our mother's getting more horizontal action than we are these days. And Will's so . . . insipid and uninspiring. A wispy kind of man.'

That did sum Mortimer up. 'I don't want to contemplate Mutsi's sex life, thanks.'

'Did you and Fabian get it on?'

'No, it didn't develop to that stage.' Fabian had pursued her with messages and gifts. She'd found him attractive, been tempted, but she'd called a halt, uneasy at his persistence and overbearing attentions that bordered on stalking.

'No one since Ed, then?'

'No one. Can we drop the subject? D'you want toast?'

'Please, with that sourdough if there's any left.' Rik lifted a little mirror from the window ledge, examined herself and groaned. 'If we were kids now with a mother like Mutsi, she'd more than likely be prosecuted for neglect, don't you reckon?'

Siv paused, slicing bread. 'More likely she'd be made to attend parenting classes.'

'That's a hoot!' Rik pulled down an eyelid, leaning into the mirror. 'D'you remember when the police came round that time we climbed on the roof of the flat?'

'*You* climbed out. I followed you.' That had always been the way: Rik leading, Siv close on her heels.

'Mutsi must have left us on our own dozens of times. How come Dad never did anything about it?'

'He didn't know. She kept him at arm's length.'

'Yes, he did. I wrote and told him.'

Siv stared, bread knife in mid-air. 'When?'

'Can't remember exactly. He wasn't the saint you believed him to be. He was so passive, always with his head in the clouds. He could have done a lot more to help us if he'd had a bit more bottle.'

Siv was about to comment that she recalled overhearing arguments between their parents, when her father had challenged their mother about her behaviour and how she spent his financial contributions. She changed her mind. It was too early in the day and she couldn't face a set-to with Rik. Instead, she asked, 'Have you told Mutsi about your job?'

'I tweeted it. She follows me, so she'll have seen it and been suitably horrified.' She mimicked their mother's accent. '*My daughter selling fast food on the streets! I'm so ashamed for her!*' Rik lifted her iPad again and chuckled. 'I might assume an alias and post snippy comments on Mutsi's blog. Or I could ask her for recommendations regarding sexual positions for the older woman.'

Siv threw her eyes heavenwards and slotted bread in the toaster. She was annoyed with Rik for stirring difficult memories and confused too by her remarks about their father. Siv had enjoyed an easy, close relationship with him. Once, when Rik had been truanting yet again, he'd remarked, 'You're the calm, safe waters close to shore. Your sister's the looming breakers on the horizon.'

* * *

Ali had slept in, not waking up until gone eleven. The late-night chips had given him terrible indigestion. He'd slumped on the sofa, rubbing his chest and imagining Nurse Keene's sarcastic comments. He was terrified of his tormentor at the diabetes clinic and often imagined her observing him like an all-seeing deity. He'd swallowed antacids and sat up watching a compilation of the best goals ever until the early hours.

He wandered down to the kitchen, yawning and scratching between his cornrows. He caught sight of himself in the hall mirror: podgy brown belly protruding over pyjama bottoms, moobs and more grey hairs invading the black. *Oh, God.*

He'd left his phone by the cooker and saw the green light winking. A text from Polly.

How was Angus's party? What kind of sentence would I get for justifiable matricide? x

There were two messages from Siv Drummond, left at 10.10 and 10.55 a.m., the second bristling with annoyance.

We have a murder. Body found at Lansdown Court, down that narrow track off Goose Lane. Meet you there.

Ali, where are you? Ring me as soon as you get this.

Bugger. Their DC, Patrick Hill, was on holiday, not due back until Monday, so Siv would be steaming at him. She'd been tetchy at times in the last couple of months, due to her sister camping out in her wagon. Ali liked the guv, found her fair and direct, but she could be crabby. He had to sympathise. She'd been widowed, and now her mother and sister were in her face, irritating the hell out of her. They were a weird trio, the father dead. Polly had commented that dysfunctional families often couldn't leave one another alone. Ali came from a loving, good-natured brood and found this too puzzling to work out. Still, the guv might be better tempered if she laid off the akvavit. He patted his paunch and grinned. Who was he to talk about self-discipline?

He poured a large glass of water and downed it, then rang her.

'Guv, sorry, just up. I slept late after a party last night.'

'I'm at the scene. It's that craft village, Lansdown Court, four miles or so south of town. Steve and his team are here.'

A bell rang in Ali's head. 'Funnily enough, I was talking to a guy who works there last night. An artist, Jem somebody.'

'Jem Calloway. The body's in his premises, but it's not him.'

'Right. Be there soon as I can.'

'Sounds as if you're still half-asleep. Get your skates on, I need you here.'

He was tempted to say, *Well, it is Saturday and technically my day off*, but didn't want to risk a tart reply. 'On my way.'

She relented. 'And don't forget to eat. I don't want you keeling over. I've got one expired person on my hands as it is.'

'Wilco.' She'd be remembering the time when he'd let his diet go west during a busy investigation. He'd suffered a hypo, frightening the life out of her, and she'd had to rush him to hospital.

He had a one-minute shower, threw clothes on, grabbed two bananas and a carton of milk and jumped in his car.

CHAPTER THREE

Ali ate the bananas and slugged the milk while he drove. There'd been a fortnight of heat, and today's intense blue sky promised more of the same. He was recalling Lansdown Court. He'd visited there on a wet Sunday afternoon with Polly when they'd been restless and fancied a trip out. It was the kind of place that people gravitated to at weekends to buy stuff they didn't realise they needed — paintings, jewellery, leather goods, pottery, rugs, throws, cushions and antiques — and maybe regretted doing so afterwards. Ali summed up most of it as *fol-de-rols*. There was a café too, although Pol had complained that the cake was bought in and none too fresh. Any cake was fine with Ali.

He pulled in for a minute and texted her, finishing the milk.

Party good. Out on a case. Stay the right side of the law. x

Ali drove on. The roads were busy with holidaymakers heading to the coast, quite a few towing caravans or in campers. Berminster didn't get inundated in the summer as it was five miles inland, but it attracted its fair share of tourists. It was a pretty town with an interesting history and the harbour was inviting. He turned on to a series of narrowing lanes with high, blossom-filled hedgerows, speeding, hoping that he wouldn't meet a tractor on the way. Then he saw the signpost for Lansdown Court Craft Centre and turned left down a grassy track.

It was three years or more since Ali had been here but it was unchanged: a large courtyard with parking spaces and single-storey stone buildings that glowed in the sun. One detached house, called the Old Dairy, stood at the head of the yard. The difference today was that a silence had replaced the buzz and bustle usually found there. Everything was closed, with police tape stretched across the entrance.

Siv was in a forensic suit, talking to Steve Wooton, the crime-scene manager. He was a short, bumptious man, very status conscious, and they often rubbed each other up the wrong way. Ali climbed into his suit and walked over.

'Better late than never,' Siv remarked, fixing her navy eyes on him. 'What can you tell us about this Jem Calloway?'

'Not much. I met him briefly last night at a party at Angus Fraser's place. It was Angus's birthday — he's Polly's boss, owns Nutmeg.'

'And Lansdown Court,' Steve said.

'That's right. Calloway seemed to want to talk about his neighbour, implied that he was maybe worried, but then his cab arrived and he left.'

'Did he say anything about this neighbour?' Siv asked.

'No. I mean . . . I'd had a few beers, he was hammered, it was late, we spoke for a couple of minutes. I assumed he meant his neighbour at home.'

'You *assumed* and he *implied*. Lovely and vague,' Siv grumbled.

'It was a party, not an interview, guv.'

Siv gestured with her head to the door behind them. 'Well, it's his neighbour who's dead, as in the next shop along in the courtyard. She's Luanna Forbes, called Lu, aged thirty-four, and she sold soaps, shampoos and other skin products. Someone stuck a blade in her neck. Come and see.'

At the door, Siv pointed at the handle. 'No forced entry.'

Ali followed her into the shop. It was airless and reeked of blood. The blinds were down and spotlights had been switched on. There wasn't much room to move, with boxes of materials stacked all around and bits of fabric and scraps of paper chucked on top of piles of magazines.

'How do customers find any space to browse?' Ali asked.

'Maybe they appreciate the anarchy of the artist's imagination at work,' Siv told him.

Three of the walls were covered with shelves, displaying a jumble of Calloway's work, all of it in vibrant colours: birdhouses, various-sized bowls and containers, flowers, necklaces, photo and mirror frames and coasters. Ali eyed the abstract art crammed together on the fourth wall: squares, circles and swirly lines. Not his cup of tea. He liked stuff you could recognise in a picture — a pastoral scene or a seascape. He wondered if the guv was familiar with the craft centre, as it was in her line of interest. She was a skilled origamist, selling her work, and she'd exhibited at the museum in town. Sometimes, he found little folded bowls containing paper fruit or vegetables on his desk, a nudge to eat healthily.

He gestured at the wall, his suit crackling. 'Calloway told me he makes all this out of recycled paper and magazines.'

'So I understand.' Siv studied the work. 'It's good. The man has skills and a distinctive style. I might have bought a few of these pieces if I had anywhere to hang them.' She moved towards the body. 'Steve says that the knife probably came from a set in a drawer in the desk, as there's one missing and the handle of the one in her neck matches the others.'

Ali had been avoiding looking at the dead woman, but now he moved towards her. Lu Forbes was slumped in a chair by the desk, a thin steel blade with a sturdy wooden handle stuck in the back of her neck. Her blood spattered the wall and desk, and her long, corn-coloured hair, tied in a ponytail, was soaked red. She wore an orange T-shirt tucked into black jeans and pretty, floral stud earrings.

'Seems like she was stabbed there, in the chair,' he said.

'Yep. Why in this shop and not her own?'

'Who found her?'

'Calloway. He says he turned up at half eight. Ms Forbes's was the only other car here. When he walked over to his shop door, he realised that it was unlocked. He opened it and saw Ms Forbes immediately. He didn't go near her, just ran to the Old Dairy for help.'

'He could have done it.'

'He could, although Steve's taken his clothes, so we should hear soon if there's any of Ms Forbes's blood or DNA on him. We need to pin down his movements. He's in the Old Dairy at present. A woman called Shona Hollis lives there. She's Angus Fraser's cousin. She saw Ms Forbes lock up and drive away just after six o'clock last night.'

'Have you met people who work here? What with the origami and all.'

Siv sounded impatient. 'Origami's a solitary pursuit for me, not a social activity. I've not been here before. Nice set-up — cutesy-quaint.'

'It's been up and running a while. There was an old house, Lansdown Manor, that got turned into a conference centre. Angus Fraser bought the land and the buildings.'

Siv was turning in a circle, taking in the room. 'There was one other shop owner here this morning, Simon Terrance. He parked just as Calloway was running frantically to the Old Dairy and shouting for Shona Hollis, so he followed him over there to see what was wrong. Uniform spoke to him before he went home. They got contacts for the other people who work here from Ms Hollis.'

'Can we get out of here now?'

'Sure, lead the way. We'll take a quick peek at Ms Forbes's shop. It's next door, to your left.'

Her shop was slightly larger, a vision of order and harmony after the chaos in Calloway's, and smelled of warm oils. It was lined with shelves holding bottles, jars, scented candles and small pots. A bench below the window had samples of

21

goods, all labelled *Forbes Natural Skincare*. To one side stood a handwritten note on a little blackboard.

PLEASE FEEL FREE TO TRY
OUR PRODUCTS ARE HANDMADE AT HOME
GUARANTEED 100% NATURAL INGREDIENTS

Ali read the labels aloud. 'Oatmeal and cocoa hand and body cream, geranium and rosewood oil conditioner, macadamia and honey soap.' He bent and sniffed. 'Heady stuff.'

Siv was scanning the shelves. 'Pricey too. Ten quid for a shampoo, twenty for a candle.' She moved to the counter and opened one of the cardboard boxes stacked on top. 'This is fresh stock, ready to unpack. Maybe Ms Forbes was planning to put it out this morning.'

'There's no sign of any disturbance in here.'

'No, and the cash register is switched off.' Siv picked up a woven bag sitting on the chair behind the counter, opened the zip and extracted a wallet. 'This is Luanna's and her linen jacket is hanging on the chair back. Looks like she unlocked and put her bag down, but before she got to do anything else, she went next door. Let's move on.'

Outside, Ali scrutinised the buildings. 'No CCTV.'

'No. Would have been handy.'

He gestured at the café. 'Have any staff arrived there?'

Siv pulled her hood down. 'Just the manager, Cherry Bolting. She sent her assistant, Malcolm Hayler, straight home, but she's staying in the café for the morning, agreed to provide hot drinks for Forensics. Steve and his team need to get back in here. You go to the house and talk to Calloway, as you came across him last night. Get his movements after he left the party, and find out what was troubling him about Luanna. And speak to Shona Hollis, ask if she saw or heard anything, find some general info on the people who work around here. She has a fifteen-year-old son, Struan. He'd left home to cycle to a football event before Jem Calloway arrived at the door this morning. I need to visit Luanna's sister, Yvonne Forbes. They share a houseboat at the harbour.' She ran a hand across the back of her neck. 'We could do with Patrick.'

'He's back soon.' Ali winked at her. 'I reckon he might be proposing to Kitty while they're away. He was dropping hints about visiting a jeweller and he had a glint in his eye.'

Siv was pulling off her suit and frowned up at him. 'Isn't that a tad old-fashioned?'

'Is it?'

'Maybe she'll propose to him, or they'll propose to each other.'

'Right, got it.' It was a minefield. He'd proposed to Polly in his parents' milking shed, on one knee in the straw. The gesture had gone down fine with her.

Siv put her jacket back on. She always wore a dark suit with a bright T-shirt underneath. When he'd first met her, she'd been dead skinny and wan. She was in better shape these days. Still pale though, with a look in her eye as if she'd lost something.

* * *

When Ali had left her, Siv stood for a few moments on the cobbled courtyard. The sun sliced across it, creating a fiery glow on tubs of trailing pink petunias. There were five shops lined up behind her as well as a café called the Buttery opposite with an outside seating area, and the Old Dairy overlooking all like a watchful sentry. It was a double-fronted, two-storey building that she presumed had once been the dairy that served the manor. Corran, her neighbour and landlord, was a weaver and knitter. She was fairly sure that he sold his wares through Terrance Textiles, the shop at the far end. He might be able to give her a picture of the set-up here.

It was so tranquil, the atmosphere serene, the buildings bathed in warm light. Hard to believe that there was a corpse behind her.

Her phone pinged. A text from Bartel.

Rik set up in her room. All fine. We go for lunch in Polska, if you can join us. Get some belly timber down you!

She texted back.

Lovely idea, but working.

It had been strange, dropping Rik's things off at Bartel's, watching her park her scooter and use the key he'd given her. The terraced house was in an area of town called Poets' Piece. Bartel had bought it the previous year and was still doing it up when he found time between his roofing jobs. Siv hoped that Rik would behave. She had form for being unpredictable. She'd been a wayward, rule-breaking child, stealing regularly, always pushing back against Mutsi, who'd divorced their father and led them a hither-and-thither life. There'd been a dizzying succession of locations, rented flats, schools and their mother's many partners, none of whom lasted long. Mutsi had a low boredom threshold. When they were teenagers, she'd tired of her daughters and stuck them on a train to Berminster, off-loading them without warning on to their father.

Siv was wary of her sister, but she owed her too. She'd been an anxious, quiet child, and pugnacious Rik had watched out for her. She'd got them into trouble as well, but Rik had been there when Mutsi was out romancing, leaving them to cope alone.

Through choice, Siv didn't have many friends, but Bartel was a good one and she didn't want Rik winding him up, which was highly likely. Oh well . . . cross that bridge, as the saying went.

She found Steve and asked him to agree the post-mortem time with Rey Anand, the pathologist, who was on his way. Steve confirmed that Lu Forbes's phone and laptop had been secured. Siv decided to have a word with Cherry Bolting before leaving. The café door was locked but Cherry answered quickly when Siv knocked.

'DI Siv Drummond. I'd like a word, Ms Bolting.'

'Sure, come on in. Would you like a tea or coffee?'

'Tea would be good.'

'Have a seat, I won't be a min.'

Some tables had wooden chairs, some armchairs. Siv chose an armchair covered with a patchwork design. The café was roomy, with an open-plan kitchen and counter. The history of Lansdown Manor covered one wall, featuring black-and-white photos of a grand house with turrets and gables. In the nearest photo, a pony and trap stood at the bottom of the wide front steps. Seated inside were two women wearing wide-brimmed hats and clutching parasols.

'Here we are. You must need a hot drink, what you're dealing with.'

'Thanks. Tea is reviving.'

Cherry Bolting was early twenties, statuesque and toned, fitted snugly into jeans and a tight T-shirt. Her bobbed brunette hair was studiedly messy and her long fringe dipped over her eyes. She blew upwards, but it settled back immediately.

'Lu was in here only yesterday for a morning coffee. I can't believe that she's dead. What happened to her?'

'I can't give any details just now. How was she yesterday?'

'Fine. I always buy her products, and she was telling me that she and Yvonne were working on a new range of hair conditioners, using apple cider and olive oil. Yeah, she was chatty.'

The breakfast tea was good and hot. 'Did you see Lu most days?'

'Yes. She often got a sandwich for lunch.' Cherry nibbled the side of a damson-varnished nail. Her lips were full and sensuous. 'This is such a lovely little community here, busy and cheerful. Everyone helps one another.' She sounded distressed and leaned her elbows on the table, a hand each side of her head.

'There haven't been any problems or disagreements?'

'Nothing like that.'

'Was Lu's business successful?'

'Yeah, the busiest shop here — quite a buzz going on. There were always customers in and out. The stuff's lovely and lots of people want natural ingredients nowadays. No parabens, alcohol or preservatives.'

'Quite expensive.'

'Not to the kind of well-heeled people who come to shop here, Inspector.'

Mutsi might well be a regular customer. It was her kind of upmarket place and she could afford pricey goods now that Mortimer was bankrolling her. Siv glanced through the window. Rey Anand had arrived, his glasses flashing in the sun.

'This buzz that Lu created — did it cause any envy?'

Cherry had an impressive cleavage, which deepened as she leaned forward. 'You mean with the other shop owners?'

'Yes. She might have thrown some into shade.'

'I suppose . . . Lu was the most recent arrival here. She took over her shop from a guy who moved to France. Before she opened up, we had a steady trade, but she did make a huge difference, created a stir.'

'The buzz came with her.'

'Exactly. I mean, she was really good at promotions, freebies, attracting customers. And she knew it. She made no secret of her success. A bit of a bighead in some ways, but then I guess a lot of successful people are.'

'That might have rankled some?'

Cherry shifted her chair, pulled at her T-shirt. 'Maybe. I can't really say. I just serve my goodies in here.'

Siv found her evasive. Cherry would surely hear and see a great deal in the café. She decided not to press her for now. 'What time did you get here this morning, Ms Bolting?'

'Around twenty to nine. I was a tad later than usual because the washing machine door was stuck, so by the time I'd sorted it, it was gone eight when I left home.'

'Can anyone at home confirm that?'

'I live alone, so no.'

'Did you notice who was already here when you arrived?'

'Lu's car was there, and Jem's and Simon's.' She blew ineffectually at her fringe again. 'The courtyard was quiet. I opened up. Malcolm arrived at nine — he's always dead on time. Then the police turned up about half an hour later and informed me that Lu had died and we could go home. I decided to stay around for a while, in case I could help in any way.'

'You hadn't had any customers by nine thirty?'

'Bit early. Does Yvonne know? She'll be gutted. She and Lu were ever so close.'

'She's been informed. Thank you for the tea.'

Cherry welled up. 'I'm learning Italian, and whenever I served Lu, she'd say, *grazie*, and I'd reply, *prego*.'

'I'm sorry. It is those small things that seem important in these circumstances.'

Siv said goodbye and reminded Cherry to lock the door after her. Time to see the grieving sister.

CHAPTER FOUR

Shona Hollis opened the door of the Old Dairy when Ali knocked. He stepped into the cool hall and blinked, refocusing after the glare outside.

'Jem's in the garden,' Ms Hollis told him. 'He said he'd rather be out in the air. He's in shock. He has a thumping head, so I gave him some paracetamol.'

'Aye, he would be shocked, right enough.' *Hungover too.*

Shona was short, with ash-coloured hair, sloping shoulders, a ruddy complexion and a large bosom. Her flowery skirt was mid-calf and her short-sleeved shirt had a lacy collar. She gave the impression of being put upon. 'I'll show you out, shall I?'

'Thanks. Are you OK?'

'Me? Yes, yes. I couldn't believe it when Jem came banging on the door earlier. This is a place where people . . . well, where they work peacefully.'

'You've had a shock too. I'll need to talk to you after I've seen Mr Calloway.'

She pushed her hair back with both hands. 'Yes, I see. Do you want to come through?'

She led him down the black-and-white-tiled hall into a light-filled kitchen and gestured to the door. 'Would you like coffee and biscuits? There's water out there on the table.'

'Water's fine, thanks.' He'd better behave after his greasy midnight feast.

Jem was sitting beneath a parasol at a metal table, his head thrown back. Ali was pleased to see that he was smoking. That meant he could light up a Gitane, the first of his three a day. (*You've misunderstood*, Polly would say snarkily. *That's supposed to be three a day of fruit and veg.*)

'Hello, Mr Calloway. I didn't expect to meet you again so soon, and in these circumstances. I'm sorry you've had such an awful shock.'

'Hi. I wondered . . . I wasn't sure if it would be you.' He had a pint glass of water in front of him, an empty coffee mug beside it.

In daylight, Calloway had a gaunter, fine-boned face. His expression was amiable, distracted, his hair pulled back and tied with a green ribbon, a ragged fringe hanging. The paper suit that Steve's team had given him was large and drooping on his shoulders. He smelled unwashed and looked as if he'd barely slept.

The chairs were cushioned, comfy. Ali lit a cigarette.

'I tried Gitanes, couldn't get on with them,' Calloway said.

'Aye, they're an acquired taste that I'd have been better off not acquiring.'

'Eh? Oh, right.'

'Last night at the party, you mentioned that you were worried about your neighbour. Did you mean Luanna Forbes?'

'Yes. How weird is that! And then I find her . . .'

'What was it you'd have told me if your cab hadn't arrived?'

'Thing is, I'm not sure. I'd had a few last night. Just that she'd been a bit weird. Acting funny.'

'In what way?'

'Some days, she'd arrive late at the shop, or leave early. Lu was always open on the dot of nine, closed at half five. She said you had to be disciplined when you were self-employed. She'd tell me off because I'm often late to work.'

That didn't surprise Ali. Calloway had gone a bit misty, so he waited a few moments. 'When did this unusual behaviour start?'

'Not sure now. Early spring.' He stroked his Adam's apple. 'I'll miss her wagging her finger at me, trying to keep me up to snuff.'

'Sounds like it was an affectionate gesture.'

'Partly. She'd get proper cross with me too when I was slacking. Anyway, one day, about a month back, she didn't turn up at all and that was really odd. I rang her, but her phone went to voicemail.'

'What about her sister? Did you call her?'

'Yvonne? No, I didn't contact her. That would have seemed a bit OTT. I raised it with Lu the next day and she just muttered something about personal business. Sometimes, I saw her walking up and down in the shop, like she was talking to herself. One day, I heard a noise and she'd thrown bars of soap against the wall. I asked her if she was OK and she just snapped, "Yeah, PMT!"' He rolled his eyes. 'Once a woman says that, I duck. Don't want my head chewed off.'

'Did anything else concern you?'

'That's it. Sounds stupid now I'm saying it out loud. But something was off with her.'

'Did you mention this to any of your colleagues here?'

'Nope. Lu wouldn't have liked it if I'd been talking about her, and I didn't want to start gossip.'

Ali wasn't sure what he made of this. Calloway could have spoken to the sister or a colleague if he was that worried. 'Ms Forbes gave reasons for her absence and moods, but you mentioned it to me last night because I'm a police detective. That indicates a pretty serious level of concern.'

'I was just worried something was wrong. I was pretty pissed at the party and I'm kind of fuzzy about what I said to you. Probably seemed important at the time. Blame it on the booze talking.' Calloway took the burning stub of a cigarette from between his lips and lit another one with it. 'See, Lu was always cool, calm, collected. So together and organised.

You could set your watch by her. So . . . you happened to be at the party and I fancied getting your opinion. You must come across all sorts.'

The water jug on the table contained slices of lemon and lime and had one of those fiddly beaded covers. Ali peeled it back and poured himself a glass. The fruit smelled fresh, sharp and a lot better than Calloway.

'Want me to top you up?' he offered.

'No thanks. I was right, wasn't I? Looks like something was wrong, very wrong.'

'You're assuming that Ms Forbes's death is connected to her unusual behaviour.'

'I suppose . . . What d'you make of it?'

'Far too early to tell.'

Calloway licked his lips and sucked on his cigarette. A blackbird flew down to the garden and pecked at the lawn.

'Lu was wary of birds,' Calloway muttered. 'She didn't like the way they swooped.'

'This day when Ms Forbes wasn't at work — can you remember the date?'

'Oh, hell, that's a tough one. Not offhand. I'll check my calendar, see if I can work it out.'

'It would be helpful. Can you think of any reason why Ms Forbes would have been in your shop this morning?'

'No. And she didn't have a key, so I don't understand how she got in there.' He gulped water. 'Shona has spares for us all.'

'What did you do when you left the party?'

'Went to see a friend and spent the night with her. I meant to go home, 'cos Saturday can be busy, but I'd had a skinful and when I woke up it was gone eight. I had to run home to fetch my car and come straight here. I've a terrible pain behind my eyes.'

'Was this friend the redhead you were talking to at the party?'

'What? Oh, no. An old acquaintance. We hook up now and then.'

31

'I'll need the name and a number to check.'

'Gail Maitland.' Jem pressed his temples and gave a mobile number.

'Whose cars were here when you arrived this morning?'

'Just Lu's. Simon Terrance rocked up right after I'd found her. He has the textile shop. He got me a cup of tea while Shona rang you lot.'

'Talk me through what you did after you left your car.'

'I walked over to the shop to open up, but it was already unlocked.' Calloway smoothed glistening slicks of perspiration from his forehead.

'The door was shut?'

'Yeah.'

'Were the blinds down?'

'Yeah, I always close them at night. I stepped in and smelled something funny and then I saw her, sitting at my desk.' He shuddered. 'That's where I work and take money. There was so much blood. I didn't go near her. Felt like I might be sick. I'm no good around blood, see. I get queasy when I nick myself shaving. I ran here for help.'

'And do you have your key?'

He patted his pocket, showed it to Ali.

'Did you notice anything else unusual in the shop?'

'No, just a bloody dead body in my chair. That was unusual enough. Listen, I'm feeling rough. Can we wind this up now? I've told you what I can.'

He did have a pasty complexion and a waxy sheen on his skin. Was that because he'd recently been violent? 'Aye, that'll do for now. We'll arrange a formal statement with you.'

'Thanks. I just want to go home and crash out.' He picked up his cigarettes. 'Tell Shona I've gone out the back gate. I can't face talking to her anymore today. She's too much like a bloody headteacher, always shouting the odds and acting suspicious.'

On his way through the kitchen Ali stopped by Ms Hollis, who was chopping vegetables. 'Mr Calloway's headed home. Do you have a spare key to his shop?'

She put her knife down and wiped her hands on her apron. 'I hold keys to all the shops and the café. I've checked, and they're all there. Would you care to see?'

'Aye, please.'

He followed her to a small office off the kitchen, next to a utility room. There was a narrow desk with a computer, a couple of chairs and a five-drawer filing cabinet. Shona took a key from a desk drawer and opened a wall-mounted metal box. There were two rows of keys, all labelled and all in place.

'Jem's is shop two, and as you can see, his key is there. Did you say he's gone home?'

'He has, yes. He's not feeling too good.'

Her mouth formed a disapproving line. 'That's often the case with Jem Calloway. There are days when he sweats alcohol. I'm amazed that he manages to run a business at all. That shop of his is always in a right state, but apparently he's a—' she raised two fingers on each hand to make quote marks — '"gifted" artist, so that's acceptable. If he's not careful, he won't have his shop for much longer.'

'Why's that, Ms Hollis?'

She stood with her feet planted apart, hands folded beneath her bosom, as if she might launch into a recital or song. 'I do the accounts and he's well overdue with the rent. He's hanging on here by a fine thread.'

'Have you told him that?'

'I was about to, but I suppose I'd better hold fire after this morning. I will be giving him an ultimatum very soon.'

Ali caught the glint of satisfaction in her eye. 'Let's sit down. I have some questions.'

'Do you mind if I just get these vegetables on first and start the pressure cooker? I'm making a casserole for when Struan gets home. He'll be hungry after a long day's training.'

It was a wintry meal for such hot weather, but routine was often important to people when they'd had a shock. 'Go ahead.'

While he was waiting, Ali texted Siv to tell her that all the keys to Calloway's shop were accounted for, and he might have an alibi for last night and this morning.

CHAPTER FIVE

The harbour glimmered on such a clear day. Siv parked and consulted the board that mapped the houseboat section. She was relieved to see that the Forbeses were berthed at the opposite end of the harbour to DCI Mortimer's boat, *Quicksilver*, so there was little chance of running into her mother. Mutsi, inevitably, referred to the boat as a yacht. She liked to impress people by inviting them aboard for morning coffee or late afternoon G and Ts. Mutsi cultivated hangers-on who were captivated by her carefully maintained appearance and style, her stories of dancing in *Hair* in the sixties — *Michael Caine came backstage one night and kissed me on the cheek* — and, of course, her blog.

Siv bought two coffees at the harbour kiosk and set off along the path balancing them in either hand. She was glad of the light sea breeze after the metallic stench of blood in Jem Calloway's shop. Seagulls screeched and dive-bombed a discarded sandwich. They always looked so angry, with their glaring yellow eyes. She recalled reading that they were descended from velociraptors, so they had form. The ones around here were huge, because of good pickings. A compact boat puttered in and berthed, a Labrador running up and down on deck, barking encouragement. The man steering saluted Siv, removed his pipe and remarked that it was a fine day to be alive. Maybe Luanna Forbes had thought the same when she was driving to work this morning. Siv continued along the path, in the slipstream of the spicy pipe scent.

The Forbeses' houseboat was in fact a large Dutch sailing barge called the *Scarlett O'Hara* and painted suitably scarlet with a black trim. The deck was covered with containers of herbs, salad leaves, courgettes and tomatoes. Shona Hollis had already contacted Yvonne Forbes, and Siv had spoken to her on the phone. Yvonne had wanted to drive to Lansdown Court, but Siv had requested her to stay put.

Siv glanced down through the open window on her way to the door and saw a woman sitting on a sofa with her head resting back on a cushion, eyes closed, earbuds in. At that moment the woman opened her eyes and stared. Siv smiled, stepped on board and tapped on the door.

'Ms Forbes, I'm DI Drummond. We spoke on the phone earlier.'

'Come in. It's open.'

She pressed the door handle down with her elbow and stepped carefully into the boat, balancing the cups. 'Here, I got you a coffee, with milk. Hope you drink it.'

'Thanks, yes. Have a seat.'

Yvonne's skin was as pale as peeled almonds. Mascara had run and pooled in the hollows beneath her tear-drenched, bleary eyes. She was barefoot, wearing a sleeveless shirtdress patterned with violets. Her curly brown hair was drawn back in a grip and she wore large round glasses. She came across as a schoolgirl, rather than a woman in her late twenties.

Siv saw that the living room was at the front of the boat, the kitchen in the middle, presumably with bedrooms behind. The living area was crammed but not chaotic, with lots of shelving and fitted cupboards. A collage of peacocks that she recognised as Jem Calloway's work hung on the wall by Yvonne. The ceiling was made of pine boards and there were two good-sized sofas. A delicious scent of oranges permeated the room and Yvonne's fingers were stained ochre.

Siv sat on the sofa by the opposite window. Yvonne lifted the lid of her coffee and had a tiny sip.

'I'm so sorry about your sister, Ms Forbes.'

'Yes. I'm still trying to take it in.'

She sounded distracted. Siv could see that she was in a fog, and recognised that feeling only too well. She opened her own coffee and drank half. It was a bit weak, but comforting. The sun was cooking the back of her neck. She slipped her jacket off and folded it beside her.

'How did Lu die?' Yvonne's voice was soft, with a wheedling note.

'We have to wait for the post-mortem result for details, but she was stabbed in the neck.'

'Oh, God. Stabbed. Shona said Jem found her in his shop.'

'That's right. Any idea why she would have been in there?'

'No. Unless she needed to borrow something, but I can't imagine what.'

'Would she have had a key to Jem Calloway's shop?'

'No. That is, I doubt it, but maybe he'd given her one. He's pretty laid-back about that kind of thing.' Yvonne sucked the side of a finger. 'I was making a batch of orange-and-mint shower gel when Shona called to tell me. I'd just pulled some fresh mint from on deck and I was grating the orange skins. Lu said it had sold well, so we needed more stock.' She blew out a loud breath. 'This is mad. I can't work it out.'

'If you could answer a few questions, it would help me. I'll try to keep them brief.'

'Yes, go on.' Yvonne removed her glasses, put them on her lap, rubbed her small, deep-set eyes. Her lashes were thick and dark.

'What time did your sister leave for work this morning?'

'She was on her way when I surfaced, soon after seven. The weekends are usually busy and Lu wanted to set out new stock. She . . . she'd had tea and a croissant. She left a warm one for me.'

'How was she this morning?'

'Fine. Yes, fine.'

'Not worried at all?'

'No. I said I'd make the shower gel and she suggested walking into town for a curry tonight. Then she was gone.'

'You've been on the boat all day?'

'Yes, I was working until I heard . . .'

'And what did you and Lu do last night?'

Yvonne screwed up her face, as if remembering was an effort. 'We were in. Lu got back about six. I'd made a chicken salad. It was a lovely evening, so we sat on deck and ate it, had some wine. Then we watched telly for a while. Lu went to bed about half ten. I wanted to finish boxing some soaps, so I turned in around eleven.' Now that she'd started talking, Yvonne seemed eager to explain. 'I make the soaps, shampoos, conditioners moisturisers and candles here in the boat, and Lu sells them at the shop. She's got the business brains. She manages online orders from there too. We bought the boat and started the shop a couple of years ago. It's doing well.'

'What did you both do before that?'

'I worked in a shoe shop in town, rented a poky flat over a newsagent. Lu was a driving instructor. She'd got divorced and they'd sold the house — she lived in Leabourne when she was married.'

Siv had heard the name but couldn't place it. 'Whereabouts is that?'

'It's a village about fourteen miles east of here. We were both fed up with our jobs, I hated my flat and Lu needed a place to live. I'd started experimenting with soaps and shampoos. I suffer with dermatitis and I was tired of trying to find decent stuff to use. My natural products were proving popular with friends and word got round. I started selling and it was taking off, but I wasn't brilliant at marketing and I preferred to focus on developing the cosmetics. So anyway, Lu and I put our heads together, we bought the barge with her equity from the house and our combined savings and we rented the shop at Lansdown Court.' She stopped, her head sinking. 'What will happen now? Lu handled the money, all that side of things.'

'It's a lot to take in. Maybe someone will be able to step in and help you.'

Yvonne gazed through Siv, far away. A couple of children thudded along the path at the side of the boat, kicking up stones and calling to each other.

Yvonne pointed. 'That was me and Lu as kids. We'd run along here, bring our fishing nets to see what we'd catch, walk to the mudflats to see what the tide had brought in.'

'It sounds as if you and your sister were close.'

'Best mates. Always have been. Lu was just . . . like my twin, even if she was five years older.' There was a quiet despair in her voice.

Siv tried to imagine such a fond sibling relationship and failed. 'Has Lu had problems with anyone recently? Jem Calloway said she might have been troubled about something.'

Yvonne frowned. 'Jem? Why would he think that?'

'He's in the next shop. I assume they'd have seen each other.'

'I've no idea why he'd have got that impression. How is he? He must have had an awful shock. He's a sensitive man.'

'Shona Hollis and my sergeant are with him.'

'That's good.'

'Did you pick up that Lu was at all troubled?'

'No way. She certainly didn't say that anything was worrying her.' Yvonne put her glasses back on. 'I've no idea whether to carry on with the shampoo now. All the ingredients are in the container. What would you do?'

She was like a child, seeking guidance. 'Do whatever's comfortable. It might help you to carry on with it. Do you have family in town?'

'There's just Dad and he's got dementia, lives in a nursing home.' She sighed. 'I'm dreading having to tell him. He won't understand.' She welled up again, pressed a tissue to her eyes.

Siv left a silence. When Yvonne was more composed, she asked, 'Do you ever go to Lansdown Court? How well do you know the other people there?'

'Shona's a good friend. She used to be a regional manager for the shoe chain I worked for. That's how we met, and then I introduced her to Lu. I've hung out with the other shop owners now and again, but I'm not as friendly with them as Lu was. Jem's mum was a friend of our mother back in the day. I go to Lansdown maybe once every couple of weeks to help Lu with stock, and I serve in the shop some weekends and at busy times like Christmas. Shona's always really kind.'

'When were you last there?'

'Monday, just gone. I took Lu some hand cream I'd made and I popped in to see Jem. His shop gets in such a state, I gave him a hand to tidy up.'

'Did Lu get on with everyone there?'

'Far as I know. I mean, she never said she disliked any of them. She'd have a coffee or lunch with Simon now and again, at the café. She admired his business skills, so she was all made up when she started getting more customers than him.'

'Lu was competitive?'

'Definitely. She won regional driving instructor of the year three years running — it was in the press.' Yvonne clasped her hands with pride. 'She was always an achiever.'

'Was Lu in a relationship with anyone?'

'No. She wanted to get over Bryan — her ex-husband. It wasn't a messy divorce, there were no kids, but he was antsy about finances and made life difficult for a while.' She gave a little smile. 'Lu needed recovery time.'

'When did they divorce?'

'Almost four years now.'

A long recovery, although who was she to say? After Ed, Siv sometimes doubted that she'd ever want to find anyone else. She wondered if the sisters had had an exclusive relationship that formed a protective shield. 'And does Lu's ex live in town? What's his surname?'

'Hendrix. Yeah, he bought a place on the Willow estate. He's got a new squeeze, apparently.'

'Yvonne, can you think of anyone who'd want to harm your sister?'

'No! It's a horrible question.'

'But one I have to ask, I'm afraid.'

'It might have been someone random, who saw her unlocking the shop and thought there'd be money in there.' Yvonne had put up a hand, as if she were in class.

'There was no sign of an attempted robbery and the till hadn't been switched on.' Siv picked up her jacket. 'If you don't mind, I'd like to take a look at Lu's bedroom.'

'Do you have to?'

'There might be something that would assist the investigation.'

'Help yourself, then. It's not as if Lu's here to object,' Yvonne replied listlessly. 'Through the kitchen, the door on the right.'

The room was bright and sunny, with a window on to the harbour as well as a skylight. It was a little bigger than Siv's bedroom in the wagon, with a single bed, built-in cupboards and drawers. Siv drew gloves on and started with the wardrobe. It was crammed with jeans, the kind of oversize linen shirts with pockets that could double as a jacket, and lots of brightly coloured scarves. Lu had liked her trainers. There were at least a dozen pairs lined up on the lower shelf. The drawers held sweaters, T-shirts and underwear, most of which was sensible cotton in plain colours. Siv glimpsed a flash of lace beneath a stack of bras and removed the top layers. There were two sets of bras and pants — one, pink and silver, still sealed in its bag with the label, Dora Larsen. The other seemed almost new, a skimpy little outfit in turquoise and lilac, mainly made of see-through lace and tulle and with the same label. Siv's interest was piqued. She slipped her phone from her pocket and googled Dora Larsen. There were similar sets on the website priced at £85. Yvonne had claimed that Lu wasn't seeing anyone, yet this was the kind of underwear that a woman might slip into when she was anticipating revealing it. Not what you'd routinely wear to work, or to go for a curry with your sister.

She took a photo of the turquoise lingerie, slipped it in an evidence bag and replaced the other items. She scanned the bookshelves, which held mainly historical fiction. There were several photos clipped to a hanger suspended from the ceiling: Lu and Yvonne with an older couple who were presumably their parents; some of the sisters at various ages; and one of the barge.

Siv knelt to check the cupboard beneath the bed. There was a plastic tray of cosmetics, a hair dryer, a back massager, wellingtons, spare bedding inside a duvet bag, several pairs of elegant shoes and a small black cardboard box. Siv lifted it out, put it beside her on the bed and flicked through Lu's birth and divorce certificates, paperwork about the company and the purchase of the barge — it had cost £210,000 — and her will, which was short and sweet, leaving her estate to her sister.

Siv made sure she put everything back as she'd found it and went back to the living area. Yvonne sat in the same spot, staring into space.

'I'll leave it there for now, Ms Forbes. We'll be in touch about the post-mortem. Are you sure you're alright here on your own?'

'I'll have to be. I'll lock the door after you. I'm going to lie down for a while.'

CHAPTER SIX

Shona brought coffee and slices of Bakewell tart into the office. Ali helped himself to one. Well, he'd tried to exercise self-restraint, but it would be rude to refuse. He'd been examining a photo on the desk. It was of a good-looking youth with striking, hazel-flecked green eyes that seemed to catch the light. His hair was thick and wavy, the colour of churned butter, and grew low on his brow, and his skin was clear and glowing. He had wide, full, raspberry-coloured lips.

'That's my Struan, my one and only.' Shona opened a tube of cream and rubbed some into her hands. She had a set, rather sour face, lacking in expression, but when she said her son's name she softened. She was in her fifties now, so it must have been a late pregnancy.

'He's a handsome lad. He's away at football training? What time did he go?'

'He left here around seven on his bike. It's a coaching day at Isbrook Academy, a prestigious event. He was one of just thirty selected for it from across the county. We have high hopes for him.' She smiled proudly. 'They were laying on breakfast, so he set off early.'

'When did he get up?'

'A quarter to seven. I'd just come down to the kitchen and put the kettle on.'

'And what time will he be home?'

'Late afternoon. I've texted him, asking him to come straight back, in case he's minded to stop off at a friend's. I need to give him the news before he hears it from anyone else. He'll be very upset about Lu.'

'He was fond of her?'

'Oh yes, they got on well. He's closer to Yvonne, but he'd often pop in and chat to Lu. He's a gregarious boy, quite the opposite to me. His dad was a cheerful, sociable type.'

From her acid tone, Ali gathered that the father might have been a tad too affable. 'You and your partner aren't together?'

Shona sucked in her cheeks. 'He left us when Struan was three. He died in an accident with his new woman a year later. Karma you might say, if you believe in that sort of thing.'

As she clearly did, Ali noted. 'I gather that you manage Lansdown Court, Ms Hollis. How did that come about?'

Shona sat up straight, holding her coffee in her sloping lap. 'My cousin Angus owns the place. When he was developing it, he invited me to run it for him. I'd been at my job for a while and I was glad to have a change. I grabbed at the chance, especially as this lovely house was part of the deal. I live here rent-free in return for my services.'

'And what does that involve?'

'General maintenance, sorting problems, arranging events, keeping an eye out, monitoring rents, finding new people if someone vacates a shop, making sure the accounts are done. Oh, and I run the website. That's the main gist of it. I have one of the shops as well. I sell preserves, jams, cakes, homemade wines and cordials.'

A thought struck Ali. 'Is there a cleaner for the premises?'

'No. Everyone does their own.' Shona drank from her cup and placed it on the desk. 'It's a happy place, Lansdown. People rub along well. This is a terrible thing.'

Ali hoovered up the last cake crumb. 'No arguments or bad feelings?'

'No.'

'Not even about Mr Calloway's failure to pay his rent? Are other colleagues aware of that?'

Shona folded her hands under her bosom. 'Not from me. I don't discuss such matters generally, but he might have told people. In fact, I wouldn't put it past him. He'd be trying to milk sympathy and get someone to lend him the money.'

'Regarding this morning, did you hear Lu or Jem arrive?'

'I don't hear cars from the back of the house. These old stone walls are very thick and they block noise. It's one of the great pluses of living here. I was in the kitchen or here in the office from when I came down until half eight, when there was a commotion at the door and I found Jem yelling about Lu. Simon was hurrying up behind him.'

'We'll need to speak to Struan, in case he saw anything when he cycled off.'

'I understand. His head was full of football this morning, so good luck with that. He lives, breathes and eats it!' She ran a finger along the edge of the desk. 'How did Lu die? Jem didn't make much sense.'

'I can't answer that for now, Ms Hollis.'

'I see . . . Oh, poor, poor Yvonne. I've told her she can stay tonight if she wants. She shouldn't be alone.'

'That's kind of you. You're good friends?'

'We met through work, we were both with Reed Shoes. We've been good friends a while now.'

'Tell me, did Lu seem worried about anything recently?'

'Nothing I'm aware of.'

'Jem was concerned about her. He told me that she sometimes opened late or closed early, and one day she didn't open up at all.'

'I didn't notice, but then I don't keep tabs on colleagues. People open up at different times on weekdays, it's completely up to them. Everyone's here on Saturdays and Sundays, our busiest times. Perhaps Lu had appointments. I wouldn't pay too much heed to Jem,' Shona added scathingly. 'He went to Cambridge University and I'm sure he had a fine mind at one time, but his brain's addled some days and he's not the most reliable timekeeper. He can be a bit of a busybody, given that he's not overwhelmed with customers. I see him wandering around bored some days, or hanging out at the café to pass the time.'

Ali noted that, despite what she said, she seemed to keep tabs on Jem. Not much would get past her. 'So, Lu was her usual self?'

'That's right. When will we be able to reopen the shops? I expect colleagues will contact me to enquire.'

'I can't say at present. We'll tell you as soon as that's possible. Have you informed Mr Fraser?'

'Yes. He's coming by later.'

'Does he involve himself here much?'

'Not really. He calls at the café sometimes and he sees me and Struan, family visits. Otherwise, he leaves the place to me.' She smiled. 'He says, "You don't keep a dog and bark yourself". That's why he's a successful businessman — he picks good managers and lets them get on with it.'

As Ali went to leave, she asked if he'd like to take cake for his colleagues at the station. 'I had a big baking session yesterday and I guess I won't be selling for at least a couple of days.'

'Thanks, but I won't. We all eat far too much sugary stuff as it is.' He patted his stomach, pleased with how virtuous he sounded.

'Oh, there's too much emphasis on skinny bodies. A bit of meat suits a man, Sergeant.'

Ali wasn't sure about that last comment, although Polly did tell him that she'd grown fond of his love handles.

* * *

Yvonne tried calling Jem again, but once again, she reached his voicemail. She was used to his evasions, but surely, today of all days, he'd pick up. Why was he telling the police that Lu had had some kind of problem? She was puzzled and desperate to hear his voice.

She hadn't seen him for a couple of weeks. They'd spent the afternoon in bed at his place. She'd had to rush back and finish a batch of soap before Lu got home. She'd been keen on Jem for ages. They'd met when they were infants, living three doors away from each other, and played together as kids. She'd worshipped him through the years. He'd been sensitive, not your usual kind of boy. *Gentle Jem*, people had called him. They'd seen each other almost every day, dressed up together as pirates, superheroes and space explorers and roamed Halse Woods, building dens.

Was it love? Yvonne supposed so, given how she longed to see him. Whatever it was, it wasn't reciprocal. Jem told her that he adored her, a catch-all expression that he undoubtedly repeated to many other women. There was no point in trying to pin Jem down or ask him about his plans. He didn't conceal his polyamory, never defended his behaviour or made promises. If she remarked on all the women he saw, he'd respond that he was just made that way, adding that he was a free-roving spirit like his great-grandmother, who'd been a gypsy. He found it hard to resist a mutual attraction. The thing was, when she was with him, he did make her feel as if she were the only woman for him. She couldn't help harbouring hopes that one day, he'd decide that she was the one.

Yvonne had kept her liaison with Jem hidden from Lu and the rest of the world. She didn't fancy being the subject of pity or gossip, and she frequently imagined the background chorus of commentary if people found out. *He's never going to settle down, she's wasting her life. Shame, a young woman like that hanging around that wastrel. He's always in town with different women. Hasn't she got any self-respect?* She saw Jem while Lu was at work, or she'd lie and say that she was meeting a friend for an evening. Her sister wouldn't have approved, would have agreed with the chorus that she was squandering her time on a no-hoper, and she'd have intervened in her bossy way. Lu had never been that keen on Jem when they were children, had always remarked that he was soppy and daft, sneering when he let Yvonne paint his nails, dye his hair or pluck his eyebrows. Jem agreed happily to the deception — anything for an easy life with him, and he didn't want trouble at work. He'd always been a bit in awe of Lu, saying that she was a formidable woman.

The problem was, Lu would have been right — Yvonne was treading water with Jem. Deep down, she suspected that she was unlikely to get a commitment from him, but she had no other man in her life and he was so sweet, tender and funny. And so talented — everyone agreed on that. She was sure that if he'd let her into his life fully, she'd be able to help him cut down on the drinking and harness his talent properly. He could be a roaring success with the right support and encouragement.

Since they were teenagers he'd called her 'Little Tree', because her name derived from the French for 'yew'. She loved the way he held her face in his hands and kissed the tip of her nose, rocked her gently in his arms and sang old Sussex songs that his gran had taught him: 'Buttercup Joe', 'Sarie' and 'The Woodcutter'. He had a light tenor voice, clear and true.

She'd never laughed with anyone the way she did with Jem. Since she'd got caught up in him, she'd understood the nature of addiction. And maybe one day, that deep bond they'd had since childhood would become as meaningful to him as it was to her. She devoured stories about childhood sweethearts who ended up at the altar. Recently, she'd read of a couple who'd been christened in the same church on the same day, and had been inseparable ever since. If she pointed out these press articles to Jem, he smiled, kissed her hand or ruffled her hair and told her she was a sentimental sweetheart.

She drifted to Lu's room and lay on top of her bed, hugging one of her pillows. Their bedrooms were adjacent with a thin partition, and every night one of them would call, 'Sweet dreams!' She'd hear when Lu switched her lamp off, blew her nose or coughed. Yvonne was a word puzzle addict and sometimes, if she was stuck, she'd shout through the wall: 'It plugs a port' or 'Stimulate the economy'. And the answers would come back: 'Cork' and 'Spend'.

Lu had redecorated this room in the spring, painting it marine blue with yellow and red cushions and curtains. She'd had a restless, dissatisfied nature and was forever altering things, moving them around. It was as if she'd always been reaching for something just out of sight. When they went blackberrying, Yvonne would point to a laden bush of glossy ripe berries, but Lu would urge her on, insisting that there must be better pickings further up the lane. *Oh, Lu!* Her dressing gown and nightdress hung on the back of the door, stirring in the breeze from the skylight. The conker-brown leather boots that she'd bought in last winter's sales stood on a shelf. They'd suited her long, slim calves.

Lu's collection of historical novels filled the tall bookcase by the bed. Yvonne reached out and ran a finger along the top row. Lu always had one on the go, and the paperback with the rich maroon cover lying on the ledge by the bed was set in Restoration London. Lu's reading habit had been one of Bryan's constant complaints. She'd mimicked his Birmingham accent: '*You've always got your bloody nose in the bloody past.*' The reading was an aspect of Lu's impressive self-sufficiency. She had moved around the world in her own confident bubble and, at times, Yvonne glimpsed how a partner might find that hard to navigate. Yvonne needed people far more than Lu had. She wasn't much of a reader, apart from magazines, but she'd liked to watch Lu with a book, and admired — envied — the way she became so absorbed, she forgot the world completely.

Yvonne wished she could do that now. She felt both numb and on fire. You could burn yourself on ice. The boat shifted on the water and settled again. It was dawning on her now that Lu wouldn't be back later, calling, 'Hiya, shipmate!' What was she going to do? Dread crept through her. Lu had always given her a lead, held the fort, sorted stuff.

She jerked as her phone rang, hoping it'd be Jem. She and Lu had selected the same ringtone, 'Sailing'. It was Shona. She lay back, the phone pressed against her ear.

'Hi, Yvonne, I wanted to check that you're OK. I'm sorry I couldn't talk for long earlier. The police were here and one of the detectives has been interviewing Jem. He's waiting to speak to me now.'

'One just left me — a woman, DI Drummond.'

'I hope that wasn't too hard.'

'She was nice, brought me coffee.'

'Did you get terribly upset?'

'A bit. How's Jem?'

'Oh, he'll survive, no need to worry about him, it'll slide off him like everything does.'

'Is he still with you?'

'Just left. I expect he'll find consolation with one of his lady friends.'

Yvonne winced. It occurred to her that he might come to the boat. He had a couple of times, when Lu had been at the shop. She was moved to defend him. 'Jem has had a dreadful shock.'

'True enough. It's been such a day. I never expected to live through one like this.' Her voice dipped. 'I hope you're looking after yourself at the boat, taking things as steady as you can.'

'I am. I always listen to your advice.'

'That's good. I don't know what else to say, Yvonne.'

'No.' Suddenly, Yvonne wanted to be in Shona's kitchen, sitting by the range, eating her scones with raspberry jam and being teased by Struan. Shona was in many ways her substitute mum. She'd often visited the Old Dairy when she'd lived alone, escaping from her poky flat and soaking up the warmth. Sometimes, if they'd been chatting and it got too late, she'd stayed over. Shona had even bought her a toothbrush and pyjamas. Lu used to joke that she was Shona's rent-free lodger. Since moving to the boat with Lu she'd rarely stayed at Shona's, but she often popped by the house. She said on a sob, 'Can I come over later?'

'Certainly, whenever you're up to it. In fact, stay the night if you want. Would you like that?'

'I'm not sure. I'll see. Is Struan alright?'

'He left early, thank goodness, to go to a football day. He hasn't heard about Lu yet. I decided it best to leave it until he's home.'

They said goodbye. Yvonne called Jem again but didn't bother leaving a message. She touched the book cover. There was a sticky stain where Lu must have smeared some jam while eating her morning toast, her novel propped against the coffee jug.

She started crying and turned her face into Lu's pillow.

CHAPTER SEVEN

Siv and Ali met back in the station at five thirty and recapped their interviews. Ali had put a diagram of Lansdown Court on the incident board and talked through it.

'Shop one is rented by Klara Boros, who sells leather and fabric goods. She's in Hungary on holiday, back next week, and her shop's been closed while she's away. Jem Calloway rents number two selling his recycled art, three was Lu Forbes's, four is Shona Hollis, trading in jams, preserves and the like. Simon Terrance is in five, with textiles. The café's run by Cherry Bolting. Shona Hollis lives at the Old Dairy with her son Struan and manages the site, which is owned by Angus Fraser.'

'So far, I'm hearing that it was a happy community,' Siv reported. 'Lu Forbes seems to have had the most flourishing business and blew her own trumpet, which might not have always gone down well.'

'I've been told it's all smiles and good cheer,' Ali agreed. 'The only fly in the ointment seems to be Jem Calloway, who's a Cambridge graduate but unreliable, drinks too much and is behind with his rent. Yet he's the only one who noticed that there might be something up with Lu. And then she's found dead in his shop, which is an interesting connection.'

'I'm not sure everything in Lansdown's garden is as rosy as it looks. No community is problem-free. Yvonne mentioned another connection, that her mum and Calloway's were friends, so they've all been close for years. She's a rather bland woman, a bit featureless.'

The room was too hot. Siv opened a window and fanned herself with an old evening paper from Patrick's desk. She propped herself on the window ledge. 'Timings. Lu left for work just after seven. She'd have got to Lansdown Court around half past, so she died within the next hour. According to her sister, she was going to sort out new stock, because weekends could get busy. She'd unlocked her shop and her bag was in there, but from the look of it, she hadn't started work. Simon Terrance says that he arrived at eight thirty, saw Jem Calloway running to the Old Dairy and went straight there to see what was up.'

'Struan Hollis left home on his bike at seven. Shona said she was in the kitchen between seven and half eight. It's at the back of the house and she heard nothing until Calloway came to the front door. He had his shop key in his pocket.'

'And Shona had the spares, all in place.'

'Aye.' Ali was noting it all on the board, rocking on his feet.

Siv flapped the paper. 'I spoke to Cherry Bolting at the Buttery. She got there at twenty to nine, her colleague at nine. According to her, the place was quiet. Too early for customers. So no one saw or heard anything unusual. I spent some time with Yvonne Forbes. The sisters were close. They bought their boat and started the business together after Lu divorced. Yvonne made the products; Lu sold them.'

'Shona Hollis is fond of Yvonne. They used to work for the same shoe company. She'd invited Yvonne over tonight.'

'Two women running a successful business in a smart shopping destination,' Siv observed. 'From the outside, it gives the impression of a quiet, uneventful life, and Yvonne was sure that her sister was in good spirits. But if Calloway is right, Lu had something on her mind, and whatever that was, she apparently concealed it from her sister.'

'According to Calloway, Lu started acting unusually in the spring. I've asked him to try to remember the day she didn't open the shop, but I'm not hopeful. The man's a flake. Wherever she was that day might be linked to why she died.'

'One other issue for now,' Siv said. 'Yvonne told me that Lu had no one in her life, but I found expensive lingerie in her bedroom, the kind that could indicate that she was seeing someone. It seems odd that Yvonne wouldn't have been aware of a love interest, as the sisters were close and lived together. Something to bear in mind. I've taken one set of lingerie and I'll send it to Forensics, see if they can retrieve any DNA.' Siv checked her email. 'The post-mortem is this evening. I'll touch base with Rey Anand about that. We need to talk to Struan Hollis, verify Jem Calloway's story about his hook-up last night and see Simon Terrance. I'll visit Terrance, you take Calloway and get a heads up on Lu Forbes's recent phone calls and online activity. We'll need to talk to Angus Fraser as well, but that can wait.' She paused while Ali yawned. 'Let's speak to Struan Hollis together tomorrow. You've got an in at the Old Dairy and I'd like to get more of a feel for it and the community there.'

'Want me to come to the mortuary with you?'

'No, I'll go solo. I can see that you're tired after last night's exertions.'

'It wasn't exactly a wild night!'

'No? But you're not as young as you were, Sergeant Carlin. These things take it out of you more as you mature.'

* * *

Siv reached home around nine that evening. She was tired and running on empty, but not actually hungry. She resisted the bottle of akvavit in the fridge, sticking to her plan of one drink every other night. After Ed's death, she'd grown too fond of the spicy, warming Scandinavian spirit, which eased down beautifully and numbed all pain, but meant a dull head in the mornings. And Rik's presence hadn't helped her resolve, with her sister pouring them both a couple of glasses in the evenings. Time for self-restraint. She found some slices of smoked cheese and tomatoes, arranged them on a plate and added a couple of sesame crackers.

The evening was lovely, with strips of crimson dappling the sky. She sat on the wagon steps with her supper, listening to the silence. Now and again, one of Corran's goats bleated. He could distinguish their voices, but Siv couldn't decide if it was Judy, Nina, Ella or Barbra sounding wistful.

She emailed Ali.

Rey Anand reported that cause of death was stab wound that pierced vertebral artery. The knife used came from the craft set in Calloway's drawer. Made of carbon steel with a flat, scalpel blade. Ask Calloway when he last saw/used the set.

She crunched a tomato and messaged Rik.
Hope you've settled in and all is well.
The reply pinged back.
Terrific. We're watching Skyfall *and eating popcorn.*
The two of them sounded very cosy. Rik had grumbled about the lack of a TV in the wagon. Bartel had a huge, wall-mounted screen. Siv found herself making a strange sound at the back of her throat that sounded suspiciously like a *harrumph*.

She took her plate in and flicked on the kettle.

It was good to have the wagon to herself again, but she automatically glanced at the window bench, expecting to see Rik stretched out, thumb in mouth. You could miss someone irritating you. She put a tea bag in a mug, watched it bob in the boiling water. *Oh Ed, here I am, the sandwich filling between Mutsi and Rik. I should be strolling in Greenwich Park with you and stopping at the café for pizza. Life goes on, but it's blurred and grey without you.* Sometimes Ed answered, but less often these days. Tonight he was silent.

She carried her tea through to the bedroom and lay on the bed. Ed's sweatshirt still hung on the wardrobe door. She didn't wear it so often now, but she liked to see it there, have his DNA in the room.

She pictured Lu Forbes leaving her car, unlocking her shop, plonking her bag on the chair, draping her stylish cream jacket over the back of it, preparing to make a start on those boxes. Someone had persuaded her to go to Calloway's shop. Like Ed, Lu had set off for work with a schedule for the day ahead. Ed had met a lorry, Lu Forbes a killer.

Sudden death was always a case of interrupted plans.

* * *

When Ali rang Gail Maitland on Sunday morning, she confirmed that Jem had spent Friday night with her.

'He rocked up about midnight and left in a hurry around eight on Saturday morning.'

'You're sure about that time on Saturday?'

'Yeah. He woke me up when he was flying around, getting dressed and causing havoc as per.'

Ali reasoned that the alibi didn't rule Calloway out as the killer, even if Gail's account chimed with his own. He could have arrived, got Lu to come into his shop and quickly stuck the knife in.

Calloway lived in a basement flat in a four-storey terrace one street away from Gail, and not far from the town centre. It bore all the hallmarks of a student house, with a couple of bikes chained outside and window stickers for Friends of the Earth, Global Footprint Network, Safe Way Home and Stop Drink Spiking. Like Calloway, the house was worse for wear, and as he negotiated the narrow steps down, Ali surmised that the man was reluctant to grow up, still inhabiting his undergraduate days. The rubbish bin was near the front door and didn't smell sweet.

Ali rang the bell several times and got no response. The curtains were pulled across, suggesting that Calloway was at home. He tried the bell again and then phoned Calloway, who picked up after the sixth ring.

'Yeah?'

'It's DS Carlin. Sorry to wake you. Can you let me in?'

'Woss time?'

'Eleven, just gone.'

'Urgh. Hang on.'

After seeing the shop, Ali expected to step into a tip, but the living room was neat, colourful and well furnished, albeit heavy with heat and stale air. Calloway's work adorned the walls, including a large, mosaic-style portrait of Frida Kahlo made from strips of colour supplements. Calloway's hands were trembling, his hair was a riot of tangles and he stank of booze. He was wearing a long yellow garment like a woman's kaftan.

'Give me a minute to brush my teeth,' he said.

'Sure. I'd say you need a hair of the dog.'

'Oh, yeah. I was drowning my sorrows about Lu last night. Lost track a bit.'

'Babe, what is it?' A blonde-and-blue-haired woman draped in a bath towel appeared. She yawned blearily.

'It's the police, about a friend of mine.'

'Oh, right.'

Ali smiled. 'Morning.'

'OK if I snag myself a coffee?' she asked.

'Go for it,' Calloway said.

'Ta.' She didn't offer to make one for them. 'I'll leave you to it, then.'

'I'll just . . .' Calloway mimed teeth cleaning and followed her, scratching his head.

Ali took the liberty of opening the curtains and the window. He studied the bookshelves, which held dozens of paperbacks of classic fiction. Calloway was well read. There must be more than met the eye to the grungy appearance. He sat in an armchair by the window and waited.

Calloway appeared, smelling minty and holding a glass of water, with his hair scooped back in an elastic band. He fell back on a sofa. The kaftan had side splits, revealing hairy legs.

'I've a couple of questions,' Ali said.

'Don't talk too loudly. My head's banging.'

'Seems to be your usual condition.' Ali couldn't help the dig.

Calloway groaned in reply.

'In your shop you have a craft knife set with twelve blades that you keep in a drawer by your desk. When did you last use or see them?'

Calloway screwed up his face. 'Thursday, I reckon. Yeah, I was trimming magazine pages and shaping some cardboard.'

'And they were all in place when you put them away?'

He nodded and then stared. 'Oh God, was one of those knives used . . . used on Lu?'

'They're part of our enquiry.'

'That's so weird.'

'Why's that?'

'Because she bought them for me last year — well, her sister did technically. I'd given them a hand with setting up displays and shifting stock, moved some heavy boxes for them. They were a thank you. Expensive too, and really precise. Oh, that's mental.'

'Who would know that you kept the knives in the drawer?'

Calloway finished his glass of water and held a hand out. 'No idea. Anyone. Sometimes I'm working at the desk with a knife when a customer comes in. The drawer might be open.' He burped. 'Mental,' he repeated, pressing his left brow.

'I asked if you could try to remember the day when Lu didn't open the shop.'

'Yeah, I checked my phone to see when I called her. It was a Tuesday, June fifteenth. She was . . . she was a kind woman and helpful. Very understanding in a "tough love" sort of way. It's only just hitting me, what's happened.'

'I gather that you, Yvonne and Lu have family links going back.'

'Our mums were friends. I've known Yvonne and Lu all my life. I played with Yvonne mainly, Lu being older. She was always like the big sister who'd tell us off for being annoying. Yvonne's a sweetie. She loves my work, tries to get me shipshape and better organised. She tidied this place up for me last week. I'm not very good at the small stuff. I get absorbed in a piece of work and everything flies out the window. When I'm not working, I get twitchy. Bloody hell, my head hurts!'

'I'll leave you to recover.' Ali stood. 'At least you have company here, a shoulder to cry on. Is that Gail? Doesn't sound like her.' It beat him, how this man attracted women, but he supposed that Calloway had a kind of lived-in charm.

'Eh? Oh, no.' He widened his eyes, pulled his mouth down. 'Actually, I can't remember her name. Met her in the pub last night and one thing led to another . . . embarrassing or what?'

'Best to stick to *babe*, like her. Sounds like she's got the same problem regarding you.'

'Right, good point.'

Ali let himself out and started his car. He couldn't imagine waking up next to a stranger. How could you face them? What would you say? Polly sometimes told him he was an innocent country boy, green behind the ears, and perhaps she was right.

CHAPTER EIGHT

Siv's first impression of Simon Terrance was that he glowed: a head covered in golden-red curls, scrubbed, glossy skin and sparkling teeth. His silk shirt had a paint-splatter pattern, as if gold and yellow had been trailed across the fabric.

When she stepped inside, the house shone too, with gleaming parquet floors and polished wood. It was a modern townhouse, and she guessed architect-designed, judging by the contemporary style: plaster-and-wood facade, huge windows and glass-and-steel stairs that led from the kitchen.

It was wonderfully cool and she heard the discreet whir of air conditioning. 'Your home is a comfortable temperature, Mr Terrance.'

'I don't know about you, Inspector, but I'm not much good in this heat. Air con is essential.'

He pulled out a custard-coloured stool for her at the white island in the kitchen and sat perched opposite. They might have been having a meeting in a trendy tech start-up.

'Do help yourself.' He indicated a cafetiere and ceramic mugs. 'We have friends in common, by the way — Corran and Paul. I had supper with them last night.'

She'd noted the classic red Ferrari parked in Terrance's drive outside her neighbours' home when she'd driven past. 'I'm very lucky to have them nearby.'

'They speak highly of you, you're their dream tenant.'

'Really?'

'Absolutely. Quiet, single, reliable lady detective.'

It sounded like the wording in an old-fashioned lonely-hearts ad. *Quiet, single lady detective would like to meet mature gentleman for walks, theatre visits and maybe romance.* 'Well, likewise, they're ideal landlords.'

'I saw your wagon after they'd completed the refurbishment, before they rented it. They're so clever, the way they worked out the space. It's dinky and gorgeous, isn't it? I almost wanted to move in myself!'

Judging by this house, there was no way that Simon Terrance would see himself in a tiny wagon with minimal facilities and an absence of air con. She suspected that he was amusing himself at her expense. His words made her uncomfortable, as if he'd been spying on her through the window. She told herself not to be ridiculous and poured coffee.

'I need to talk to you about Lu Forbes.'

He grew solemn. 'It's so appalling. I can't process it at all. I arrived for work and as I got out of my car, I saw Jem running like a headless chicken to Shona's. I hurried after him and heard him gabbling that Lu was dead.'

If she'd only heard him on the phone, she'd have imagined Terrance to be late middle-aged, yet she'd read in the record that he was twenty-seven. He had the voice of a much older man and his manner was old-fashioned — courteous, formal, smooth.

She decided to see if she could shake up his easy composure. 'Did Lu Forbes have any enemies?'

He carried on pouring his coffee without missing a beat. '*Enemies* is a strong word.'

'Murder indicates strong emotion.'

'True. I can't say that Lu provoked any such antipathy.'

'What was she like?'

'Determined, a bit humourless. Perhaps she caused a little envy at times.'

'Why was that?'

Terrance crossed his legs, his linen trousers creasing at the knee. 'Lu ran a highly successful business with a healthy turnover. She was skilled at selling and growing her clientele. Hers was the busiest shop in terms of customers.'

'And that didn't go down well with some people?'

Terrance stirred cream into his coffee. 'Her success was good for Lansdown Court because it attracted interest and footfall. In that sense, everyone there was pleased. But she could brag about her prowess, shall we say. We often heard about how many sales she'd made in a week, or the amount of orders that had arrived online. Maybe at times she implied that colleagues needed to up their game.'

'Did you resent that?'

He smiled, his chin dimpling. 'I didn't, because I had no need to. I have a shop in the Lanes in Brighton. That's my major outlet, where my profits are made from direct sales, but I also trade online and export. I'm doing very well. The shop is really an extra interest for me. I bore easily, so I enjoy having different showrooms. I open four days a week there and sales are good. I like the artisan nature of Lansdown Court and the way it's woven into the locality. It pleases me to have a presence there.'

He sounded pretty boastful himself. The Lanes was a fashionable area of Brighton and it would be costly to have a shop there. Terrance must be doing well to be able to indulge himself with his local shop. 'You have a manager for your Brighton shop?'

'I do, and I visit it at least once a week.'

'Who was Lu aiming her criticism at, if not you?'

'Colleagues would have to speak for themselves.' He pulled at an eyelash, blinked.

'I'm asking your opinion.'

He looked offended. 'I don't want to talk out of turn and cause offence.'

Siv pushed her mug away. 'Mr Terrance, murder is offensive. Please answer the question.'

He recrossed his legs. 'I would venture that Shona and Jem were occasionally exasperated by Lu. She found Shona's homely produce a little ordinary and unexciting — a bit WI for the Lansdown image. She certainly felt that Jem needed to buck up his ideas, although she cut him a lot of slack because his stuff is so highly rated.'

'Did they fall out with her?'

'I really can't say. Shona tends to stand on her dignity. She's conscious of her status as manager of the court and her relationship to Angus Fraser. Jem gets by on his roguish smile and air of helplessness. He's a bit of a waster, a Peter Pan, and there's no harm in him. He does have huge talent. If he could exercise some self-discipline, he has the potential for real success. I can't see that happening, though.'

'Did you like Lu?'

'Absolutely. I admired her drive and energy, and the way she and her sister had turned an idea into a viable business, which is no mean feat. We got on well, had lunch in the café sometimes.'

'And Yvonne?'

'I met her now and then, when she was at Lansdown. Nice woman, a bit in her sister's shadow. Lu was in the driving seat, Yvonne very much the passenger, but she works hard behind the scenes on all the products. Is that all, Inspector? I'm due at a brunch.'

'Not quite. What time did you leave here yesterday morning?'

'Around eight.'

'Can anyone verify that?'

'Hardly. I live alone. I suppose a neighbour might have noticed.'

'Thanks. I'll leave it there for now.'

Siv got up and he moved quickly to lift her jacket from where she'd hung it on the back of her chair. He flapped it gently and held it out for her. Again, she couldn't help speculating that he was amusing himself.

When she stepped outside, the heat clung to her and the car was a small oven. Terrance was a man at one with his home: cool, urbane, sophisticated. She didn't like or trust him, and wasn't sure why. Maybe just one of those things, an irrational prejudice or simple envy of his air con.

* * *

A woman with streaks of blue hair and figure-hugging yellow jeans came out of Jem's flat as Yvonne reached the bottom of the steps.

She grinned, leaving the door open and gesturing with a thumb. 'He's in there. Has he got a rota running or something? I mean, he's got his good points, but he's not that fit!'

Yvonne blushed and slammed the door shut. Jem was sitting on the sofa in shorts and vest, drinking coffee and brushing his flowing damp hair.

'Hi, Little Tree! I wasn't expecting you.'

'Why haven't you called me? Didn't you get any of my messages?'

'Sorry. I switched my phone off and I've been in shock. I've had the police here this morning.'

'Not just the police. I met your other visitor on my way in. She's kind of bargain basement.'

'Yes?' He smiled, holding her gaze. 'Come and sit beside me, sweetie, brush my hair for me. You have such gentle hands.'

She sat next to him, took the brush. 'Jem, I can't believe you didn't phone me. Lu's dead and you found her. I've been beside myself. I was expecting you to come round.'

'I'm sorry. I was traumatised yesterday and the police were in my face. I'm no good with difficult stuff. I was all over the place, shaky and confused. I wouldn't have been any help to you in that state, would I? I'd have been a burden and made everything worse.'

He had a way of turning every situation around. She wanted to say, *You weren't too traumatised to get a woman into your bed*, but understood that if she did, he'd say it was nothing, just a mindless sort of therapy and she'd have made a fool of herself.

'I was thinking about you all day,' he added, 'sending you positive vibes, willing you to keep strong. Are you managing?'

'Not really. My sister's dead. I'm miserable and frightened.'

'I'm so sorry, Little Tree. I'm such a klutz. Come here. I'll try to make it better.' He cradled her face in his hands, rubbed the tip of his nose to hers. 'I'm gutted about it — I'd known Lu for ever. You must be truly heartbroken.'

Mollified and comforted, she rested her cheek against his.

'Forgiven?' he whispered.

'I suppose.'

'You're so lovely. I don't deserve you in my life. Do my hair and then I'll do yours. It will soothe you.'

Brushing each other's hair was one of their routines. Sometimes they tried out different styles. One day, they'd plaited strands of their hair together and lain in bed, attached. She knelt beside him on the sofa and drew the brush through his thick locks, stopping to untangle densely knotted strands.

'Did you tell the police that something was wrong with Lu?'

He looked up at her. 'I mentioned that she'd been a bit odd recently.'

'How, odd?'

'Sometimes she missed work or was in a mood.'

Yvonne stopped brushing halfway through a hank of hair. 'Why didn't you tell me?'

He stroked the back of her hand. 'I didn't want to worry you, and when I asked Lu, she talked about PMT. So, probably nothing to fret about.'

She pulled the brush through. 'She seemed fine to me.'

'Well, there you are. Just me, imagining things. I'm always fizzing with silly ideas. And I was so upset yesterday, finding her like that, I didn't really understand what I was saying to that podgy detective.'

She sat back on her heels, tears spilling. 'What am I going to do without her, Jem? I'll never be able to manage the shop on my own. She did all the management. I don't even understand the systems she used.'

'I'll help you, Little Tree. No need to get in such a state. I'll help out.'

'Will you? Would you really do that for me?'

'Do my best, honest. You're always sorting me out, coming to my rescue. Remember that time I sprained my ankle and you let me lean on you all the way home?' He kissed her tenderly. 'Least I can do is lend a hand.'

'Oh, you're so lovely. That means so much to me. Takes a weight off my mind.'

He lifted the brush, shushed her and got her to sit on the floor between his legs. He eased the band from her pony tail and spread her hair out, lifting it through his fingers. Then he sang 'The Ploughboy' while he brushed and eased her. She closed her eyes, safe between the warm pressure of his legs.

* * *

Shona Hollis showed Siv and Ali into a high-ceilinged living room with comfy furniture covered in red, green and blue tartan. The fireplace had a stone surround and a copper hood over the fire, which was set with logs.

'Can I get you coffee, Detectives?' She stood, smart in a navy skirt and white shirt.

'We're fine, thanks,' Siv said. Ali had told her about Shona's hospitality yesterday and she didn't want to get cosy.

'Struan will be down in a minute.' Shona took a chair opposite them. 'I'd like to sit in with him.'

'Please do,' Siv told her.

'He was terribly upset when he got in last night and I told him about Lu. I've never seen him so shaky. I let him lie in this morning.'

'We understand that this is difficult,' Ali said.

'Yes. Will it take long? Our lunch should be ready at two and it's beautiful beef, so I wouldn't like it to go over.'

'Half an hour should do us for now,' Siv answered.

'Thank you. Yvonne's coming by later, although she told me she's no appetite.'

'Did she visit you last night?' Ali asked.

'She did, but she didn't stay. She wanted to be in her own bed, which I could understand. I've noticed that people who've been bereaved have a nesting instinct. Ah, here he is now, the man of the house.'

Struan Hollis was like a walking advertisement for healthy youth. Siv could see him featuring in a promotion for vitamins or energy drinks. He was lithe and tall, in a white polo shirt and dark jeans. A bloom feathered his cheeks and his blond hair bounced from recent blow-drying. He exuded confidence and an awareness that he was handsome.

'Hi.' He was carrying an orange smoothie in a glass with a straw. 'Thanks for making me this, Mum, it's delicious.'

Siv made introductions. 'We need to check a few things with you, Struan. We realise that this is a sad time for you.'

'Yeah, I can't get my head round it.' His phone pinged. He hitched it from his back pocket and checked the screen.

'When did you last see Lu?'

'Thursday. She was locking up when I got back from school. We said hello, that was it.' He held the smoothie between his knees and typed on his phone with two thumbs as he talked.

'And yesterday morning you left on your bike at seven a.m. for a football event at Isbrook Academy.'

'Yep.'

'You cycled straight there?'

He sucked through his straw. 'That's right.'

'Did you see anyone around here as you were leaving?' His phone pinged twice again and he reached for it.

'Could you leave the phone for now?' Siv asked.

'I suppose.' His eyes were sleepy below thick brows. 'No, no one was here at that time. I mean, nobody would be here that early.' He rested his drink on the arm of the chair.

'Careful with that, Struan,' his mother cautioned. 'I don't want it all over the place like last week.' She smiled at Siv. 'For a boy who's so deft with a football, he's all thumbs with drinks.'

Struan knit his brow at the intervention, but picked the glass up again and smoothed the chair fabric. 'This is a sacrosanct Clan Fraser tartan, ye ken,' he announced in a mock Scots accent, downing the rest of the smoothie in one long draw.

His mother simpered as if he'd uttered a profound statement. 'It's a good while since we left Scotland, but it's important to remember our roots and heritage. I expect you find that too about Ireland, Sergeant.'

'Aye, you can take the boy out of Derry, but you can't take Derry out of the boy,' Ali said. 'I'm not aware we have a family tartan, but we have a Carlin motto: *Felis demulcta mitis*, meaning "A stroked cat is gentle".' He saw Siv's raised eyebrow and focused on Struan. 'Now, Struan, tell us about your friendship with Lu and Yvonne.'

'They're both really nice. I'm friendlier with Yvonne because we've known her longer. She used to stay over quite a bit and she'd help me with my homework. I sort of knew Lu to chat to now and again. Saw her in the café, stuff like that. She gave me the odd sample of shampoo, told me my hair was my crowning glory.' He sighed. 'She was alright, was Lu.'

'You didn't hear that she'd fallen out with anyone, or notice that she was upset at all?'

'Nope.'

'So, how did your training day go?' Ali asked.

'It was cool — really good, thanks. Yvonne likes footie. She comes and watches my matches.'

'I go to as many as I can, but Yvonne understands the game better than me.' Shona laughed. 'She's always trying to explain it to me, but I still struggle with some of the tactics.'

'It was pretty weird, getting back and seeing the police everywhere,' Struan said. 'Your Forensics people are cool. I was chatting to them, told them I'm wondering about it as a career.'

'That's the first I've heard of it.' His mother sounded astonished.

'It's interesting, I've been reading up about it. It's my plan B if I don't make it as a professional footballer.'

'Well, it's good to be kept in the loop,' Shona told him. 'Now, I'd better check my roast, and if you're finished with Struan, he's going to make the gravy.'

Siv decided to leave them to their domestic tasks and wrapped it up. Outside, the sun was beating on the courtyard.

She nudged Ali. 'Is Polly back yet?'

'No, still stuck with her mum.'

'Fancy lunch, then? We could go to the Horizon café, sit outside and catch a sea breeze.'

'Sounds good to me, guv.'

CHAPTER NINE

Siv and Ali sat beneath an umbrella on the café terrace, surrounded by families with noisy children. A toddler was banging a toy bus on the next table while her sibling cackled.

'Maybe this wasn't such a good idea after all,' Siv apologised.

'I don't mind the wee ones, they have to blow off steam and this grub's good.' Ali was tucking into his chicken-and-leek pie.

Siv loaded Camembert on her baguette. 'Struan's a confident young man. Quite the mummy's boy.'

'Aye. I'd say he rules the roost. Older mother, father gone, only child.'

'Where is the dad?'

'He left and he's dead now. I gathered he was a rover.'

'Like Jem Calloway, from what you've told me.'

Ali swallowed a mouthful. 'The man's a mystery to me. I get the impression he has a harem. Why would any woman find him attractive? Can you explain?'

'I've only met him briefly so far. I can see that for some women, he might have an urchin charm.'

'Give me a break.' Ali snorted. 'The man went to university, so he has to be bright, but he just drifts around aimlessly, living in a tatty flat. Maybe he's a lot cannier than he pretends.'

'Explain.'

'Well, all this stuff about Lu Forbes having been worried. No one else has told us that. He could have killed her and he's coming up with those details to confuse us.'

Siv crunched cucumber. 'That would mean it was premeditated, because he sought you out at the party the night before to mention his concern. Why draw attention to himself like that? Seems a bit far-fetched, and how was he to know you'd be there?'

'Aye, I get it. I just don't quite buy his "absent-minded artist" shtick and the way everyone refers to him as ineffectual. We should keep him in our sights.'

Siv waited while the toddler screamed because the bus had been taken away. 'Agreed. I'm interested in the day when Calloway claims that Lu Forbes wasn't at work. If her car's got satnav, we might get something on where she went now that you have the date. We'll meet first thing in the morning, at eight. I'll text Patrick.'

Ali finished his pie and sat back, patting his stomach. 'I used to be as slim as Struan, if not slimmer. Then, when I was around fifteen, I started to pile on the weight. It was like adulthood added layers. Mammy used to say it was puppy fat, but I'm a bit of an old dog for that excuse now.'

Siv didn't want to comment. Anything she said might be taken the wrong way. She wriggled out of it by directing his attention to the toddler. Negotiations had taken place with her and she was now enthusiastically chucking a squeaky duck on the ground. It landed near Ali's foot. He picked it up and handed it back to her, asking her if she had a licence to fly it. She glared at him and then roared with laughter.

Ali finished his Diet Coke. 'Want me to do anything else today, guv?'

'No, have some home time. Let's get out of here before you have to play fetch the duck for the rest of the afternoon.'

She glanced at him, head to one side. '"A stroked cat is gentle." Did you make that up?'

'I did not! We have a wee sampler in the kitchen back home that my great-granny stitched. Are you jealous because the Drummonds don't have a motto?'

'I've no idea whether we have or not. I've never felt the need of one.'

'Definitely envious,' he gloated, bending to pick up the toy duck and hand it back.

* * *

Yvonne and Struan were watching TV, a nature programme about Newfoundland. Shona put the kettle on and finished stacking the dishwasher. Yvonne was so pallid, her eyes scrunched and raw. When she'd arrived late afternoon, she'd cried for a good half an hour. Struan had slipped away with his skateboard while Shona had comforted her, holding her hand.

Shona wouldn't miss Lu. She'd been a bossy, interfering madam with a high opinion of herself and quick to comment on others. Once she'd divorced her husband and bought the boat with Yvonne, Shona had seen much less of her friend. She'd missed Yvonne and her regular stays at the Old Dairy, and now Lu was gone, they could be close again.

Shona blew down the front of her top and sprinkled cold water on her face and the back of her neck. She was always too warm these days, and this weather was a persecution. The doctor had prescribed HRT patches, reassuring her that they would improve her sleep, her hot flushes and her foggy brain. She'd been using them for several months. The hot flushes had improved a little, but there were still days when her brain seemed to have wandered off on holiday and she had an overwhelming need to lie down. It took so much effort and energy to conceal her wooziness and her cotton-wool head from everyone. She was still boiling. She took a pack of peas from the freezer, stuck it in her bra and stared out of the kitchen window.

She was unsure what to do. She and Struan loved living here, and Angus had been very kind to offer her the house and the management of the yard. She'd been over the moon. At the time, they'd been living in a two-bedroomed semi on an estate, a house with paper-thin walls and a poky garden. The Old Dairy was her dream home, a kind that she'd never have been able to afford on her own, and a great place to raise a child. On the day they'd moved in, it was as if she'd won the lottery. But there were downsides to this good fortune. She'd learned that being Angus's tenant and indebted to him wasn't always a comfortable niche, and brought its own stresses. Angus was a forceful, driven man, unafflicted by random sweats and a haphazard memory, and who didn't like to hear about people's problems. He'd made it clear from day one that he expected Shona to run a successful operation and sort out any difficulties before they became crises. When she was around him these days, Shona felt clumsy and addled.

Things had been ticking along until Simon Terrance had brought unwanted attention. Simon was a difficult man to deal with, bland and slippery. The first warning she'd had was when she'd noticed two men arguing with Simon outside his shop. Some weeks later, a furious woman had knocked on Shona's door, asking where Simon was as she had a bone to pick with him. 'He doesn't respond to phone calls, so I've tracked him to his little lair here,' she'd hissed. When Shona had told her that Simon's shop was closed on Mondays, she'd ranted on about organising protests before stamping away.

Simon later explained that he'd bought the leaseholds to a group of kiosks at Minster Beach, and he'd given notice to the tenants, who weren't happy. He was planning some sort of development there. Lu wasn't helping, he'd added, by getting involved in a petition against his plans. Shona could tell that he was irritated by her questions. Like Lu, he had a high opinion of himself. He'd called his annoyed visitors professional whingers, adding that if they caused any further trouble at Lansdown, he'd contact the police.

Shona had been fretting that someday soon, the story might blow up. The angry woman had mentioned going to the press. Lansdown Court might be dragged into disrepute, especially if Simon had to call the police to deal with the protestors, and Angus would be asking questions. Now, after the murder, there was police tape everywhere and forensic staff in suits. Customers might be put off. She had no idea how Yvonne was going to run the shop as well as making the products — she was highly strung and no businesswoman, and she'd relied on Lu to front the sales.

Shona was beset by difficulties. To cap it all, Angus had called in earlier, a fleeting visit, giving the impression that she had somehow allowed a horrible crime. He'd frowned, tapped his teeth and instructed her to make sure the shops were reopened pronto. As if that were within her power!

The peas had worked their magic. She popped them back in the freezer and placed cups and milk on a tray. One thing that she could resolve that *was* within her power was tackling Jem Calloway about his rent. Her menopausal stupor had caused her failure to notice his rent arrears until they'd become a huge sum. She'd inadvertently cut him too much slack. She would put him on a warning that he'd get notice at the end of the month if he didn't pay up. Yes, time to take a leaf out of Simon's book and act decisively.

She gave a satisfied nod and filled the teapot.

Struan appeared, weaving around the kitchen, opening the fridge door and peering in. 'What cake are we having? I'm starving!'

'Apple. You can't possibly be starving, you ate a huge lunch.'

'I'm growing, I use up a lot of energy.'

Shona laughed. 'You've hollow legs, that's what it is.'

Struan's phone pinged. He checked it, laughed and sneaked a slice of beef from the fridge. 'Loads of people from school and footie are contacting me, wanting the lowdown on what's happened. It's been on the news.'

Shona's mood dipped. 'Be careful what you say and don't encourage gossip. Don't forget this is our workplace where I make a living, as well as our home.'

'No need to burst a blood vessel. You can't blame people for being interested. Who d'you reckon did it?'

'The murder?'

'Yeah.'

'Goodness, I have no idea! No one we know, I'm sure of that.'

Struan's eyes lit up. 'I might have cycled past whoever did it yesterday morning, near enough to hear them breathing. Maybe they were watching me.'

'Stop, Struan! You make me nervous. And for heaven's sake, don't talk like that in front of Yvonne or mention that people are curious. How is she?'

'Dozing. Shall I wake her up?'

'Let her sleep on for now, she's exhausted. You bring the tray. I expect she'll wake soon enough and she'll enjoy a slice of cake. She always loved my baking, it's a pleasure to watch her eat.'

* * *

Cherry Bolting paced up and down her messy living room. She ought to tidy up, but she couldn't be bothered. Standards had slipped in recent days, and no wonder. She was eating baked beans from a can. It was a disgusting thing to do, and if her mother could see her, she'd fold her arms, tap a foot and ask what on earth was going on. Cherry was hungry and too distracted and worried to cook. Should she anticipate the worst, see Shona and tell her what had been happening?

She stopped by the open window and watched the woman next door clipping her front hedge. *Snip-snip*, the shears went. Cherry dipped her spoon into the beans and sank down on to the wide window ledge.

How could she face Shona? She liked her, and Shona had always been friendly and fair. If Cherry confessed, she'd be furious. She'd probably throw her out and ring the police. That's what she'd do in Shona's place. She'd lose her job and her name would be in the press. Why had she been such a fool?

She put the empty can on the floor. She still felt hungry. Funny, how food didn't fill you up when you were living on your nerves. She followed the shears slicing across the top of the hedge and tried to calm herself. She was only this alarmed because the police were swarming all over Lansdown and asking questions. She'd been careful. There was no reason why they should find out about her.

Best to stave off the panic, carry on going to work and keep her head down. With any luck, the police wouldn't be around there for much longer. Why anticipate trouble that might never come? One thing she knew for sure: she was going to behave herself from now on and not take any more stupid risks.

The neighbour looked up, smiled and gave her a wave. Cherry waved back, reassured by this little touch of normality.

CHAPTER TEN

On Monday morning, Siv parked at the station and decided to buy coffees for the meeting. She was intercepted by DCI Mortimer as he headed to his car. Her heart sank, but she stuck a smile on. She tried to keep contact with him to a minimum and communicated by email when she could. Now that her mother was living with him, she was uncomfortably aware that her boss was also a kind of stepfather. She'd had a surfeit of those in childhood, although Mutsi had usually coyly referred to them as *uncles*, and she had no desire to have one as an adult. Sometimes when they met, Mortimer alluded to her mother, or aired the possibility of social get-togethers with an awkward laugh.

'Walk with me, DI Drummond. Thank you for last night's email about the murder. Any progress?'

'Ali and I worked the weekend, interviewing. The PM confirmed that Luanna Forbes died from a stab wound to the neck. She appears to have been well liked. Steve and his team will finish at the scene today, so I should get fingerprint results soon. We've done a press release.'

Mortimer's step was jaunty, his jacket slung over a shoulder. Mutsi had been giving him a gradual makeover. His hair was a richer tone and better cut, and his skin had improved.

He had new aviator-style sunglasses with thick tortoiseshell frames and his face was sun-bronzed. He and Mutsi would have been sailing on *Quicksilver* over the weekend.

'Good, good. Is DC Hill back today?'

'He is. We're about to meet.'

'Keep me updated. Lansdown Court is a lovely place. Your mother and I bought a kilim there last month and we lunched in the café. The food was very good, although Crista commented that they should do more salad options. I have to admire the care she always takes about what she eats.' They'd reached his car. He squinted skywards. 'Goodness, this weather!'

She seized on the reliable, safe topic. 'It's going to be another scorcher, that's for sure. In fact, I must get out of this sun!'

She hurried to Gusto, the local café, where she bought coffees, mini croissants and mango slices. The sun already felt intense on her face as she walked back. The station was a handsome listed building, originally part of the corn market. The foyer would be cool, but the south-facing team offices on the first floor baked in this weather. The ancient building had dodgy heating and plumbing, shabby decor and intermittent plagues of mice. For some time, there'd been rumours that they would move to a modern set of offices, and every now and again, people with clipboards and iPads appeared, scrutinising floor plans and making notes.

Ali was opening the windows wide as she walked in. 'It was too hot to sleep last night. I couldn't get comfortable at all. I had a shower only half an hour since and I've sweaty oxters already.'

'Translation of *oxters*, please?'

'Armpits.'

'Too much information.' She could tell how much he was missing Polly. Ali was habitually benign and reliably good-natured. She was usually the prickly one, and had been especially so in the first months after she'd arrived, grieving and thin-skinned. 'Have some chilled fruit, it will cool you down.'

Patrick hurried in, natty as usual in a slim-fitting suit. 'Hi, I'm back and raring to go!'

Ali welcomed him with a clap on the shoulder. 'A sight for sore eyes, all suntanned and relaxed!'

'Good holiday?' Siv asked.

'Terrific. Rhodes is amazing. The Acropolis and the archaeological museum were fascinating.' Patrick was a history buff, with a particular passion for Hannibal.

Siv handed him a coffee. 'I hope you spent some time with Kitty and not just traipsing around old ruins.'

Patrick raised his left hand, waggling the silver band encircling his ring finger. 'We got engaged at the Acropolis in the moonlight. Old ruins can prove romantic settings, thank you very much.'

'Congratulations!' Ali said. 'When's the big day?'

'We haven't decided on that yet. Maybe next year. Kitty's parents were engaged for almost five years before they got married, although we're not planning on waiting that long. Noah's delighted. He's agreed to be best man.' Noah, Patrick's brother, had been a wheelchair user since he'd had a stroke. They shared a house on the coast road that had been adapted for him. Patrick held out a bag. 'I got you these. They're almond-and-walnut pastries, called *kataifi*.'

'Get thee behind me, Satan,' Ali groaned.

'I'm sure you're allowed one, they're only small.' Patrick grinned and pointed at the incident board. 'So, what's been happening behind my back?'

Siv stood by the board, where Ali had added photos of all the people so far involved. 'Let's get started.' She pointed to the photo of Luanna. 'Luanna Forbes, aged thirty-four, left home just after seven on Saturday morning, July ninth. As far as we can tell, she didn't stop off anywhere, so she'd have arrived at Lansdown Court about half seven. There's no CCTV there to help us. For some reason, she got access to Jem Calloway's shop and she was stabbed in the neck there between her arrival and eight thirty, when Jem Calloway states that he found her dead. Lu ran Forbes Natural Skincare in the shop next door with her sister, Yvonne, who makes the products on their houseboat in the harbour. Lansdown is owned by Angus Fraser, but managed by his cousin Shona Hollis, who lives on-site in the Old Dairy with her teenage son, Struan. To date, we've been told that Lu was a successful, competitive businesswoman with no enemies.' She went through the people who ran businesses on the site and paused for coffee. 'What have we learned so far? Ali, you first.'

'Jem Calloway's a man who likes alcohol and women. Appears disorganised, and he's behind with his shop rent. The woman he spent Friday night with confirmed that he left her at just gone eight on Saturday morning, which fits with his account of arriving at his shop at half eight. We should get forensics back on his clothes later today. He claims that he didn't go near the body, so those results should be clear. He says that Lu was troubled about something, and hadn't been at work as regularly as usual. Nobody else has mentioned that.' He pulled his shirt away from his chest and flapped it. 'Shona Hollis states that Struan cycled off to footie training at seven on Saturday, and she didn't see or hear anything until half eight, when Calloway came banging on the door with Terrance on his heels. Her sets of spare keys to all the premises were locked away, all present and correct.'

'What about the Buttery café? Was anyone there?' Patrick asked.

Siv tapped Cherry Bolting's photo. 'Ms Bolting, who runs it, says she arrived at eight forty and opened up. No one can confirm her movements. Her assistant, Malcolm Hayler, came in at nine. She saw Lu regularly, didn't think she seemed worried at all. I visited Yvonne, Lu's sister. According to her, everything was fine on the work and home fronts. Lu was divorced and single, but I'm waiting for forensics on some new-ish, expensive lingerie I found in her bedroom.' She scrolled to the photo she'd taken of it and showed it to Ali and Patrick.

'Looks designer,' Patrick commented.

'Yes,' Siv agreed, 'and may indicate that Lu did have a male friend who her sister was unaware of. I also met with Simon

Terrance — Mr Smooth lives alone, so no one can corroborate that he left home at around eight on Saturday. He noted that Lu was sometimes critical of Shona's produce and Calloway's work ethos, so she could have stirred resentments.' She hooked a chair towards her and sat, marshalling her thoughts. 'We have no suspect. We need to wait for forensics on Calloway's clothes, but I'd say he's an unlikely killer. If he'd wanted to murder Lu, he'd hardly have invited her to his shop, and why put himself in the limelight by saying she was worried? So far, nothing much in Lu Forbes's life is signalling concern, other than Calloway's vague concerns about her occasional moods and a day's absence from work. There's also Terrance's view that she could be a bit boastful about her success, and critical of others if she believed they weren't making the grade.'

'Calloway acknowledged that Lu told him off some-times, but he described it as tough love,' Ali added. 'And when he asked her about any problems, she alluded to PMT, so he backed off.'

'Was the killer trying to implicate Calloway by using his shop?' Patrick asked. 'Maybe it was someone with a grudge against them both.'

'Fair point,' Siv agreed. 'So, to tasks for today. Patrick, I want you to find out if Lu Forbes had satnav in her car. We need to establish where she went for the day on June fifteenth. Talk to Bryan Hendrix, Lu's ex, and arrange fingerprints for all the names on the incident board apart from Calloway — Steve and team have his. Ali, check out Malcom Hayler from the café and confirm what time Struan Hollis arrived for his train-ing. I'm going to speak to Angus Fraser. Once Steve's team have finished at Calloway's shop, I'll see you there and we'll do a proper search. We'll meet back here around half five.'

* * *

Bryan Hendrix had said that it would be easiest for him to come to the station. He was a building inspector for the local council, out on site visits all day, so he could call in.

While Patrick waited, he brought himself up to speed with information and found the Lansdown Court website. It was basic, with a general description and some pretty photographs.

Lansdown Court is an attractive arts and crafts centre, offering a unique and peaceful rural shopping experience and free parking. There is a café, the Buttery, where you can relax over morning coffee, lunch or afternoon tea. Do come and browse in the fascinating variety of shops within these historic, converted manor buildings, where you will find special gifts for any occasion.

Shona Hollis's details were on the contact page and another gave location details. The website was efficient but dull, and could be made a lot more eye-catching and interactive, Patrick thought.

When the front desk rang to say that Bryan Hendrix had arrived and was in an interview room, Patrick skipped down the stairs, refreshed by his holiday. It had been terrific on all fronts. Kitty was happy to move in with him and Noah, and his brother was content to have her there. It was good when life's cogs moved smoothly. They hadn't always for Noah, especially when he'd been involved with a woman who'd fleeced him. At one time, Patrick had been weighed down by responsibility for his brother, but Noah now had a girlfriend, Eden, and a decent social life, and he helped out at a community centre two days a week.

Bryan Hendrix had made himself at home in the interview room. His laptop was open on the desk, a notebook beside it, jacket on the back of a chair, and he was standing by the window, busy on his phone. He was dressed in a short-sleeved shirt, jeans and lumberjack boots. He glanced at Patrick, gave a finger wave and continued talking about roof timbers. Patrick was unimpressed and made plenty of noise pulling out a chair and shifting the table.

Hendrix took the heavy hint. 'Have to go, I'll be there around four and we can discuss further.' He put his phone away and sat down. 'Really busy right now.'

'So am I. Thanks for coming in. I'm sorry about your ex-wife.'

'Yes. Terrible. I'm still pinching myself.'

He did have puffy eyes and a baffled expression. Patrick modified his tone. 'When did you last see Ms Forbes?'

'Around Easter. We bumped into each other at the shopping centre and had a quick chat.'

'You were on friendly terms?'

He gripped his bare forearms with stubby hands. 'Absolutely. It's not that huge a town. If we came across each other, we exchanged pleasantries.'

Patrick had skimmed through the guv's interview with Yvonne Forbes. 'But the divorce was tricky?'

'Who told you that?'

'It was mentioned. Was money a stumbling block?' Patrick saw Hendrix tightening up. 'I'd imagine that can easily happen. Finances would be hard to disentangle.'

'We had some differences of opinion, but we worked it out through our lawyers, and we both came away with a satisfactory agreement. That was a while back, you understand, the dust had settled. We'd moved on, bought properties, shaped new lives.'

He made it sound easy, but any divorce Patrick had heard about was messy and damaging. 'Can you tell me your whereabouts on Saturday morning, seven to nine?'

'I was at home, having a lie-in. I got up at half nine. Before you ask, I was on my own. I do have a partner, Zara, but we don't share a home.'

'Can you give me her full name and address?'

Hendrix bridled. 'Why? I don't see why Zara should be bothered. She'd never met Lu and I don't want her upset.'

'Just for our records,' Patrick said easily. He expected him to refuse, but Hendrix crossed his arms and gave the details. 'Thanks for that. When you saw Ms Forbes at Easter, did she indicate that she was worried about anything?'

'Quite the contrary. She was upbeat, pleased with the way the business was going.'

'After the divorce, she bought a houseboat with Yvonne, her sister, and they established the shop. Did they get on well?'

'I assume so, as they chose to live and work together.'

Patrick tapped the table. 'Oh, come on, Mr Hendrix. You were married to Lu, you must have an opinion.'

Hendrix made a soft, exasperated noise. 'Yes, they were good mates, got on well. Yvonne leaned on Lu a fair bit, depended on her for direction in life. She'd gone to college and got a teaching qualification, but she ended up working in a shop. Then she was making cosmetics at home, just selling to friends. The business was Lu's idea and she encouraged Yvonne to set it up with her. Classic older and younger sister, I suppose. I'm an only child, so I don't understand much about these things.'

'You can't think of anyone who might wish Lu harm?'

'No. This is astonishing. She'd never hurt anyone.' He clenched his fists and looked down, as if keeping a grip on strong emotion.

Hendrix agreed readily to have his fingerprints taken. When he'd gone, Patrick nipped out to the small garden at the rear of the station for a breath of air while he tweeted on his popular police page.

@DCBerminsterPolice
We are seeking information about a murder at Lansdown Court on the morning of Saturday, 9 July. Ms Luanna Forbes, who ran a shop there, was found dead. If you saw anything unusual, or can provide any detail that might help us, please contact the station. We rely on your help to fight crime and bring people to justice.
#keepingberminstersafe

Patrick stood in the shade. It wasn't as hot as Rhodes, but the air had the same still, intense quality. His thoughts went to Bryan Hendrix. There was a tension, an off note to the man. He and Lu Forbes had been divorced for a while, but his distress had seeped through the detached front he'd tried to maintain. Patrick filed that away for future reference.

CHAPTER ELEVEN

Ali wasn't in the best of moods. The heat was syrupy and oppressive, and Polly had just texted him to say that after a meeting with the medics, she'd have to stay at her mum's for at least another fortnight.

> *Mum's hip not mending as well as hoped, and she's still in a lot of pain and unable to do much. I'll have to stay around, but I will get carers in as soon as feasible. Hope you haven't already emptied the freezer! Xx*

She'd warned him that might be the case on their call the night before, but it was still a blow. The bed was so empty, the house so cheerless, and she wasn't there to tell him his shirt wasn't tucked in properly.

When he called Malcolm Hayler's number, his mood didn't improve. An older woman answered, saying that she was Malcolm's mum. He explained why he was ringing, and she spent some time commenting on the dreadfulness of the murder, how appalling it was that criminals were on the loose, and what a terrible society we lived in when a young woman wasn't safe at her place of work.

'Aye, it is shocking. I do need to have a word with Malcolm, if he's available.'

'Oh, I see, Sergeant. Well, Malc's left his phone at home and gone out for a walk. He's making the most of this glorious weather and an unexpected day off. He lives here with me — it's easier on him financially. Well, it's a big house and it's so handy, having him around to lend a hand.'

'Maybe you can help me. Did you notice what time Malcolm left for work on Saturday morning?'

'This Saturday just gone?'

'That's right.'

'Oh, no. I take medication for my arthritis and it knocks me out. I never wake until about ten. He's so kind, he always leaves my breakfast ready in the kitchen. I do feel spoiled, but he tells me I deserve it.'

'Aye, I'm sure you do. How does he travel to work?'

'He borrows my car. He loves it at the café, thrives on it, and he's ever so fond of Cherry, says she's a lovely boss.'

Ali ended the call, asking that Malcolm ring him as soon as he got home. He checked his blood sugar on his watch and saw that it was reasonable, so sneaked one of Patrick's pastries from the bag. Sheer bloody bliss, and the sugar rush made the world seem kinder. He tackled the next item on his list and rang Isbrook Academy, where he was told that Saturday's football training had been run by a company called Sports Mad, who'd used the academy's facilities. When he called their number, he learned that Karin Herron had been in charge of registrations and general administration on the day, but was now on two days' leave. He demanded her phone number and address from a reluctant receptionist and was given them after she'd consulted a manager. 'Like bloody drawing teeth,' he muttered to himself.

Ms Herron's phone went to voicemail. He left a message and then checked her address. She lived in Aldmarsh, not far from town. He'd escape this sweltering office and drive there, enjoy whatever hint of breeze he could find in the country lanes. He found his car keys, still tasting almonds and honey, and palmed a second pastry on his way out.

* * *

When she met Angus Fraser, Siv immediately saw Struan Hollis's resemblance to his uncle — similar build and shape of head. He was an imposing, handsome man with a large face, full mouth and jutting chin. His hair was dark and thick, swept straight back from his high forehead. They sat in his office on the ground floor of his huge house. A housekeeper had brought in a tray of coffee and thin cinnamon biscuits.

'Anything I can do to help, Inspector. This is too awful.'

'Thank you. How well did you know Luanna Forbes?'

'I suppose I'd sum it up as a casual acquaintance. I saw her occasionally when I visited Lansdown. I believe I once bought some hand cream from her as a gift.'

'Her shop's been successful, drawing in customers.'

'So I understand.'

He had a stolid, deadpan presence. His functional office, with no photos or pictures, gave little hint of his personality.

'Do you have much involvement with Lansdown Court?' Siv asked.

'Minimal.' He held up a thumb and forefinger a couple of centimetres apart. 'I placed it in Shona's hands and she gets on with it.'

'You have no particular interest in arts and crafts?'

He smiled. 'I'm a philistine, Inspector. My hobby is collecting vintage cars and motor racing. Lansdown is purely a business interest.'

Siv didn't want the coffee, but sipped some to leave a pause. 'Have you been aware of any tensions or problems at Lansdown, particularly concerning Lu Forbes?'

'If there were, I'd be the last person to find out. Shona's your best source for that. She hasn't mentioned anything to me.'

'But you wouldn't expect her to, because you leave her to manage things.'

'Exactly so.'

'Where were you between seven and nine o'clock on Saturday morning?'

He didn't hesitate. 'Here, at home. Friday night had been a late one, what with the party. Ali Carlin came along and enjoyed himself — I hope he had a clear head the next morning. I got up about half eight and started tidying.'

'You were doing that yourself?' She'd have expected staff to deal with menial stuff.

'Sue, my housekeeper, arrives at ten. I wanted to shift some of the debris for her.' He crossed his legs and hooked his hands behind his neck, flexing his wide shoulders. 'I might have staff, but I like to be considerate and I'm not incapable of a bit of housekeeping.'

'Can anyone corroborate that you were here between those times?'

'I was on my own. I can assure you that I wasn't sneaking out to kill Lu Forbes.'

'Noted. Do you see much of Shona and Struan?'

'Now and again. I go there for supper and we catch up. Struan's a fine lad — and talented. I was glad to be able to give them a home at the Dairy. Shona's husband abandoned them and life was a struggle for a while.'

'It was generous of you. The Dairy is a handsome property.'

'My generosity pays off. Shona is a reliable presence there, she's hardworking and loyal.'

'Lansdown is a good investment for you?'

'Absolutely. A sound part of my portfolio, generating reliable income.'

'What do you make of Jem Calloway?'

'I'm told that his work is highly rated and recycling is a very *zeitgeisty* activity. As a man . . . he certainly plays the part of the shambolic artist.'

It was the first interesting thing he'd said. 'Do you mean he's less disorganised than he appears?'

'I'm never quite sure. I'm not that friendly with him.'

'Friendly enough to invite him to your party,' she pointed out.

Fraser inclined his head. 'He's interested in vintage cars. We chatted about them one day at Lansdown. He promised he'd do me a portrait of my Citroen Cabriolet, but it never materialised. Still, there's something likeable about him, so I invited him along.'

'Shona didn't attend?'

'I did ask her, but she's not keen on parties and noise. And she wanted to ensure that Struan got to bed in good time, as he had a training day on Saturday. He has huge potential.'

'Thanks, that'll be all for now. Our crime-scene manager has advised that the shops can open again tomorrow and he'll advise Ms Hollis. Mr Calloway's will need to stay locked until it's cleaned. Yvonne Forbes can have access at any time now, as it's her business also.'

He stood and offered a brisk handshake. 'I'm glad that people can get back to work, it's for the best in this situation.'

For them, or for your income? Siv suspected he knew the answer.

CHAPTER TWELVE

The address in Aldmarsh was an end terrace on a row of six cottages. Karin Herron's was called Barna and had a pretty wreath of flowers on the white front door. Ali parked on the verge opposite and rang the doorbell. When there was no reply he tried again. Still no answer, yet the front top and bottom windows were open.

When he pressed the handle on the side gate, it gave way. He called, 'Hello?' and walked down a paved path, past a glazed side door and a water butt. Ahead, he could see a patch of lawn and flowerbeds with striped geraniums.

When he rounded the corner, he froze. A naked woman lay sunbathing on her front on a lounger, a visor shielding her forehead. Her head was turned from him, her ears plugged with the buds that trailed from the phone on the decking beside her. As he gaped, she raised her right foot and scratched the back of her left calf with it. He backed on to the side path, rubbing the sweat slick on his neck. Thank God she hadn't seen him. He'd have been in deep shit. At least he'd only had a back view, although that wouldn't have sounded convincing if she'd sensed him there and turned round. What to do? He could just slink away, but that would be a wasted trip, which wasn't acceptable in a murder investigation. He was rescued from his quandary when a snowy cat brushed past him and trotted round the corner. The next moment, the woman's voice sounded, fond and exasperated.

'Bloody hell, Boo, you gave me a fright. Pull those claws in, you little bugger!'

Ali seized his chance. 'Hello? Is anyone at home? Ms Herron? Karin Herron?'

'Stop! Don't come round here. Hold on!'

'I'll wait here, by the side door. I'm DS Carlin, from Berminster police.' He wiped his brow with his forearm.

She appeared after a few moments, barefoot, the cat in her arms. She'd thrown on a loose red beach dress with thin straps. Her expression was cross. 'It's usual to ring the doorbell.'

'I did, twice. I've tried phoning you as well.' He cleared his throat, which had become tight and sticky, and held out his ID. 'I saw windows open, so I guessed you might be in the garden on such a day. Best to lock your side gate if you don't want to be disturbed.'

'Oh. As you can see, I'm relaxing on my day off.'

Ali was suddenly glad of the glaring sun. She wouldn't clock his blushes. 'That's grand. Could I have a quick word? We're investigating the murder of Luanna Forbes.'

She fondled the cat's ears. Her visor cast a blueish tint on her face. 'I heard about that — awful. I didn't know the woman, so I don't see how I can help you.'

'I want to speak to you about Struan Hollis. He was at the football training day on Saturday. I called Sports Mad and they told me you're the person I need.'

She put the cat down and it sauntered under a bush. 'We'd better get out of the sun. Come round the back, to the kitchen.'

'Thanks,' Ali said gratefully.

The kitchen was small and cool, with exposed beams, a pine table and two chairs. A tall jug of cornflowers stood on the window ledge.

Karin took off her sun visor, fluffed out her dark, crinkly hair and opened the fridge door. 'You're on fire. Cold drink? I've apple juice, or water?'

'Juice, thanks.'

'Take a seat.' She poured two glasses, popped a tray of ice from the freezer and splashed cubes shaped like polar bears in each. 'Here.'

Ali held the cold glass in both hands. 'I'm sorry to interrupt your time off work. I understand that you organised the football training at Isbrook Academy on Saturday.'

'That's right. I set it up: venue, registration, programme and refreshments. It was a successful day.'

'How many people attended?'

'Thirty teenagers from schools across Sussex.' One of her straps slipped down her shoulder and she flipped it back.

'And did you check attendees in as they arrived?'

'Yes. Arrival time was from eight o'clock, with a continental breakfast between eight and nine. I handed them their name badge at reception, details of their group and a paper programme. I sent those out via email, but adolescents being forgetful types, half of them had forgotten to bring them.'

Ali reached for his phone and found a photo of Struan Hollis, which he showed Karin. 'This is Struan. Would you have a record of when he arrived?'

'Oh, him,' she replied drily. 'Cocky young man. He was late. I pointed out to him that he was the only person who hadn't arrived on time, and he came out with something smart about how he was worth waiting for.'

'How late was he?'

'I can tell you.' She reached for an iPad on the worktop and tapped the screen. 'He turned up at almost half eight. Told me he'd had a puncture that delayed him, but there was no apology. I was tempted to say that he was too late for breakfast, but I decided that'd be mean.'

Lansdown Court was about seven miles from Isbrook Academy. It shouldn't have taken more than half an hour for a fit young man to cycle. Ali had mended a fair few bike punctures in his day, and a running repair wouldn't take long. That left a lot of time unaccounted for. 'How did Struan seem? Was he upset at all?'

'No. A tad breathless, but then it was hot and he'd have been cycling fast to make up for lost time.' She scooped an ice cube from her glass with a finger and sucked it. 'Why are you asking about him? He's just a young lad who's full of himself. Attractive, very talented and knows it.'

'We have to confirm details of everyone who knew the victim.'

'Right. Struan is a skilled footballer. I watched him play. His is one of the five names we've put forward from the day, recommending extra coaching. He's on our "ones to watch" list.'

'You reckon he could make it professionally?'

'Oh yes, a strong likelihood — as long as he puts in the time and effort and winds down the conceit.'

Ali drained his juice. 'Many thanks. I might come back to you if we need any further information.'

'Sure, but that's all I can tell you. I'll get back to my garden now, but I'll take your advice and lock the gate.'

Ali's cheeks were growing hot again as he hurried to his car. Wait until he told Polly about his unexpected encounter. She'd laugh her head off.

* * *

Luanna Forbes's shop was stifling. Siv raised the blinds and opened the windows while Ali relayed his news about Struan Hollis.

'We'll catch up with him when we've finished in here,' she said.

They worked methodically through the shelves and drawers, finding nothing of interest.

'Just creams and lotions,' Ali commented. 'She must have kept all her accounts and stock records online. There are leaflets in this drawer — stuff about the company ethos and how the products are made.'

Siv came over to the counter as Ali flicked them like a deck of cards. A small card fell to the floor and she picked it up. The front featured an illustration of a tree, a bottle and a stack of newspapers, and printed down one side: *RECYCLE TODAY FOR A BETTER TOMORROW*. Inside was a handwritten message: *Let's continue recycling, we're benefiting the planet! xx*

She showed it to Ali and examined the back, but there was no information about the publisher.

'A message from an environmentally minded friend?' Ali suggested.

'Possibly, but it seems a bit odd to find it tucked away, as if it's significant. And why the kisses?' Siv bagged the card. 'Could be from Jem Calloway. We'll ask him and show it to Yvonne.'

Ali pointed. 'That's easily done. Here she comes now.'

When Siv opened the door, Yvonne was standing outside, seemingly a little lost and staring up at the sign over the shop. She stepped back, hand to her throat.

'Hi, Ms Forbes,' Siv said. 'We've just been checking the premises, but we're about to leave.'

Yvonne was coolly dressed in a cotton sunhat with the brim turned up, a pink crop top and loose Bermuda shorts. 'I wanted to visit, realised I'd better make myself. It's like I owe it to Lu or something. I need to do this and I want to check over the stock.'

Siv moved aside to let her in. Yvonne entered and paused by the bench holding tester samples. She opened a bottle, closed her eyes and sniffed. 'This grapefruit and rosemary was one of Lu's favourites. She liked more pungent notes.' Her voice cracked and she leaned on the bench. 'Don't mind me, I'm all over the place.'

Ali moved some testers from the bench, creating space. 'Sit down for a minute.'

'Thanks. I've been building up to this and reckoned I was ready.'

'Would you like us to get you a drink?' Siv asked.

'No, no.' She cupped her hands around her knees. 'I'll be fine, honest.'

They needed to speak to Yvonne again, so Siv decided to seize the opportunity and distract her from her grief. 'Could you do me a favour and look at this card? I'll hold it out for you. Please don't touch it. Do you recognise the handwriting?'

Yvonne stared. 'No. Where did you find it?'

'In the drawer over there. Was your sister particularly interested in recycling?'

'Only inasmuch as we tried to recycle as much as we could. Sorry, I can't help you.'

'When we first spoke, you told me that Lu wasn't seeing anyone, wasn't in a relationship. You're quite sure about that?'

'I'm sure. She'd have told me.'

'It's just that when I was searching in Lu's bedroom, I found some expensive lingerie tucked away. The kind that you might wear if you were meeting a lover.' Siv found the photo she'd taken and showed it to Yvonne.

She reddened. 'I could do with a drink now. There should be some water under the counter. Lu always kept bottles there.'

Ali found a bottle and brought it over to her. She unscrewed the top and gulped, spilling some on her neck.

'Did Lu mention the lingerie?' Siv prompted.

'No. I never saw it. Maybe it was from when she was with Bryan and she kept it as a memento.'

'Seems unlikely after a divorce,' Ali commented.

'I suppose . . . I've never been divorced so I can't say.' Yvonne dribbled water on her wrists and rubbed them together.

Siv flicked a glance at Ali. Something was making Yvonne uncomfortable and it was more than the heat or talk of lingerie. She crossed to the counter and rested against it. 'Jem Calloway told us that Lu didn't open the shop on June fifteenth and wasn't around at all that day, a Tuesday. Any idea where she was?'

Yvonne took off her hat and fanned her face with it. 'I don't recall her saying anything. Hold on.' She slipped her phone from her pocket and scrolled. 'I've nothing on my calendar for that day.'

'Lu didn't have any medical appointments, anything of that nature that might account for her absence?'

'No. I'm not much help.'

'We need to push on,' Siv said. 'Are you sure you're up to being on your own here?'

'Sure.' She gave a feeble smile. 'I'm calling in to see Shona when I've finished. She'll make me tea and patch me up.'

'We're just going there now, so give us some time.'

* * *

Outside, Siv turned to Ali. 'Yvonne seemed embarrassed when I mentioned lingerie and the possibility of a lover.'

'Aye. I'd say she's holding back.'

'We won't put any more pressure on her for now. It's gone four. Let's see if Struan's home from school. You can do the talking.'

Struan was home, sitting bare-chested at the table in the garden. He was busy on his phone and eating a large bowl of muesli. Ali reflected that he was seeing a lot of flesh today. Shona was hovering behind them as she showed them out to her son.

'Why do you want to see him again so soon? You've got what you needed, surely?'

'Sit with us,' Siv told her, 'and you'll find out. Hi, Struan.'

He raised a hand, still focused on his screen.

'I don't understand why the police are back, but they want to talk to you.' His mother sat next to him. She was flustered, her forehead shiny, and she kept tweaking the neck of her cotton dress.

'Right, yeah.' His phone pinged, he laughed and tapped the screen.

Ali reached over, snatched the phone from his hand and placed it on the table beside him.

'Hey! That's mine!'

'And you'll get it back as soon as we've finished.' Ali smiled. 'We need you to concentrate.'

Struan gave him a hostile stare. 'You sound like a teacher.'

'Teachers, cops . . . we're a pain. Just to recap. You left here on your bike at seven on Saturday morning, yes?'

'Yeah. I told you that. Have you got a poor memory?'

'And if my poor memory serves me right, you stated that you went straight to Isbrook Academy.'

'Yeah.'

'About a thirty-minute ride, yes?'

'About that.'

'I'd say you're the one with memory problems,' Ali threw in casually.

Struan fingered the golden down on his chest. 'Sorry?'

'I saw a Ms Herron today. She ran your training day on Saturday and she recorded that you arrived at half eight. You told her you'd been delayed because you had a puncture.'

'You didn't mention that, Struan,' his mother said anxiously. She turned to Ali. 'I expect he forgot after the excitement of the day, and then the shock when he came home and heard about Lu.'

'Well, Struan?' Ali tilted his chair forward and leaned on the table.

'Yeah, like Mum says, I must have forgotten. I got a puncture — a nail in the tyre, and I had to stick a patch on.'

'Where did that happen?'

He hesitated for a few seconds. 'About four miles from town — yeah, that's right.'

'Did anyone see you, anyone stop?'

'Dunno. Nobody stopped. It was by trees, a side road.'

'Struan always has a puncture kit with him, in a little rucksack,' Shona explained. 'I've always made sure of that, with the miles he cycles.'

'Almost an hour late. That's a long time to mend a puncture,' Ali commented.

'Fuck's sake! It was fiddly, all right?' Struan fidgeted, pushed his chair back, the legs grinding. 'Then I sat under some trees and had a drink of water, chilled for a bit, spent time on my phone.'

'Even though you'd be late for an important day?' Ali raised both eyebrows.

Struan drew himself up. 'There was no great emergency. The actual training didn't start until nine.'

'You'd been selected for this day,' Siv carried on. 'I understand that was quite an achievement. How come you weren't keen to get a wriggle on and show up?'

'No biggie. I was only going to miss some pastries and I was sure I'd ace the day.' He smirked. 'Why all the fuss?'

'Because you lied to us.'

'Misremembered surely, Inspector,' Shona leaped in.

'Yeah, you're right there, Mum,' Struan agreed. 'A lot happened on Saturday, my head was all over the place and I was, like, stunned after I got home and heard the news. Mum was upset. It was tough. I'd like my phone back now, *pretty please*. Don't want to accuse the police of theft.'

'I'm expecting Yvonne, so if you've finished your questions, I'll show you out.' Shona's mouth was a grim line.

'I want to see the puncture repair first,' Ali told her.

'And there is something else, Ms Hollis,' Siv said. 'Was Lu Forbes sometimes rather critical of your business?'

Shona bristled. 'How do you mean?'

'Homemade cakes and jam and the like. Someone commented that Lu found it a bit "Women's Institute". Is that correct?'

'Ouch, Mum,' Struan sniggered.

'I've no idea who's been saying such nasty things.' Shona was visibly upset. 'My produce is popular and sells well. If Lu had those opinions, she never shared them with me.'

'She did reckon your marmalade was a bit bitter,' Struan remarked slyly. 'I heard her tell Cherry.'

His mother stared at him. 'When was that?'

'Can't remember. Don't fuss, it was hardly headline news!'

'Well, all I can say is, it sold out and I had to make another batch, so it pleased most people. Bitter, indeed!'

Siv decided to leave the dissent over preserves there. Struan showed Ali the repair on the back tyre of his bike, smirking with hands on hips as the sergeant bent over it. They walked back to the car through the hot, sleepy yard.

'The tyre's been repaired, all right, and fairly recently, but that doesn't mean it was done on Saturday. I'd bet that Struan's a lying toerag, and he used the puncture from another day as a cover story.' Ali lit up a Gitane.

'Hard to prove. It does beg the question, what was he doing during that time? Perhaps he didn't leave straightaway on Saturday morning, but waited around and stabbed Lu, then set off.'

Ali leaned against the car bonnet. 'He could have accessed his mum's keys, got a copy of Calloway's. He might well have known about the set of knives and where to find them.'

'But with what motive? There's no indication that he had any quarrel with Lu Forbes and he seems wrapped up in himself. I'm baking. Let's head back.'

CHAPTER THIRTEEN

At the station, Siv checked her email and then waited while Ali poured water and Patrick propped the door open to let the air flow. She regarded them fondly. They were a tight little unit. Ali sometimes wound her up with his food obsessions, but he was a solid detective, and despite his laid-back persona he could act bad cop when needed. She'd enjoyed Struan's dismay when Ali had taken away his phone. Patrick was more mature and reliable since meeting Kitty. The improvement in his brother's life had also stabilised him. He could still be hasty, and she suspected that his ambitions lay outside of routine police work. He was tech-savvy and requested any training going on data analysis. She'd no idea what they thought of her, but they seemed to tolerate her and cooperate, which was all she needed.

'I've heard from Forensics,' she said when they were all seated. 'Jem Calloway's clothes are clear, so we can eliminate him as a suspect. He might be a womanising slob, Ali, but he's not a killer. The only decent fingerprints they found in the shop were Calloway's, Yvonne's and Lu's. We've established that all three of them had been in there. There were traces of others on items for sale, but that's to be expected from customers picking up stock. Patrick, what have you got for us?'

'Lu Forbes's car has no satnav. Bryan Hendrix stated that he and Lu had a civil relationship on the odd occasion when they met. He lives alone and was on his own on Saturday morning, although he has a new partner. There was something he wasn't saying, but I can't put my finger on it. I'm going to check in with Zara Lennard, his partner.'

'I got hold of Malcolm Hayler,' Ali said. 'He told me that he left home at eight forty on Saturday, driving back roads, and arrived at the café just on nine. There's no one to corroborate the time he left. He lives with his mum and she was asleep. He didn't notice anything out of the ordinary, and he wasn't aware that Lu Forbes had any problems. Struan Hollis is hiding something about Saturday morning, but unless we can prove otherwise, he was fixing a puncture and hanging out. Like all teenagers, he's surgically welded to his phone.'

'What's he like?' Patrick asked.

'Well up himself, talented at footie, could make it professionally,' Ali replied. 'Mum worships him and he enjoys pressing her buttons. He could do with better manners.'

Siv downed water. 'Struan bothers me. Even if he had a puncture, why would he loiter around after he mended it? Football is hugely important to him. I'd have expected him to push on, given the training day potentially offered big rewards for him, rather than playing on his phone, hooked on porn or gaming.'

'He is arrogant, though,' Ali said. 'He'd be the type to believe that he'd coast the training. How did you get on with Fraser, guv? Polly rates him.'

'Successful, poised man of business, beautiful house. He was home alone on Saturday morning, recovering from the party. He'd seen Lu occasionally, and meets Shona and Struan monthly for a meal. He expressed confidence in Shona — I'd guess that the relationship is that of benefactor and grateful recipient. He implied that Jem Calloway might not be as disorganised as he appears.' She gestured at the board. 'Day three, and we've just a lot of general chat and an impression that Lu saw herself as top dog at Lansdown Court. That could have riled someone, and although Shona denied it, she might well have felt undermined. We've no idea how Lu and her killer accessed Calloway's shop, or why. We need to dig much deeper into Lu's life and establish where she went on the fifteenth of June. Ali, can you show the card we found at Lu's shop to Calloway, and speak to Klara Boros, who should be back home now. Also, I want you to get Struan Hollis to take you to where he had his alleged puncture and talk you through how he spent his time. See if you can puncture his arrogance. Patrick, please chase the techies about Lu's laptop and phone, and get car registration numbers for all these people staring down at us, see if ANPR picks up any of them heading towards Lansdown Court on Saturday morning. Bearing in mind your impression of him, scrutinise Hendrix's movements and check with his neighbours. I want to ask about Lu's previous job as a driving instructor and revisit Cherry Bolting. I'd say she has more to tell us.'

* * *

Siv found Corran on his own when she called in on her way home. She'd apparently disturbed his supper, seeing a half-eaten plate of food beside a newspaper and an open bottle of wine on the huge elm table he'd made in his workshop.

'I've interrupted you, I'm sorry.'

'Not at all. Who likes to eat alone? Paul's having dinner with a friend in Brighton. Have you had supper?'

'Not yet.'

'Do stay and have some, then. Chicken-and-mushroom pasta. I made plenty, as always, so you'll be helping me out.'

There was sliced ham, wrinkled tomatoes and drying bread in her fridge. Corran's food was always delicious, his hospitality infectious. 'Well . . . if it means I'll be helping you.'

He laughed. 'Sit yourself down and I'll fix you up.'

She sat at the table, tracing a finger around a whorl in the wood. Corran and Paul aimed to be as self-sufficient as possible, making their own bread, growing fruit and vegetables and chopping logs in their acres of woodland. The pasta would be homemade. Corran ferried a large dish of steaming food over and then returned with a plate, cutlery and a glass. He was a small man with a neat beard, light on his feet and muscular. She had privately named him 'Nature Boy', because whatever the weather, he often walked around in shirt sleeves, oblivious to the elements.

'Help yourself to wine and dig in,' he invited.

She spooned food on to her plate, poured a glass of tawny wine and tasted it. It was rich and full-bodied, just what she needed. After a few mouthfuls of succulent chicken she exclaimed, 'This is wonderful! How are your girls?' It was how he referred to his goats.

'In fine voice and eating for England. I had a long chat with them earlier. They were very talkative.' Corran tapped the paper. 'I was just reading about Lu Forbes. Nasty business.'

'My other motive for visiting, as well as cadging supper, was to ask you about Lansdown Court. Did you know Lu?'

'We met now and again. She had a stall on the market on Saturdays at one time, selling her skincare products. It was how she got started, before she and her sister established the shop.'

Corran still sold his goods at the market every weekend. 'I wasn't aware of that. Was she on the market for long?'

'Just a couple of months, then she set up shop at Lansdown. Our paths crossed from time to time. She was a smart woman with a real talent for keeping up with her market. That shop was a great success.'

'Likeable as well as successful?'

'I liked her.' Corran always chose his words carefully. 'She was vocal about her achievements at the shop. I did wonder if that might grate with some. Her sister's quite different. Under the radar, self-effacing, but that's possibly why they did so well. A yin-and-yang set-up.'

Siv forked up the last of her meal. 'Thank you, I needed that.'

'I haven't made pudding, but there's fruit if you'd like some.' He gestured to a heaped fruit bowl.

'I wouldn't say no. And I'll have another glass of this amazing wine, if there's some going. It tastes expensive.'

'It is. Our friend Simon brought it with him the night before last. It's a Syrah, from the Valais, as he was careful to point out. Simon's a connoisseur. He'd be terrified to drink our homemade plonk.'

'I met him yesterday and enjoyed his air con. He told me that he rated Lu.'

Corran picked a peach from the bowl and quartered it deftly, holding a chunk out to Siv on the point of the knife. 'He did. He saw her as a real asset to Lansdown. Simon's pretty condescending towards some of the other traders there.'

'For example?'

'He reckons that Jem Calloway squanders his talent, and I have to say I agree. It's not much good when customers are put off by the alcohol on your breath.'

The peach was the taste of summer, fragrant and delicate.

'Simon's sniffy about Shona too,' Siv commented.

'Simon's a snob. He's a friend, but a little of him goes a long way. I make sure I get on with him because he sells my work, and very effectively. He isn't kind about Shona's home produce. He's always regarded Lansdown as an upmarket destination, and in his view, Shona lowers the tone.'

Siv savoured the last of her wine. The lights were dim, the dusky sky outside fading to damson and red. A moth danced around a candle in the centre of the table. She was drowsy and relaxed now. She pushed upright, blinking. 'Have you ever heard of any problems at Lansdown?'

'Nothing, and my grapevine's pretty healthy. Simon has been a bit concerned about another business venture. He mentioned it the other night.'

'What's that?'

'He bought some beach kiosks and he's fallen out with the people leasing them, because he's ending their tenancies.

He has plans for some kind of development. Actually, there's quite a lot on the Berminster Neighbourhood Facebook page. I was reading it earlier. The stream of comments must be making him hot under the collar.' He picked up his phone and scrolled. 'Here, see for yourself while I put the kettle on. Tea or coffee?'

'Tea for me.'

'Camomile, mint or builder's?'

'Builder's, thanks.'

Siv read through some of the Facebook posts.

CASSIA WADE AUTHOR

Please sign our petition to Berminster Council to save our Minster Beach kiosks and stop Simon Terrance from ruining our lovely heritage. The kiosks have been there since the 1930s. Mr Terrance wants to knock them down and build a 'well-being hub'. We need your support to prevent this appalling vandalism.

SUE MCKINTY

Signed! Awful plan to create mayhem on a peaceful beach!

DAN SINEK

Minster Beach could do with a bit of livening up. I like the description of what he's planning.

JESS SCHEPP

My mum always bought us lollies at the kiosks and I take my kids there now. Part of our heritage, so leave it alone.

LEWIS PAYNE

To be fair, the kiosks are a bit scruffy and an eyesore, seen better days.

DAN SINEK

Like you, mate!

CASSIA WADE AUTHOR

The kiosks are not scruffy! The tenants keep them well maintained. If you mean they're old-fashioned, that's deliberate and in keeping with the seaside ambience. Attached some pics of our recent protest on the beach. I'll be posting details of our next very soon.

TERRI ROSE

Petition signed. Just another businessman wanting to grab a piece of our heritage to make himself richer.

STEVE HEMMING

What's a 'well-being hub' when it's at home?

CINDY STAFF

That's my childhood, leave it alone!

And so it carried on, with comments running into the hundreds. Most seemed to side with the petition. Siv swiped through the photos and stopped at one, enlarging it. She forwarded it to Ali with a message: *Isn't the guy on the left holding a banner Malcolm Hayler?*

The group of kiosks was at one end of Minster Beach. Siv had been a frequent visitor to them in her youth and fondly recalled their pastel colours and striped awnings. They sold seafood, beach goods, ice creams and teas. They had a jolly, slightly ramshackle air, with a distinct whiff of nostalgia.

She clicked a link posted by Cassia Wade to a press article.

MINSTER BEACH DISPUTE

The tenants of Minster Beach kiosks are up in arms at the proposals of local businessman Simon Terrance. Mr Terrance bought the leases to the kiosks in 2021 and has given the tenants notice to vacate. Mr Terrance has applied for planning permission to knock down the kiosks and the Tide restaurant behind them, which he bought in 2019. His

*proposal is to build a well-being hub, which will comprise a
juice bar, yoga, tai chi and meditation studios, a children's
activity room and an arts workshop area, where musicians,
photographers and other creatives can hold classes.*

*When we approached Mr Terrance for comment, he
stated: 'The kiosks on Minster Beach are in poor repair
and have had their day. Many people comment that they are
unsightly. This is an opportunity to provide the area with a
modern, thriving, year-round hub that will offer huge benefits
to the community. The focus will be on well-being and self-de-
velopment. I appreciate that the tenants are disgruntled, but
I believe that my scheme will enhance the seafront and be
popular with visitors to the beach.'*

*Spokesperson for the tenants, Cassia Wade, whose
mother runs one of the kiosks, told us: 'These kiosks are
part of the Berminster landscape and heritage and in keeping with the seaside attractions of Minster Beach. They don't
just cater for visitors. Many local people come to the kiosks
every day. They are a focal point for older folk and those who
are lonely — a place to meet and pass the time. The proposed
centre will charge for access and deprive many of a much-
loved, inexpensive resource. Plenty of people like to meditate
and relax while they share a cuppa or an ice cream, they
don't need to pay a developer for the privilege! We intend to
fight this all the way and we urge people to sign our petition.'*

*We contacted Berminster Council for comment. Their
spokesperson advised us that the proposed plans can be
viewed on the council website or at the town hall, and the
public can register their views.*

'Simon Terrance isn't very popular,' Siv observed when
Corran handed her a mug of tea.

'I doubt that bothers him. He bought the leases with a
view to development and didn't expect to run into so much
opposition — "old-fashioned diehards who can't stand progress", he called them.'

'Did Lu have a view?'

'No idea. Maybe they'd discussed it.'

They chatted for a while and then went to see the goats, who jostled and butted them. Siv inhaled their feral smell and allowed Barbra to nibble at her sleeve. Corran spoke fondly to each of them in turn. Siv watched him and pictured his measured, predictable days, spent weaving, cooking, goat-tending and working the land.

There was a lot to be said for such a life.

She'd die of boredom.

CHAPTER FOURTEEN

Shona went to Jem's shop during her lunch break. She was awash with flushes today. They were like a constricting corset. She'd not slept well and she'd had a dizzy spell when she got up, but she needed to tackle him. She'd already left this for too long and Jem was no doubt laughing behind her back.

He was sitting in his usual disorder, ripping thin strips from a *Daily Telegraph*. Horrible, guttural music with a heavy bass thump was coming from his phone. The air smelled cheesy. His sleeveless vest had holes in. She had to tap him on the shoulder before he noticed her. No wonder his sales were so poor. He wouldn't be aware if customers were clamouring for attention.

'Could you turn that awful racket down, Jem?'

'Sure.' He switched it off. 'Sorry, I was miles away. I'm making a paper gun and it's fiddly.' He grinned up at her. 'What's your cake of the day? I might come and snaffle a slice.'

'Never mind that. You still haven't paid your rent.'

'Yeah. What with Lu and everything that's going down — kind of slipped my mind.'

'It hasn't slipped mine. I've given you several warnings.' It was hard to confront him while she was so self-conscious, aware of sweat sliding between her breasts. She could see herself reflected in his eyes — a fussy, red-faced, middle-aged nuisance.

'Yeah, so you have. Tell you what, I've nearly finished a collage for someone and that'll bring in three hundred.' He gestured at a piece of board standing against a wall, featuring a seated nude in profile, with his legs dangling over the side of a chair. It was half-covered in splashes of mixed colours.

'It doesn't look anything like finished to me.'

'I got distracted by this idea. I have to go where the flow takes me.'

He infuriated her. People indulged him and fell for his 'naughty boy' act. He coasted and did whatever he liked without a care in the world while she grafted hard, working her fingers to the bone and worrying about keeping all this ticking over. She ground her teeth and wiped her brow with the back of a hand. 'You owe three thousand pounds. Finishing that collage — if you ever do, if you don't keep getting *distracted* — won't begin to cover it.'

'Don't get worked up. I'll find a way. Don't worry, Shona, it'll sour your cake mix.'

'Don't speak to me like that! Just because some people here humour you, you needn't assume I'm going to wait and wait. I'm not taken in by your nonsense. I'm warning you that if you don't pay the full amount by the end of next week, you'll get a formal, written notice.'

He put the paper down, placed a hand across his chest and said meekly, 'I'll do my best, honestly.'

'Unless your best is what's owing, I'll be giving you notice to quit. I'll have no trouble renting this shop to someone who pays on time and doesn't mess me about. Understood?'

'Yeah. Can I get back to my work now?'

She glared at him and opened the door.

'You never told me what today's cake is!' he called.

She ignored him.

* * *

Klara Boros lived on the top floor of a six-storey block of flats encircled by dusty grass and dried-up flowerbeds. Inside the foyer, Ali eyed the staircase and pressed the button for the lift, reasoning that it was too hot to benefit from the exercise of climbing upwards. At least there was no chance of finding Ms Boros nude in the garden. Music vibrated through her front door, a rippling piano accompanied by lush strings.

A small woman with heavy eyebrows and strong shoulders answered his ring and invited him in. He followed her bow-legged walk into a small living room.

She turned the music down low and gestured to an armchair. 'It's so bloody hot! You want water?'

'No, thanks.'

She moved a chair to a slight angle and sat, her loose cotton skirt billowing around her. Her feet were browned and bare, with strong toes. She had the build of a gymnast past her prime. The air smelled vinegary and a bit off, although the room was neat and the windows had been thrown wide open. A little cloud of fruit flies drifted above her head and she batted them away.

'Blasted flies. I forgot to get rid of a couple of bananas before I went on holiday. I came back to them rotting in the bowl and these critters having a field day.' She laughed. 'I've been on a killing spree, but a few always escape.'

Ali brushed one from his hand. 'I need to speak to you about Luanna Forbes.'

'Can't believe it, frankly, coming back to this news. I mean, Lu was a life force.'

'Tell me about her.'

'She was bright, determined. Brimmed with energy. From the first day she moved into her shop, she fizzed with ideas about the business.'

'How did that play with everyone else at Lansdown Court?'

Klara eyed him. 'Is that a trick question?'

'Why do you ask?'

She smiled. 'I'm sure you've already been told that Lu didn't rate Shona's produce and thought that Jem was lazy.

She didn't hesitate to state her opinions. Lu told Jem to his face but she was more circumspect around Shona, given that she's related to Angus Fraser. Shona keeps tabs on everything, not much gets past her. She always seems to hear every little bit of tittle-tattle going around.'

'Did anyone dislike Lu enough to kill her?'

Klara clapped her hands over a fly. 'Hardly. Lansdown is a pretty sedate place — well, *was* until this happened.'

'How was Lu recently — did she mention any troubles to you?'

'No, but then we weren't mates, just swapped ideas now and again, bounced stuff off each other.' She folded her hands under her chin. 'I wasn't supposed to talk about this, but given what's happened, you'd better be aware . . . last month we had a discussion about me taking over her shop.'

'Lu was considering giving up the business?' It was the last thing Ali was expecting to hear.

'She seemed to be. I'm keen to expand mine, and she mentioned that she might move on later this year.'

'Did she say why? She was successful and her sister's involved with the shop.'

'I was really taken aback when Lu mooted it. I got the impression that she hadn't discussed it with Yvonne, which was odd. She didn't give a reason, and when I sounded surprised, she commented that she was getting a bit bored with it. She warned me not to say anything to anyone else while she worked it out. I didn't get my hopes up because it was just a chat, and I could see that she was weighing up the situation and testing the waters with me. I was keeping my fingers crossed, though, that she would decide to move on and I'd be able to have a second shop.'

'And she gave no indication about her reasons? It wasn't to do with anything being wrong at Lansdown?'

'She didn't say so. Seemed like a case of itchy feet. That was the only time she talked about it.' Klara wrinkled her brow and held up one finger. 'Lu did say something in passing about Struan a while ago, that he needed to be kept in line and his mum was too lenient with him. She was right, he is conceited, sees himself as the Adonis of Lansdown Court. His mother worships him, which doesn't help.'

Ali leaned forward. 'Was Lu referring to any particular incident?'

'Not that I recall. Struan swaggers around. He'd get on her nerves now and then.'

Ali could appreciate that. 'Did you see much of Yvonne Forbes?'

'Nice woman, a quiet sort. She works hard at making all their stuff. Bit of a lonely life for her, on her own all day. She's very proud of the shop, so I did wonder how it would affect her if Lu moved on.'

'She and Lu had a good relationship?'

'As far as I could tell.' Klara scratched the tip of her nose. 'I didn't see them together that often but, yes, they rubbed along well.'

The flies were bugging Ali. He swatted one away from his eyes and showed Klara a photo of the card they'd taken from Lu's shop. 'Do you recognise this handwriting?'

She reached for a pair of glasses and focused. 'It's not familiar. Is it important?'

'Possibly. Thanks, anyway.'

Klara saw him to the door. 'Hang on, Sergeant.' She reached up and flicked the top of his head. 'Sorry, you had a bug trapped in your hair. I'll have to get a spray. These flies are a real pest and they're everywhere.'

Ali made his escape, shaking his head in case any more fruit flies were opting to hitch a ride with him.

* * *

Patrick didn't usually mind door-knocking, but it was no joke in this heat. He'd had no luck with finding any of Bryan Hendrix's immediate neighbours at home. He downed half a bottle of water before he crossed the road and showed the photo of Lu Forbes to the thirtyish man who opened the door opposite. He was relieved to see a nod.

'I recognise her, yes. She's the woman who was found murdered, isn't she?'

'That's right. Have you noticed her around at all?'

'I saw her leaving from over the road a while ago, and I remembered buying shampoo from her on the market. It was a bit pricey, but lovely stuff, really gentle.'

The man had an intensity about him, a gleam in his eye that made Patrick step back a pace. 'When you say over the road, where do you mean, Mr . . . ?'

'Bhatt, Nilan Bhatt. She was coming from Bryan Hendrix's place.' He pointed.

'Can you remember when that was and what time of day?'

'Was she a friend of Bryan's?' Bhatt folded his arms and leaned against the door.

'If you could just try to remember . . .'

'Difficult to be precise. I'd say around early May, late afternoon. I was putting up a new blind at the front window and I saw her come out and get in her car.'

'Did you see Mr Hendrix?'

'Just her. Are you the DC Hill who tweets?'

'That's right.'

'Great to meet you. So, is my seeing her important?'

'It's hard to say. Was it just the one occasion?'

'That one time, yeah.'

'Did you happen to notice Mr Hendrix around last Saturday morning?'

'I was at a stag do in London Friday night, didn't get home until early afternoon on Saturday.' Bhatt grinned, showing sharp little teeth. 'Is Hendrix a suspect? This street could do with a bit of livening up!'

'Just making enquiries. Thanks for your time.'

Patrick beat a hasty retreat, this nugget of information warming him as much as the sun. Bryan Hendrix had some questions to answer.

* * *

Keira Durham had spent a couple of days debating with herself. Maybe she should tell the police. It might mean something or nothing, but given the circumstances, this kind of thing might backfire. She still got shivers when she recalled that evening, which was ridiculous. She was twenty-eight years old and he was just a kid, albeit a tall, muscular one. Keira had been terribly fond of Lu, and was deeply upset by the violence that had ended her life. The shock of hearing about Lu's death gave her a nagging headache and made her absent-minded. She kept burning food and forgetting where she'd put things.

The decision was taken out of her hands when the inspector turned up at Come Drive With Me on Tuesday morning. It was stuffy in the office, which smelled of plug-in air freshener. (Customers were often nervous while they waited for a lesson, some of them a bit whiffy; BO and bad breath were the driving instructor's burdens.) Keira had switched on the fan and the percolator and just despatched the first two lessons when a woman came in. Tall, in a dark-grey suit and amber T-shirt, with a green leather bag hooked over her shoulder. She introduced herself as DI Drummond in a clear, precise voice.

'Are you the manager of the driving school?'

'That's right. Keira Durham.'

'I need to speak to you regarding Luanna Forbes. Have you heard the news about her?'

'Yes. It was an awful shock.'

'I understand that she used to work here.'

'She did, yes.' Keira glanced at her watch. 'I have a lesson booked at ten thirty. Should I postpone?'

'That's up to you, but I doubt that you need to.'

The inspector smiled and Keira was reassured. She realised that she'd been standing with her hands clenched and opened them, flexing her fingers. 'Please, sit down. Would you like a coffee? I've just brewed some.'

'Thanks.' She sat, placing her bag by her feet. 'Did you know Ms Forbes when she worked here?'

'I joined the year before she left. I'd just qualified.' Keira poured coffee into two mugs. 'Please help yourself to milk and sugar. I'm afraid I'm out of biscuits.'

DI Drummond added milk and stirred her drink. Keira watched her long fingers gently agitate the spoon in the mug. She had the impression that the detective would take her time. The fan was stirring wisps of dark hair across her forehead and she nudged them back.

'Would you prefer it if I stopped the fan rotating?'

'No, it's a relief. Who else worked here with you and Ms Forbes?'

'Baz Barnes. He owned the school. Baz retired a while back and I bought him out. I employ two instructors, but they didn't work here in Lu's day.'

'How did you get on — you, Baz and Lu?'

'Fine. We were a good team. Baz had heart problems, so he left most of the training to me and Lu. She was an ace instructor with this amazing energy. I learned loads from her. She won awards.'

DI Drummond put a hand over some papers on the desk that were fluttering in the breeze from the fan. 'You didn't find Lu bossy or arrogant?'

'Here, let me move those papers, they're a nuisance.' Keira switched the fan down. 'Lu was direct and spoke her mind. I liked that.'

'How about the customers? Did they always like that?'

Keira felt a bit cornered, as if her words had been misconstrued. 'No one complained about Lu, if that's what you mean.'

'A person learning to drive might be quite nervous. They might benefit from a subtle approach.'

'Well . . . yes, you have a point. Lu was fair but firm. All I can say is that the customers appreciated that, and she had an excellent record for passes at the first attempt, almost one hundred per cent. And that's what people want, isn't it? To pass their test.'

'I passed the second time. Sounds as if I needed Lu as my instructor.'

The inspector smiled again, a tired lift of her mouth. She'd be working all hours. The sun was at the back of the office, so it was still in shade and the fan hummed steadily.

'So, Ms Durham, as far as you're aware, Ms Forbes hadn't fallen out with anyone when she worked here.'

'That's right.'

'And did you maintain a friendship after she left here and started her cosmetics business?'

'We kept in touch, yes. We had lunch now and again, and I bought my moisturisers from her.'

'I'd like a contact for Mr Barnes, if you have it.'

'Oh, Baz died only months after he retired. That seemed so unfair, that he had no time to relax and enjoy life.'

'Perhaps his work kept him alive.'

'His wife said that to me.' Keira's mouth was dry. She sipped her lukewarm coffee and licked her lips. 'Inspector, there's something I should mention.'

The detective folded her hands in her lap and nodded encouragingly. Keira listened to the comforting *whump* of the fan and eased her shoulders down.

'I was at Lu's shop one evening last year, just before Christmas, buying gifts. There was a little event at the court — mulled wine and mince pies, that kind of thing.'

'The season of good cheer and retail therapy.'

'Exactly. A young man, a teenager, came in while I was choosing gifts. He started trying out the testers and asking me which scents I preferred, holding out his wrist for me to sniff. He was knocking back mulled wine. I asked if he should be drinking alcohol and he winked. He was engaging and friendly, and told me that his name was Struan. We chatted for a bit and he helped me take my stuff to the counter. Then I started talking to Lu and he vanished. When I'd put my purchases in the boot of my car, I found him beside me, asking if I needed a hand. I said, no thanks.' Keira was flushing with heat, thinking back. She reached a hand out towards the fan. 'It was dark, around five o'clock. Before I knew what was happening, this boy was kissing me roughly,

116

his hands clamped on my bottom. I shoved him away and told him to leave me alone — something like that, anyway.'

'And did he?' Inspector Drummond asked.

'Yes, but he laughed in my face, he wasn't the slightest bit apologetic. He was nasty, quite threatening. He said—' she shook her head — 'he said that I tasted good, but he'd had better. Then he sauntered away. I got into the car and drove home, not quite believing what had happened. I've had men come on to me with unwanted advances, but never a boy!'

'Did he try to contact you?'

'No, thank goodness! The whole thing was so strange. I did wonder about seeing if I could find his parents, but in the end I decided I'd rather forget about the experience. He'd been drinking and perhaps that had made him act in that way. I mentioned it to Lu sometime later when we met for lunch. She explained that Struan had just turned fifteen and lived at the Old Dairy with his mother. She told me that he was spoiled and indulged. She was very cross about it, and said that if I wanted, she'd raise what had happened with Struan's mum, but I told her not to. I'd persuaded myself by then that he was a young, testosterone-fuelled boy, a bit drunk, experimenting and being foolish.' She touched her hot cheeks. This was so excruciating. 'I didn't want to cause trouble, and it occurred to me that he might attack as a form of defence, turn the story around and say that I'd grabbed *him*. There was something deeply unpleasant about him there in the dark, quite different to the charmer who'd joked with me and helped me with my shopping. It was as if he'd had a personality change. If he decided to turn the tables on me and claim that I'd made sexual advances to him, I'd be in a pickle. I mean, you read about such instances, where allegations are made, and even where they're unproven or found to be false, the adults concerned lose their jobs and reputations.' She slumped back, drained now that she'd relived the incident.

The inspector straightened her mug, tracing a finger down the stripes. 'Might Lu have mentioned this to Struan's mother, despite your wish that she shouldn't?'

'The last time I saw her was in April, for a coffee. She didn't refer to it, and neither did I. I decided that I should tell you in case it was of any significance.'

'You were quite right to. Did Lu seem troubled about anything in April?'

'No. She looked well.'

The inspector stood and moved closer to the fan. 'Did Lu ever discuss her divorce or her ex?'

'Not recently. She'd refer to seeing solicitors sometimes when we worked together, but she didn't tend to refer to her home life.'

'Was Lu seeing anyone? In a relationship?'

'She didn't say that she was. She seemed to be focusing all her attention on the business.'

The detective sat down again, fixed her eyes on Keira's. 'You could still make a complaint about Struan Hollis's assault if you want to. It's not too late.'

'Oh . . . no . . . that's the last thing I want to do.'

'Up to you, naturally. I'd encourage you to consider it.'

'I realise why you're saying that, but I just want to put the incident behind me, forget about it.'

The inspector widened her eyes in a way that communicated, *We both know that's not likely to happen anytime soon*. She placed a card with her details on the desk as she was leaving, saying to contact her if anything else came to mind. Keira blew down the neck of her blouse, pulled the fan nearer and closed her eyes for a few minutes. She didn't feel as relieved as she'd expected. Keira had never been convinced by the commonly held wisdom that talking about problems eased them.

CHAPTER FIFTEEN

Siv chucked her jacket into the car. She'd parked in the shade of a tree and rested against its trunk for a moment, reflecting on what she'd learned about Struan Hollis. If he'd assaulted Keira Durham, it was likely that he'd behaved similarly with other girls and women. She emailed Ali and told him to check if Struan's school had any concerns about him. She was lost in thought when her phone buzzed and she read a text from Bartel.

Can you come round? Your mother and Rik are here shouting at each other and I can't get them to stop.

Her worst fears realised. She replied quickly.

On my way.

She drove straight to the house, gripping the hot wheel tightly, wondering what she was going to walk into. She'd witnessed many fights between Mutsi and Rik over the years and she'd hoped that those days were long gone. When she rang the bell, she heard Bartel thudding down the stairs. He opened the door and drew her in, his huge hand on hers.

'Madame, thank goodness!' He was dressed in work clothes — stained jeans, old denim shirt and stout boots — and he smelled tarry.

'What's going on?' She could hear raised voices from the back of the house: 'Fucking bitch' from Rik, followed by Mutsi yelling, 'How dare you!'

Bartel was built like a tank and his powerful bulk filled the narrow hallway. He gripped her hand in both of his huge paws, the calluses on his palms ridged against her skin. She'd never seen him agitated before, his English fracturing under the strain.

'I work here today, insulating the loft. I'm minding my own business when I hear screaming. I come down and Mutsi and Rik are in the kitchen, rowing. I try to get them to stop, but they don't listen.' He grasped his pointed beard. 'If men fight, I know what to do. But women . . . I go back and hide in loft.'

'Maybe I can join you.' She heard something smash. Instantly, she was taken back to childhood and the regular ding-dong battles between her mother and sister: she quaking in a corner with nausea filling her throat, while Rik needled and her mother grew shriller and broke something. 'Mutsi throws things when she's angry,' she explained, hoping that it wasn't one of Bartel's beautiful stoneware plates.

'Can you get her to stop? I like my kitchen.'

'I'm so sorry about this. I did try to warn you that you might be inviting trouble into your home.' She pressed his fingers. 'I can try.'

He raised her hand and kissed it. 'My angel of rescue. I wait upstairs.'

Siv went through to the kitchen and yanked open the door. Both women were standing, Rik with her back to the sink, Mutsi gripping the table. The room was filled with her mother's heavy scent and the heat of anger. Siv was glad to see the shards of a cheap white china mug on the floor.

'What's going on?' She immediately corrected herself. 'No, I don't want to know. I just want you to stop this.'

'Your sister has been posting nasty, sarcastic comments on my blog,' Mutsi hissed. 'Hiding behind some silly name, being hurtful. Same old Rik, unable to grow up. She's come back here to cause trouble.'

'Hang on, isn't that your forte?' Rik asked.

'What do you mean?' Mutsi was flushed, some of her golden hair escaping its chignon.

'You turned up here from Finland and all you've done is swank around, making waves for Siv. You always did do your best to torment her and she could never stand up for herself. I mean really, shagging her boss! Tasteless or what?'

'How *dare* you!'

'Oh, play a different tune,' Rik told her, the joy of battle lighting up her eyes. 'Why don't you bugger off back to Scandinavia and leave us in peace? We always had to look after each other as kids and nothing's changed. You're older, with more wrinkles, but you're still a nasty piece of work.'

Siv tugged the back of her hair. It was as if she'd walked on stage to reprise her role in a familiar drama, one that had been running for years. The Drummond family version of *The Mousetrap*. And as usual, she was the mouse.

'You should show me some respect,' Mutsi cried.

'I can't come up with one reason why.' Rik folded her arms.

'For heaven's sake, because I'm your *mother*!'

'We all have our crosses to bear,' Rik goaded with pure malice.

The two of them were capable of keeping this up for hours. Neither had ever been willing to cede ground. Arguing fuelled them. Siv's own anger sparked. All those long years of watching these two and listening to them tear pieces out of each other. How blissful it had been when they'd lived on separate continents! How foolish of her to believe that her peace would last.

She could hear her phone ringing in her bag. *Enough.*

'You both need to show some respect.' She stepped forward, keeping her voice low. 'Bartel is my friend and this is his house. I'm ashamed that you're here, rowing and embarrassing him. Take it somewhere else. You can beat each other's brains out for all I care. Just don't do it here.'

Her mother's mouth dropped. '*Sivvi!*'

Rik stared at her, then clapped slowly. 'Good for you, and about time.'

'No, don't do that, Rik,' Siv said sharply. 'Don't pretend I'm taking sides here. You need to leave, Mum. Rik lives here — for now, anyway. If I was Bartel, I'd tell you to pack your bags. Why aren't you at work?'

'Day off.'

'Skiving, more like,' Mutsi spat. 'You never could hold a job down, Rik.'

'At least I make a living working, rather than lining up sugar daddies and earning a crust on my back.' Rik sniggered.

Mutsi shielded her face with her hands. 'How can you speak to me like that?'

'Truth hurts, Mother,' Rik replied with mock sadness.

'Stop!' Siv pointed to the front of the house. 'Go home, Mutsi. I've work to do, even if neither of you have.'

'You are both just . . . *ungrateful*,' her mother said. 'I can't believe that my daughters have grown into such selfish, uncaring women.'

'We had you as a role model,' Rik threw at her. She opened a cupboard, found a dustpan and brush and bent down to sweep up the smashed china.

Mutsi put her hands up to tidy her hair, picked up her bag and left without another word, slamming the front door so hard, the house quivered.

Rik emptied the shards of mug into the rubbish bin and poured herself a glass of water. 'Didn't mean to piss on your chips, sis. Mutsi stormed in with all guns blazing about her sodding blog. She never could take a joke. It's just too easy to press her buttons. The good old days, eh?'

Rik had always got round her, cajoling, enlisting her in the fight against their mother. Siv didn't want to be on that battleground again. She opened the back door and breathed the viscous, drowsy air.

'Maybe it's time to grow out of your jokes, Rik. What does it say about you, that you need to wind her up? She's such an easy target, it can hardly be satisfying. Do me a favour and apologise to Bartel.'

'He's cool, nothing rattles him,' Rik said airily. She saw Siv's expression and held her hands up. 'Fine! I'll make it up to him.'

Siv went upstairs. Bartel was sitting in the loft opening, his feet resting on the ladder, his bald head shining in the dust motes floating down. He resembled a Norse god who'd wandered into suburbia.

'Mutsi's gone, it's safe to come down. You'll have noticed the house shivering.'

'Thank you, Madame. I'm so sorry to have called you from your work. I had no idea what to do. I suppose I could have just left them to fight it out, but it didn't seem right.'

'No, I'm sorry. That was awful. I worry that I've helped to bring a horrible blight into your home.'

He peered down at her, turning one of his gold earrings. 'Took you back to your childhood?'

'And some! Do you really want to let Rik stay on now?'

'Families. They quarrel.' He shrugged. 'I like Rik, we get on well. And to be fair, you did tell me I might be taking on trouble.'

'If it's any consolation, I doubt that Mutsi will come here again. Rik always bested her in these kinds of arguments and she'll need to lick her wounds.' She crossed her fingers behind her back.

'She should learn not to call the wolf out of the woods.'

Her phone was ringing again and she needed to see Cherry Bolting. 'I have to go. Catch up soon?'

He raised a thumb and shuffled back into the space above.

* * *

Struan Hollis idled out of school pushing his bike, chatting to a girl who was flicking her hair back and giggling.

He'd taken his tie off and tied it around his head, pulled his shirt outside his trousers and was dangling his blazer from one shoulder. Ali reflected on Siv's message about the boy's behaviour with Keira Durham. The head of the school had reported no concerns about him, no complaints from pupils or parents. Some teachers found him egotistical, even for a teenager, that was all. But there might well be girls here who were too nervous to speak up.

Struan's animated expression switched to surly when he saw Ali waiting. 'What's this? You stalking me or something?'

'If I was inclined to stalk someone, I wouldn't choose you. I want you to come with me and show me where you mended your puncture on Saturday.'

'I told you that already!' He rolled his eyes for the girl's benefit.

'You gave a vague account. I need specifics.'

'*Specifics*.' He mimicked Ali's accent. 'What about my bike?'

'In the boot. Then you can cycle home.'

'What if I say no?'

'You'd be in trouble for obstructing a police enquiry and it wouldn't play well for your footie prospects.'

Struan preened to the girl. 'If I vanish, make sure you tell everyone I left with this threatening paedo.'

In the car, Struan just grunted when Ali checked where they were heading and started playing a game on his phone.

'Put your phone away and pay attention,' Ali ordered after a few minutes.

Struan muttered but slid the phone in his pocket and glanced around. 'Turn left at the next crossroads.'

Ali turned and drove along a narrow road bordered by grassy strips and deep hedges. Struan hummed, clicking his fingers.

'D'you not get tired, playing to the gallery all the time?' Ali snapped.

Struan narrowed his eyes. 'What's that mean?'

'Doesn't matter.'

'Just there.' Struan pointed. 'By those trees.'

Ali pulled in. 'Out of the car, then, and talk me though it.'

Struan left the door hanging open, clasped his hands behind his back, planted his feet apart and adopted a monotonous tone. 'I was proceeding towards the training day on my bicycle, Officer, when I became aware that I had a puncture. I dismounted from said vehicle on the verge, just about here. I mended the aforementioned puncture and then I adopted a seated position under that tree, where I played on my phone and partook of a liquid beverage. Then I continued on my journey to Isbrook Academy.'

Ali refused to react to the mockery. 'And no one passed by during that time?'

'That's correct. No pedestrians and no vehicles.'

'Seems a bit unusual.'

'This is a quiet cut-through, that's why I use it.' Struan gestured and grinned. 'There are cows in that field. One of them might have seen me, but I doubt that they're reliable witnesses.'

Ali stared at him. 'Struan, this is a murder enquiry and the woman who died was a friend of your family. Your manner's a tad distasteful in the circumstances.'

'I'm fed up of you lot going on at me. It's not fair. I've told you what I can.'

Ali had had enough of him. He told him that he could go home and watched him cycle away. He didn't believe him. Struan might well have mended a puncture around here at some time, but not last Saturday.

Ali fetched a bottle of water from the car, sat under a tree and drank. A cow's head appeared over the hedge, chocolate brown with cream markings. It munched steadily, observing him.

'If only you could talk,' Ali called.

CHAPTER SIXTEEN

Siv sat with Cherry Bolting under the awning outside the Buttery. They both had glasses of freshly squeezed carrot juice with ginger. Siv was trying to make the most of the zing on her tongue, hoping it would keep her alert. Her head was still full of the scene at Bartel's house and she was struggling to focus. She pictured a brush sweeping through her brain, clearing out the Mutsi and Rik debris. It helped a little.

She opened her notebook, more as a prop than because she needed it. 'Have you worked here since Lansdown Court opened?'

'That's right. In at the beginning.' Cherry was wearing a short, skimpy dress with a lemon pattern and chain straps. Her upper arms were plump and freckled. She was smiley today, her generous lips, outlined in dark plum, curving upwards.

'And you said it's generally a happy community, a good place to work.'

'Yeah. I'm very happy here.'

Siv recalled the message from Patrick about Lu Forbes's visit to her ex. 'I get the impression that Ms Forbes was more complex than people have been saying.'

Cherry hit the pause button on her smile. 'How do you mean?'

'Did she ever mention Bryan Hendrix?'

'Her ex? No . . . I mean, only in passing. I gathered that she was divorced.'

Siv had an intrusive image of Mutsi's tight knuckles gripping Bartel's table. She sipped some juice and rolled her neck. 'What about other relationships? She was young and single.'

'She didn't talk about seeing anyone. Yvonne would be able to tell you about that, I suppose.' Cherry was eyeing two women who were strolling around, pausing by shop windows. 'They've been here for a while now, but they haven't bought anything. I'd say they're rubberneckers, rocking up to absorb the drama.'

'That's inevitable, I'm afraid. Has Struan ever caused any problems here? Any complaints about him from colleagues or customers?'

Cherry continued to monitor the women. She pulled at one of her straps. The chain had left little oval indents like thumbprints in her skin. 'He's a bighead, no doubt about that. He caused a bit of nuisance with his skateboard one time, but he only uses it around here now when the shops are closed.'

Siv sensed a headache growing. It was shady under the awning, but the sun was baking and the tension she'd absorbed earlier was pulsing in her temples. Had Rik apologised to Bartel? What if Mutsi had already returned for another bout? She cleared her throat. 'Did Lu have an opinion about Simon Terrance's beach development? I'm sure she must have. It's causing quite a stir locally.'

Cherry turned back to her, her smile in place again. 'Ah, you've heard about that. Simon's not popular with some. I reckon it's a great proposal.'

'And Lu?' Why did she have the impression that Cherry was avoiding direct answers?

'She was giving Simon an earache about it one day, saying that it would disrupt the traditional atmosphere of the beach. I could see he was taken aback. I was surprised that she wasn't keen on it, given that she was all for business opportunities, but then Lu grew up here and she was dead proud of the town, so I suppose she was sentimental about it — "hands off my childhood territory", kind of thing. Simon and me are blow-ins, so we have a different take on it.'

Siv hadn't noticed Lu's name on the Facebook page, but there were hundreds of comments. 'Did Lu sign the petition against the development or add to public debate?'

'No idea, but she might well have. She was upfront with her views, so it would be in character.' Cherry blew her fringe up. 'Wow, it's too hot to think!'

Siv took the hint, privately agreeing that the heat was distracting. She wasn't finished yet, though. Malcolm Hayler had been on a protest at Minster Beach and had posted several comments on the local Facebook page, so she told Cherry she had some questions for him.

He appeared quickly, deftly wiping a table on his way past. A small man, suntanned, wiry and cheerful, wearing a T-shirt saying *Reading the Waves* teamed with black Bermuda shorts. He'd brought two packets of crisps out and waved one at her enquiringly. She waved a hand.

'I need the salt, or at least, that's what I tell myself. Really, I love the vinegar.' He pulled a bag open and started crunching.

'Are you a surfer?' Siv pointed at his T-shirt.

'Well detected! Not round here that much, though. The surf's not so great. I go to Brighton mostly.'

'I suppose there's more of a buzz there.'

He suppressed a yawn. 'Sorry, been a long, warm day. Sure, Brighton's livelier.'

'But you want to maintain sedate Minster Beach as it is.'

He looked puzzled, and then snapped his fingers. 'Oh, you mean the protest against Simon's development.'

'You've attended demonstrations about it.'

'It's not against the law. Why are you bringing that up? I presumed you wanted to talk to me about Lu.'

'You're vocal in your disapproval of the development, and so was Lu. She'd signed the petition. Did she attend any protests?'

'I didn't spot her at the one I went to. We didn't discuss it that much. Lansdown Court wasn't united on the issue, if that's what you're getting at.'

'How did Mr Terrance react to your opposition?' Siv finished her juice.

'He didn't raise it with me, but he did get antsy with Lu about it.' Hayler paused, pulled a tissue from his pocket and blew his nose.

'Go on. How antsy?'

'Lu had copies of the paper petition in her shop and Simon got to hear about it. I heard him telling her that it wasn't appropriate to have them in her workplace and if she didn't remove them, he'd complain to Shona. She got miffed with him, but in the end she agreed to lose them.'

'Sounds like that was heated.' The crisp-crunching was getting on her nerves. Siv was relieved that he'd almost finished them.

'Yeah, it was one of those hissed, angry conversations.' He grinned. 'I quite enjoyed it. Things are usually staid and unruffled around here. They were in the yard by her shop one evening when I was leaving work. There was no one else around and they were so into it, they didn't notice me. Simon's pretty stubborn and so was Lu. Two immovable forces. I was surprised when she caved.'

'Why was that, in your view?'

Hayler blew his nose again. 'Sorry, hay fever. I talked to her the next day. She'd weighed it up, and it was more important that the business ran smoothly and she kept good working relationships here. Lu was canny like that.'

'When was this argument?'

'A few weeks back. I can't remember exactly. Simon might have complained to Shona anyway. The woman who heads up the petition came here one day, wanting to speak to him. He wasn't in, so she was moaning to Shona about him.'

'Is there anything else that you can tell me?'

'Like what?'

'Someone was so mad with Lu Forbes, they killed her. Any ideas?'

'None.'

'How did you and Lu get on?'

'Fine.' He held the end of his nose and sniffed. 'I served her coffee and sarnies, we'd pass the time of day. We touched on the Minster Beach issue now and again.'

Siv let him go back to his duties. Hayler had no alibi for Saturday morning, but she couldn't see that he had any motive for killing Lu. If anything, they'd had a cause in common.

She stretched and headed back to the station for a meeting.

* * *

Patrick was on the phone, making rapid notes, swivelling in his chair. He grinned and made a victory sign to Siv as she came in. She swallowed a couple of paracetamol while she waited for him to finish the call.

'What's he so excited about?' she asked Ali.

'Sounds like useful information. Got a headache?'

'Hm.'

'It's this heat. Everyone's knackered and grumpy.' Ali's forehead was shiny and his shirt was hanging out, with damp patches around the armpits.

'Are you telling me I'm grumpy?'

'A bit. But join the club.'

'Patrick's annoyingly cool and alert.'

'Oh aye. That's his genes. Or maybe his hair gel.'

Patrick slammed the phone down and punched the air. 'We've got Struan Hollis nicely boxed. That was a Ms Alfonso, a Tesco delivery driver. She saw Struan talking to Lu Forbes around seven fifteen on Saturday morning. Well . . . she identified Lu from the images she's seen, and she reported that a young, tall, blond guy in a navy tracksuit with a bike was with her. Lu was standing by her car and he was sitting on the bike.'

'Where was this?' Siv asked, forgetting her throbbing head.

'On Goose Lane, about five miles from Lansdown Court. Ms Alfonso was travelling in the opposite direction.'

'I could tell he was a wee liar,' Ali said.

'I'll enjoy seeing how Struan deals with this when we confront him with it. Let's sit and go through what we have.' Siv recounted her conversation with Keira Durham. 'We've learned that Struan can be sexually aggressive. Anything from his school, Ali?'

'Zilch. Just the usual story of arrogance. I got nothing more from him when we went to the site of his supposed puncture. Just the usual load of cheek. But now we've established why he was delayed, or at least part of the reason.'

'Yes, part of it,' Siv agreed. 'Did they quarrel about something during that meeting on Goose Lane? Perhaps he followed her back to the shops and stabbed her. But he's not the only male that Lu Forbes was meeting, is he, Patrick?'

Patrick went through his encounter with Bryan Hendrix's neighbour. 'Bit fishy, Hendrix not mentioning that Lu visited his house. I contacted Zara Lennard, his current partner. She confirmed that they've been seeing each other for about eighteen months and she made it sound as if everything's sweet between them.'

'Where does she live?' Ali asked.

'Near Hove.'

'Not exactly on the doorstep, then. She wouldn't be aware that Hendrix was seeing Lu again.'

'Recycling!' Siv's head had suddenly cleared. 'Has anyone recognised the handwriting on that card we found?'

'No luck so far,' Ali said.

'I bet it's Hendrix's and refers to them meeting up again, and the relationship being recycled. Why else would Lu have been at his house?'

'The flame was reignited?' Ali looked doubtful.

'It can happen.'

'Bennifer, for example,' Patrick declared.

'Who?' Ali asked, mystified.

'A famous Hollywood couple who've got back together. You need to keep up with celebrity gossip,' Siv told him. 'Thank goodness, we're making headway now. What else have we got?'

'Nothing suspicious on cars travelling on Saturday morning,' Patrick chipped in, 'but I've checked and there are quite a few side lanes that you could use to drive to Lansdown, avoiding cameras. So that can only take us so far. I'm still waiting for Lu's phone records and access to her laptop.'

'I saw Klara Boros,' Ali told them. 'She said that Lu Forbes had been disparaging about Struan's attitude, so it certainly sounds as if there was bad feeling there. Also — and this could be a major headline — Lu told her a while back that she might give up the shop later this year, because she was getting bored. Klara was interested to hear that, because she'd like to expand her business. It was nothing definite, but it's the first we've heard of Lu having any doubts about staying at Lansdown.'

'That would have had huge implications for Yvonne,' Siv said. 'She relied on Lu's marketing acumen and the way she fronted the business. She's given no indication that she was aware that Lu felt that way.'

'It seems to have been under wraps.' Ali popped chewing gum in his mouth. 'Klara told me that Lu asked her to keep shtum about the conversation, so she did. We have Lu considering a major life decision without sharing it with her business partner. Has to have been about more than being jaded with the shop.'

'Yes,' Siv agreed. 'Especially as everything else we've heard has indicated that she was passionate about the place. It must have been connected to the second time around with Hendrix. This is certainly an important line of enquiry now. And we have another interesting bit of info.' She reached for a bottle of water and described Simon Terrance's proposed development at Minster Beach and the opposition to it, including that of Lu Forbes. 'There's a lot of traffic on the Berminster Neighbourhood Facebook page.'

'Noah's been involved in that,' Patrick said. 'He was at a demo on the beach — "hands off our kiosks" and handing out leaflets. He waxes on about it. Personally, I reckon those kiosks are a bit of an eyesore, but Kitty agrees with Noah.'

'So, Patrick, could you go through the Facebook posts and see if Lu contributed? According to Ms Bolting, she and Terrance disagreed over it and he chose not to mention that to us. Malcolm Hayler overheard them arguing about Lu promoting the petition in her shop.' Siv rubbed her hands together, energised. 'Good, we have a sudden glut of information concerning Struan Hollis, Terrance and Hendrix. The three of them have been concealing things from us. Busy day tomorrow. Let's sort out our next moves and escape from this oven.'

When they'd wrapped up the meeting, Siv decided to head for home and lie on the riverbank under the green canopy of the trees. She'd paddle in the Bere and cool her feet and brain. She checked her email before leaving and saw that Forensics had found no DNA traces on Lu's lingerie, which had been laundered. She'd just picked up her bag when her phone rang and DCI Mortimer said he needed to see her.

She climbed the stairs, aware that she was flushed and grubby. Mortimer had a portable air-con unit in his office and was parked at his desk, staring at his computer screen. It was so cold in the room, she shivered at the startling contrast. Siv assumed he wanted an update on the investigation, so delivered a quick summary of progress so far. He listened, nodding and pushing back a cuticle. He was proud of his shapely hands and kept a manicure set on his desk.

'Thank you, DI Drummond, that all sounds productive. Ahm . . . well . . . let's see . . . I had a call from your mother a little while ago. She sounded terribly upset. Distraught, in fact.'

'Oh dear.'

'Yes.' He gave one of his trademark sniffs. 'She said that she'd visited your sister, who'd been horrible to her and, ahm . . . your mother seemed to believe that you'd sided with Rik.'

Siv's headache was inching back. Mortimer was moving things around shiftily, avoiding her eyes. She couldn't help feeling a flash of pity for him, ending up in the Drummond family soap opera. He was like an innocent wanderer in the dark forest, one of those victims who featured in a book of Finnish tales that Mutsi used to have. Ajatar, an evil spirit, would lie in wait in the dense, forbidding trees and devour unwitting prey: lost children, woodsmen, hunters. She wanted to tell her boss to run while he had the chance, board *Quicksilver* and steer over the horizon. She was hot, tired and utterly fed up. Not in the mood for diplomacy.

'I don't want to get involved in this, sir. My mother and sister were arguing at Bartel's house. He was keen for me to intervene. I did, through embarrassment at the insult to his hospitality. I don't take sides. They're both as bad as each other. I preferred Berminster when neither of them were here.'

'Oh, goodness, that's quite . . .' Mortimer reddened. 'I realise that your family has its problems . . .'

'With respect, sir, you have no idea.' Siv got up. 'I've had a long day and there's lots of possible breaks in this case. I'm not responsible for my mother or my sister. Maybe they should just book a boxing ring and slug it out.' She'd never spoken so plainly to him and she'd regret doing so.

He opened his mouth, closed it, turned his face to his flickering screen. 'Thank you, DI Drummond. Have a good evening.'

'And you, sir.'

In her car, she consoled herself with the fact that she was heading home to the flowing river, the quiet of a solitary evening and a tall glass of iced akvavit. Mortimer would be facing tears, recriminations and sulks, especially if he didn't demonstrate enough sympathy.

She definitely had the better deal.

But when she reached home, she found it hard to settle, the row she'd witnessed earlier replaying in her head and stirring memories. She had a cool shower but still felt hot and restless. Had Rik really written and told their father about

134

Mutsi's neglect of them? If so, why had he failed to act? Rik lied so much and so easily, she could have made that up on the spur of the moment, or wanted to believe that she had informed him. Now she'd planted the seed in Siv's mind, suggesting that their father, who Siv had adored, had been less than honest in his dealings with them.

She opened the fridge, stared at the akvavit, decided no. Instead, she soothed herself by focusing on the origami project she was making for the main reception at Berminster hospital. She hadn't been able to work on it while Rik was staying. She had to be alone to fold. The project comprised of a series of twenty amino acid chains. She worked late into the night, her fingers making minute twists and adjustments, her mind fully occupied with translating paper into shapes.

CHAPTER SEVENTEEN

Struan Hollis came to the police station for a voluntary interview, sporting a smart school uniform and smelling of cypress.
His hair and skin gleamed. He'd opted to have Angus Fraser
present as an appropriate adult. Siv wondered how that had
played with his protective mother. Perhaps Struan had decided
that she'd be more of a hindrance than a help in this formal
setting, or that Fraser would be an influential presence. She'd
told Ali to lead on the interview, wanting to exploit his and
Struan's mutual antipathy.

'Now, Struan, can I make sure that your phone is
switched off for this interview?' Ali smiled.

'It's off. My fans will have to wait.'

'That's the ticket. We needed you to come and talk to
us in case there's anything else you'd like to tell us about last
Saturday morning — something that maybe slipped your
mind when you were upset?'

'Like what?' Struan stuck his hands in his pockets.

'That sounds like a trick question.' Fraser was sitting
close to Struan, a stolid figure in grey linen.

'Not at all.' Ali was genial, soft-voiced. 'Struan did say
previously that he was worn out by Saturday's events and

hearing about the murder. It's important to set the record straight, if that's needed at this point.'

'Fine, but no need to go round the houses,' Fraser replied.

Struan's smile had faded to half-beam. 'Ask me a proper question and I'll answer it, if I can. No promises.'

'Try this, then,' Ali said. 'What were you wearing when you left home on Saturday morning?'

'A navy tracksuit. From Diesel.'

'With a green stripe across the shoulders?'

'Yeah.'

'Were you wearing it when you got home?'

'No, I kept my football kit on after training.'

'Where's the tracksuit now?' Ali asked.

'I put it in the laundry basket for Mum to wash.' Struan's tone indicated boredom.

'You see, it's not too painful to just give straightforward answers,' Ali commented. He leaned back, crossed his legs. 'And what were you discussing with Ms Forbes around a quarter past seven on Saturday morning?'

Struan went to speak, then paused. 'I wasn't discussing anything with her. Like I keep telling you, I was on my way to training.'

'Not according to a witness who's come forward. You were seen on Goose Lane with Ms Forbes. She was standing by her car, you were sitting on your bike. The witness described you.'

Struan's lips morphed into a scowl. 'They must need glasses.'

Angus Fraser shifted in his chair but stayed silent.

Ali referred to his notebook. 'Our witness reported, "He was a young, tall, blond boy in a navy tracksuit with a green stripe on the shoulders." Unless you have a twin who was out riding his bike at the same time, this sounds like you, Struan. If necessary, we could arrange an ID with the witness.'

'What if it's someone lying and trying to cause trouble for me?' Struan pouted his lips.

'Why would anyone do that?'

'Could be some loser who doesn't like me. Maybe jealous of me for some reason — could be 'cos of my footie achievements. I dunno. It's weird.'

Ali said patiently, 'The weird thing here is that you'd come up with someone fabricating such a story. This witness isn't one of your school friends, Struan. It's an adult who's never heard of you.'

There was a silence. Fraser looked at Siv, his mouth twitching. She maintained a blank expression.

Fraser turned towards Struan. 'If you need to tell them something, best to do it now.'

'Good advice,' Ali said.

'No need for the drama. It wasn't like it was anything important.' Struan huffed. 'I didn't mention it because it was just Lu being bossy and stupid.'

'Expand on that,' Ali invited.

'What a fuss about nothing! I was cycling along, minding my own business and she was coming towards me and she stopped.'

'This was on Goose Lane.'

'Yeah. Lu pulled in and got out of the car, yelling that she wanted a word. She started banging on about one weekend when I was playing my music around the place, griping that it was too loud and a couple of customers commented. I promised to be a good boy in future, and she told me I'd better or she'd speak to my mum. Then she drove on to Lansdown.'

'How long did this conversation take?' Ali asked.

'Five mins, max.' Struan glanced up at the ceiling. 'Then I had the puncture and I had to stop to fix that.'

Siv leaned forward. 'You do understand, Struan, that lying to the police is a serious matter. Tracking Ms Forbes's movements on Saturday morning is crucial to our investigation.'

He stuck his chin out. 'I told you, it was all a load of nothing. Lu wanted to have a moan about my music. So what? It didn't seem to matter much.'

'I'm sure that Struan does realise that he was wrong not to have mentioned this.' Fraser straightened his tie. 'He's young and I suppose he's been rather foolish regarding the matter, but that's no excuse. I expect he'd like to apologise. Yes, Struan?' He put a hand on Struan's arm.

'Yeah, sorry. Didn't mean to mess you about,' Struan muttered.

'Is there anything else that you haven't considered important enough to tell us?' Siv asked sharply.

'No. Can I get back to school now? I've got exams soon and I might miss important stuff.'

When they'd gone, Siv and Ali went out to the garden and stood in the shade.

'Struan wouldn't know the truth if it bit him.' Ali lit a cigarette and drew on it deeply.

'I agree, but we've got nothing to place him at the scene of the murder. We can check his tracksuit, but I'd bet that his doting mum has washed it by now. I'd like to discover what he and Lu were talking about. I'd wager it wasn't music.'

* * *

Angus Fraser dropped Struan at school, maintaining a stony silence during the journey. He then drove to the car park near the coastal path. He changed into shorts, T-shirt and trainers, pulled on a hat and set off towards Cliffdean Point. The sea was glassy and there was the faintest whisper of a breeze.

Like Edith Piaf, Angus didn't really do regrets. Life was too short, and his personal mantra was 'ever onwards'. However, nowadays he had growing misgivings about Shona. He'd told DI Drummond that all was rosy at Lansdown because you didn't air family problems or give yourself a bad review. The reality was less upbeat.

When he'd offered Shona the management of Lansdown Court, he'd ignored the golden rule of never mixing family with business. Angus usually resisted the temptation to get involved in other people's lives or do good, and he cursed the day he'd given in to it. He'd been sorry for Shona and overestimated her abilities, assuming that as she'd been a successful manager at Reed Shoes, she'd have transferable skills. And she wasn't a bad manager, just blinkered and pedestrian. Sometimes she had a stupefied look, as if she were elsewhere. Her homely products weren't really what Lansdown was about. Lu had collared him on the subject when he'd visited, commenting that Shona's shop wasn't exactly high end, and Simon Terrance had indicated similar sentiments.

Lansdown was ticking along, making modest profits when it should be a gold mine. It needed drive and initiative, a manager with edge and vision. Shona had turned out to be a competent plodder. Angus's problem now was that he'd dug himself a hole and he was annoyed at his stupidity. Shona loved living at the Old Dairy, never stopped singing its praises. Uprooting her would be tricky, but he'd have to do it. That business could soar in the right hands.

Angus stopped to watch razorbills swooping to their cliff nests, reflecting on the visit to the police station. Classic Struan. His fingers had itched to clip the lad around the ear. What a disappointment he'd turned out to be. Angus didn't care for him, or the way his mother spoiled him and let him get his own way. When Shona's husband had done a runner, Angus had entertained ideas that he could be a substitute dad, a male role model. Struan had been an engaging, bright child with a cheery take on life. Angus had never found a woman he wanted to settle down with and fatherhood seemed an unlikely prospect, so he'd focused on Struan. It had helped that the boy looked so like him, and, at first, mentoring him had been a satisfying endeavour — pleasurable even. But as the years went by, Struan had turned into a self-serving young man, full of himself and insolent. *Entitled*, that was it, and slippery too. Angus disliked Struan's guileful smile and his expectation that everything would fall into his lap. Yes, he was a gifted football player, but Angus doubted that this would come to anything because Struan didn't put the gruelling work in. Angus had tried a pep talk with him now and again in recent years, explaining that hard graft was needed to back up natural talent, and citing his own road to success as an example. He had an aptitude for commerce, but he'd started with a tiny bank loan and put in long hours to build his businesses. Struan always listened quietly, smiled his polite, languid smile and thanked him for his advice, saying that he'd take it on board. Angus suspected ridicule.

He walked on, pulling his hat down further over his neck where the skin was beginning to tingle. Angus was aware that we all lie many times every day; it was human nature, and he could fib as easily as the next man. But Struan's lying bothered him. It was on another level. The lad was bright enough to realise that you shouldn't mess with the police, yet he hadn't told the truth until he was cornered, and even then, Angus wasn't convinced that he'd been totally honest. He'd seen the same impression in DI Drummond's eyes. What was Struan concealing? It was bad enough having a murder at Lansdown. The possibility that a relative might be involved was the stuff of nightmares.

Angus picked up his pace despite the heat, trying to sweat away his irritation at the predicament he'd got himself into.

CHAPTER EIGHTEEN

Patrick accepted a glass of iced fizzy water from Bryan Hendrix. He was working from his living room, his laptop on the sofa beside a pile of drawings and diagrams. It was a spacious, square room, painted milky white and teeming with plants. Hendrix noted Patrick's gaze.

'I'm a sucker for houseplants, a bit of an addict. I can't drive past a garden centre without checking them out — I'm like a kid in a sweet shop.'

Patrick smiled politely. He'd never given much attention to indoor greenery, although he had memories of his mother polishing the glossy leaves of a huge plant that blocked a corner of the kitchen. When Patrick was little, Noah had told him that the holes in the leaves were caused by mice who nibbled them at night — hence its name, cheese plant. Patrick had believed that story for years, and sometimes he'd get up in the early hours and creep down to the kitchen to see if he could spot the mice. His mum had found him early one morning, crouching by the table. She'd taken pity on him and explained that the holes were how the plant grew. Suddenly the plant wasn't so interesting.

He dragged himself back to the present. 'Mr Hendrix, we've received some information about Ms Forbes that I need to check with you.'

'Oh? How can I help?'

'She was seen leaving your house one afternoon in early May. That doesn't fit with what you told me previously.' An ice cube bobbed against Patrick's lip, making it ache deliciously.

Hendrix had a sip of his water. 'Ah. That complicates things.'

'In what way?'

'Nobody likes being caught out.'

'It happens quite frequently when the police are doing their job.' Patrick didn't bother concealing his impatience. He had no truck with time-wasters.

'Fair point, DC Hill. I suppose that, deep down, I anticipated this. I'm a pessimist and I'm right to be.'

Patrick left a useful silence. A woman pulled up in a car a few houses down. A loud rhythm thudded for half a minute or so until she turned the music off.

'Full disclosure, then.' Hendrix smiled weakly.

'It's usually for the best.'

'Right. Lu *was* here. We'd got back together. It was completely unexpected. I hadn't seen her for ages and then we crossed paths in the shopping centre at Easter. We had a coffee and . . . it's hard to explain . . . something just clicked. We fell in love all over again. Crazy but true. We were both blown away by it.'

'That must have been overwhelming.' Patrick was trying to imagine it. It would, as Ali might well say, mess with your head.

'Yes. Not in the life plan at all. Maybe we'd both grown up a bit, or realised subconsciously what we'd been missing. Who can tell? We tried to analyse it, but in the end love isn't explicable. I couldn't see Lu at her home, for obvious reasons, so she came here when she could, or we'd meet at a hotel. We didn't like deceiving them, but we wanted to tread carefully. Just before . . . before Lu died, we'd agreed that we'd tell Yvonne and Zara later this summer.'

That ticked off the lingerie and strange moods, Patrick thought, and the times Lu had been missing from work. 'Did you send Lu a card at her shop, saying that you should continue recycling?'

Hendrix's face relaxed. 'Yes, that was from me. She enjoyed the pun.'

'What were your plans for the future?'

'We wanted to move away from here, make a fresh start by the coast. Kent, hopefully. Lu was getting pretty jaded about Lansdown Court. She didn't rate Shona's management or the stuff she sold, and she said that Jem Calloway's shop let the side down. Lu had had big plans when she opened there, but despite her own success, the venue wasn't living up to her expectations.' He winced. 'Lu did agonise letting down Yvonne, because she'd need her share from the boat and she'd be giving up the business. That's why I didn't tell you, you see. I didn't want Yvonne to find out now, or Zara. It hardly seems fair — cruel and pointless too, in the circumstances.'

And it saved your skin, Patrick reflected. Was Hendrix going to carry on with Zara now? There might be a different version of this tale, one where Lu had been keen and rushing to make plans, whereas Hendrix had developed cold feet and decided to rid himself of a problem.

'Did either of you tell anyone else about this rekindled relationship?'

'Goodness, no! We tried to be circumspect, to spare people's feelings. We wanted Yvonne and Zara to hear about it from us. Clearly, we weren't careful enough.' He grimaced. 'I'm sorry I wasn't honest with you before.'

'Do you know anything about Ms Forbes's death?'

'No! I've been racking my brains, going over the last few months, in case Lu said anything that might have indicated any problems, but nothing comes to mind. I may not be showing it, but I'm lost, completely lost. The woman I truly loved has gone after we were offered a second chance. That's hard, especially as I can't talk to anyone about it. Except you.' He leaned forward, hands dangling between his legs. 'Zara has been sympathetic about Lu's death and I'm being such a shit. I don't have a clue what to do about her. I am fond of her but . . .'

Patrick peeled himself off the chair. His shirt was sticking to his back. 'I expect we'll need to talk to you again.'

Hendrix walked him to the door. His breath was sour and hot. Up close, Patrick could see the exhaustion in his face.

'Will Yvonne have to find out?' he asked.

'I can't say at this point. I'll be in touch.'

* * *

Siv answered Patrick's call as she parked at the harbour.

'Guv, I've just seen Hendrix. He and Lu had rekindled their relationship in recent months. She was planning to leave the business and move away with him, but she hadn't told Yvonne.'

'I'm just about to visit her.'

'Will you mention it?'

'I'll work around it for now. Thanks.'

She walked slowly along the path to the *Scarlett O'Hara*. Lu's plan would have been devastating for her sister. Had Yvonne somehow got wind of what she was up to? There was nothing to suggest that.

On the boat, she watched Yvonne decant shampoo into bottles. She worked carefully, steadily, nudging her glasses up her nose with her inner arm.

'I'll just finish this, if you don't mind,' she said.

'That's fine. It's a lovely scent. What is it?'

'Eucalyptus and pine.'

Siv was enjoying the shade. All the blinds were down, blotting out the glare. 'How have you been?'

'Hard to answer. Bit absent-minded. I almost forgot to add the almond oil to a soap mix yesterday. I made a rainbow soap, first time.' She leaned down to a box. 'Here, have one.'

It was oval, in layers of red, orange, blue, green and yellow. 'How pretty, thanks. Is it very complicated to make?'

'Not really. You just have to be patient and let it set properly.' She sighed. 'Lu had the idea that we should do a small range for kids. She canvassed customers and they were keen. The rainbow soap was the first product we agreed. I kind of made it for Lu, in her memory.'

'That's lovely.'

'Have you any idea who killed her?' There was a tremor in her voice.

'We're working on it.'

Yvonne capped the bottle, wiped around it and ran the cloth through her fingers. She sat, folding her legs beneath her, lifting the hair off her neck.

Siv made a careful approach. 'Did you and Lu see the business as a long-term prospect?'

'Yes, we were in it long haul and both really hopeful. I was the happiest I've been in a long time. I hated my job at the shoe shop. Working on my own here suits me, and it's been satisfying to produce stuff that's so popular.'

She sounded earnest and honest. Siv said gently, 'Someone we've spoken to suggested that Lu might have been contemplating giving up the shop.'

Yvonne raised washed-out eyes. 'That's nonsense. Who's been saying that?'

'Lu hadn't indicated anything like that to you?'

'Definitely not! She was always developing new ideas — we discussed them constantly. Whoever told you that must have got the wrong end of the stick. I hate the way people gossip, especially at a time like this.' Tears welled, trembling on her lower lids.

'I'm sorry that you find this upsetting. There's another thing I need to check. Did Lu see anything of Bryan Hendrix?'

'I told you before that she'd moved on from him, made a new life. Why would she have wanted to see him?' Yvonne shifted her legs to the other side of the chair. 'Lu didn't have a good word to say about him during the divorce. She said he was a bore.'

'What did you make of him?'

'I didn't spend much time in his company. He was pleasant enough. A bit bland. Why are you asking about him again?'

'We have to check everything. Did Lu ever talk about Simon Terrance's proposed development at Minster Beach?'

'She wasn't keen on the beach being developed. She didn't say that much to me about it. I didn't have strong opinions either way. Why, is it important?'

'It's part of the picture.'

Yvonne chewed at a nail. 'Lu loved the beach and the way it's not been commercialised with loads of tat. She was upfront with Simon about it.'

'How did he take it?'

'Not sure. Lu remarked that he hadn't expected such strong opposition. He's trying to push it through, though. Simon won't back down, he's not the type.'

'What type is he?'

'A slick operator, according to Lu, and used to getting what he wants. I'm not sure he'll be successful about the beach plans, there's lots of people up in arms about it and the council's pretty keen on conservation.'

Siv had a couple of final questions. 'Tell me a bit more about Struan. You've been friends with him a long time.'

'He's like a little brother to me. I'm so fond of him. I've always loved hanging out with him and Shona. We have a lot of fun.' Her voice dripped with nostalgia. 'Winter's always been my favourite time with them, when we hunker down in the living room with the fire burning, playing board games.'

Siv was once again struck by Yvonne's lack of maturity. She could picture her and Struan larking around while Shona cosseted them, ferrying scones and cakes. 'I've heard that Lu told Struan off sometimes.'

'She could come across as a bit strict. She'd grumble about his music and his skateboard. I'd tell her to lighten up. He's still a kid, after all.'

Siv left her to finish her shampoo. Back in her car, she raised the soap Yvonne had given her to the light. It was

147

delicate and precise with even layers. Her distress about her sister was apparent and it must be hard working in the place where they'd lived together, surrounded by memories.

* * *

Siv bought a raspberry lolly at Sunny Sam's kiosk on Minster Beach. Her father had favoured Sunny Sam's, saying that their ice cream was perfectly soft and rich. She'd often stood in the queue with him on summer days, struggling to choose between a strawberry cone with chocolate sauce or a minty tub. Her dad always had a basic vanilla; *no need to gild the lily*. He'd been a man of simple tastes, liking plain food, his academic books and rambling. Siv had often speculated on how the bespectacled scientist and the flamboyant dancer had ever got together, and she always settled on the same image: her father had been a rabbit, caught in Mutsi's headlights. She had no memory of Rik being with them on the beach. Her sister would have been busy shoplifting or smoking pot with her mates. Siv clocked the message chalked on the blackboard next to the cold shelves.

PLEASE SIGN OUR PETITION TO STOP THE DESTRUCTION OF OUR TRADITIONAL KIOSKS. YOU CAN ALSO SIGN VIA FACEBOOK, ON THE BERMINSTER NEIGHBOURHOOD PAGE.

'How's your petition shaping up?' Siv asked the woman serving her.

'It's going well. Over ten thousand signatures last time I checked.' She indicated a clipboard on the counter. 'Have you signed?'

'I'll do it online.'

'Make sure you do, otherwise our lovely beach might be ruined.'

'Have you met Cassia Wade? I've seen her name on Facebook.'

'She's my daughter. She's heading up and coordinating our protest. She's a real trooper!'

Siv ate her lolly sitting on the sea wall. She understood why people were up in arms. This was a traditional family beach, unchanged for generations. It shelved gently to the waves and it had a genteel, timeless quality, a contrast to the clamour of Brighton. The kiosks were part of people's families, familiar and reliable, like cousins or aunts you visited occasionally.

Her phone pinged with a message from Simon Terrance, informing her that he was available now. She finished her lolly and licked her fingers. Terrance had been in meetings at the Tide restaurant all afternoon, and she'd agreed to speak to him there, wanting to gauge him in different surroundings.

She walked up to the restaurant, having to admit that it had seen better days and lacked the whimsical charm of the kiosks. She'd never eaten there. Polly Carlin reported that it served awful microwaved rubbish. The white cladding was stained and worn, the windows were spattered with salt and grime and the door handle was tacky to the touch. Inside, it was almost empty. Just a couple of pensioners, a woman with a baby in a pushchair and tinny country music in the background. All the furnishings were a marmalade-coloured fake oak.

Terrance was in a warm office off the kitchen, looking startlingly out of place in tan linen and tasselled loafers. He hadn't exactly lost his cool, but his curls were limp and his mouth dipped grumpily. A fan was redistributing the smell of fried food.

'No air con here,' Siv remarked, sitting on a worn plastic chair.

He grimaced. 'I won't offer you a coffee, it's dire.'

'If your plans come to fruition, that situation will improve.'

'And it can't be too soon! It's embarrassing, having my name on the deeds of this place.'

'That's why I wanted to see you. Your proposed development is causing feathers to fly.'

'That's to be expected. I'm confident that I'll win. But why does that interest you?'

'Because I've heard that Lu Forbes was against it, and had told you so. At one point, you had a heated argument about Lu placing the petition in her shop for customers to sign. You didn't mention it.'

'I didn't see any reason to. We had an exchange of views, and afterwards, Lu saw sense and removed it.' He steepled his fingers. His pale eyelashes made his eyes seem naked.

'I did ask if there were any problems at Lansdown Court.'

'Inspector, it wasn't a problem. I was taken aback that Lu didn't favour my scheme. I suppose I'd taken it for granted that she'd be all for it. She made her views clear, I told her I was disappointed and we left it at that.'

'Very civilised.'

'Yes, as it should be among colleagues.' He crossed his legs. 'I respect that some people want to keep the beach unchanged. Brits do have this odd hankering for the past. Those sunny days when you could leave your door unlocked, everyone was a good neighbour and the local bobby stopped for a natter. Days when tinned fruit salad and evaporated milk were a big treat. Nostalgia.' He dragged his fingers through his curls. 'I don't buy into it, and I believe that there are more people like me than the yesteryear brigade.'

Despite his assertion, he was growing rattled, his voice shriller. Might be worth goading him.

'I wouldn't underestimate the swell of opinion. Berminster's a town with a traditional heart.'

He pointed at her. 'What's *your* opinion?'

'I'm here as a public servant. I don't have an opinion. So, you and Lu Forbes didn't fall out any further over the issue?'

'No. Once I was reassured that she wasn't encouraging protestors through her shop, I accepted that she had her own views.'

He was plausible. 'You must be investing heavily in this proposal, what with buying the buildings and getting plans drawn up. Will you make a big financial loss if the development isn't approved?'

'Some, but that's the nature of risk-taking. In the end, I can still turn this restaurant around or submit altered plans. There's always another option.'

He had an answer to everything. 'What do you make of Struan Hollis?'

'Can't say I've ever paid him much attention. Handsome, and knows it. Very confident and chatty. That's about it.'

'Did you ever have the impression that he'd fallen out with Lu?'

'Seems unlikely, as Yvonne's a close friend of his mum's. She used to stay overnight at the Old Dairy quite often at one time.'

Siv couldn't come up with any more questions, so she wrapped things up and headed to her car, wrinkling her nose at her T-shirt, which now reeked of cooking fat. Ali phoned as she got behind the wheel.

'Guv, Cherry Bolting appears to be missing. She left the café around one o'clock, telling Malcolm Hayler that she needed to pop out for an hour. She hasn't been back and she's not answering her phone.'

'Who contacted you?'

'Hayler. Cherry didn't give any reason for going, but she had a phone call about half an hour before she left, and she seemed worried. Hayler closed the café as usual at five and went home.'

Siv checked the time. Just gone half five. Cherry hadn't been gone for long, and would hardly be classed as missing in usual circumstances. But she might be involved in a murder. 'Get Patrick to contact her phone provider and see if we can get a trace on her. I'm on my way back to the station. Are you there?'

'Aye.'

'We'll phone around the other people at Lansdown, see if any of them can throw light on where she's gone.'

* * *

Siv called it a day at 10 p.m. Cherry Bolting's phone was switched off and the last signal had been around the town centre. No one at Lansdown Court could say where she'd gone and none of her friends had heard from her. Uniform constables had visited her home and reported that her car was parked outside, but her flat showed every sign of being empty. Siv contemplated Ali and Patrick, who were both worn out and listless from the heat. A fly was circling a dried wedge of the takeaway pizza they'd ordered mid-evening.

'We can't go down the official misper route just yet,' Siv said. 'Let's hope she's surfaced by the morning. If not, it gets formal.'

After they'd gone, she tidied up, turned the lights off and stood at the window, opening it wide to catch the breeze. It was laced with the marshy tang of low tide. There was still a dim, rosy glow in the sky. She ran over what they'd learned about Lu Forbes. An independent, focused woman, skilled at business, not big on humour. Apparently devoted to her sister, but deceiving her and making plans that would affect her life. Lu had argued with Simon Terrance, disapproved of Jem Calloway's habits and told off Struan. But this was more of a silhouette than a full picture. Was Lu's murder connected to Cherry Bolting's vanishing act, and if so, how? A car horn blared in the street below, followed by loud laughter. She roused herself, gathered up her things and headed home.

Back at the wagon, Siv tried Cherry Bolting's phone once again, with no luck. The wagon was suffocating, her pores clogged. She threw off her clothes, wrapped herself in a towel and headed through the purple dusk to the silent river. The Bere was so shallow now, there was just a foot of water. She stepped out of the towel and lay down at the edge in the cool flow, resting on grit and sand. One of Corran's goats bleated, a faint complaint. Her mind roamed to Rik and Mutsi, wondering what trouble lay in store. *Leave it, Sivster*, Ed murmured. *There's nothing you can do about those two.*

She smiled. A tear slipped from the corner of her eye. Maybe she could sleep here, washed all night by the gentle current.

CHAPTER NINETEEN

Thursday morning, nine thirty, and no one had seen or heard from Cherry Bolting. Her phone was still switched off. Patrick was busy activating missing person enquiries. Siv and Ali drove to her flat, which was on the ground floor of a double-fronted Victorian house. They collected the key from the neighbour, donned protective gloves and let themselves in. The flat had high ceilings, original cornices, covings and sash windows and was a complete mess, littered with clothes, books and magazines. Judging by the empty packets, Cherry was a fan of spiced nut mix. The kitchen, by way of complete contrast, was sparkling.

'Maybe she ate at the Buttery.' Ali nudged an empty bean can on the floor by the window with his foot. 'I reckon she just leaves stuff where it drops, the manky article.'

'It's smaller than you'd imagine from the outside.' Siv was doing a swift scan, making sure the place was empty. 'One bedroom. Let's see what we can find.'

'It'll be hard to find anything in this lot.'

'Stop moaning and open a window, it's airless in here.'

Fifteen minutes later, they'd retrieved Cherry's passport and noted around ten pounds in change in a bowl in the kitchen.

'The wardrobe's full,' Siv said, 'and there are two luggage bags under the bed. Doesn't look as if Cherry took anything with her.'

'Maybe she parked the car but didn't come in. If so, she was in a rush.'

'Or scared and panicking. This flat isn't giving up any secrets, it's just a distraction from the investigation.'

Their phones pinged in unison with a message from Patrick.

Hendrix called me. He remembered that about eight years ago, Lu Forbes was involved in an accident when she was a driving instructor. There was a court case. I found a news story. Worth a read. Also, Cherry's mum lives in Tunbridge Wells and hasn't heard from her.

He'd attached a link to the *Berminster Herald*, dated November 2014. Siv sat on the sofa and Ali propped his bum against a window ledge while they read the article.

LOCAL DRIVING TRAGEDY

A learner driver who killed a child has been spared jail at Berminster Crown Court.

Fiona Epsom, 18, panicked when Isaac Garman, aged 10, ran out between parked cars.

The court was told that on 9 July this year, Isaac was going to the Tesco Metro on Brighton Road to buy snacks. Ms Epsom was having a lesson with her instructor, Ms Lu Forbes of the Come Drive With Me school, Berminster. Isaac Garman suddenly ran into the road from behind a parked van, right in front of the car. Ms Epsom mistakenly put her foot down on the accelerator instead of the brake and hit Isaac. He was killed instantly.

Summing up, the judge said, 'This is a tragic case, where a young boy lost his life. The learner driver unfortunately pressed the wrong pedal in panic and confusion. Isaac Garman was wearing earbuds and listening to music, so he may have been distracted and unaware of the danger. Ms Forbes has an exemplary record as a driving instructor and an excellent reputation, with several awards to her name.

She did not have time to react before Ms Epsom pressed the accelerator, and cannot be held responsible for this terrible accident.'

Ms Epsom's sentence was a community order lasting one year and fifty hours of unpaid work.

'Interesting angle, guv,' Ali said.

'Isn't it? And the accident happened on the same date as Lu's murder. We need to find Fiona Epsom and the Garman family.'

* * *

Angus arrived at the Old Dairy at 8.10 a.m., just after Struan had cycled off to school. Shona was still in her faded cotton dressing gown, not yet showered and with her hair uncombed. Angus was clean-shaven, exuding vigour. His unexpected appearance did nothing for her bleary brain.

'I hope you don't mind the early call, Shona. I wanted to catch you before you open the shop.'

'Come on in. I was just finishing my breakfast.'

They sat in the kitchen. He accepted a cup of tea, but left it to one side, ignored. She was conscious that she smelled of sweaty sheets. With his dark suit, solemn expression and mouth set grimly, he had the air of an undertaker and she feared that he'd come to bury her dreams.

'Thanks so much again for accompanying Struan to talk to the police. I really appreciated it.' She heard how ingratiating she sounded.

'So you've said. No need to keep mentioning it.' He tapped the table. 'It should never have been necessary, and it wouldn't have been if Struan had been honest in the first place.'

'I agree. But Struan has been terribly shocked—'

Angus's hand shot out in a stop gesture. 'Shona, the boy's a liar. I was ashamed of him. He sat as brazen as you like in front of those officers and lied. And he was downright rude.'

155

'I'm terribly sorry, I—'

'I didn't trust myself to speak to him afterwards. What's happened to him? He used to have some manners.'

Angus wore a heavy, masculine scent, woody and pungent. It dominated the room. Shona took a drink of tea, but it was lukewarm and bitter. Her half-eaten poached egg congealed on its raft of toast. She longed to climb the stairs and crawl back into bed.

'The teenage years are tricky, Angus. Struan's flexing his muscles, pushing boundaries. All adolescents do it.' She hated the pleading note in her voice.

'This goes beyond what young lads get up to.' Angus was staring at the teapot as if it offended him. 'There's something about him that's not right. You're too slack with him. He gets away with far too much. What's his punishment for lying to the police?'

'Well . . . I've told him he must tell the truth in future. He said he was sorry and promised he will. He was confused and he panicked.'

'Confused! Shona, listen to yourself! You need your head examined. He's running rings around you. You must exercise some discipline here, make him understand who's in charge.'

'I do my best.' *What would you know about it? You've got staff waiting on you hand and foot. It's no walk in the park, trying to run this place, make a living, deal with rogue hormones and keep tabs on a boy who's almost a man and has a mind of his own.* She tugged her dressing gown away from her clammy neck, filled with a desperate longing to run.

Angus folded his strong hands on the table. 'Shona, I realise that you work hard, but I'm not sure that this arrangement is working out quite as I anticipated.'

There it was, the statement she'd been dreading. Her head was swimming and she couldn't speak.

'Honestly, it seems to be too much for you. And now with Struan testing you like this — it's a lot for you to handle. I've gone through the accounts and there isn't as much revenue here as I expect or need. Also, I see that Jem

Calloway owes thousands in rent. Why have you let him backslide like that?'

She coughed, a grating noise. 'He's such a slippery character. I've tackled him about it.'

'So I should hope! It doesn't sit well with me, having to come here like this, and it pains me, but this is a business and I have to take prudent decisions. I don't see how you can continue in this role.'

'But where will we go? This is our home and our livelihood.'

She noticed his look of distaste as her tears welled, and she blinked hard. It was a bad move to show weakness in front of Angus.

'There's no call to get upset. I'll help you find somewhere. You can continue with the shop if you wish.' He didn't inject any enthusiasm into his words. He shoved his chair back. 'I'll let things lie until the police have resolved their investigation and then we'll talk again. Get Calloway to stump up his rent. Stop letting people play you. And I recommend a punishment for Struan — grounding or stopping his allowance, whatever suits. I'll see myself out.'

She sat after he'd gone, unable to move. The sulphurous smell of the egg turned her stomach and she shoved it away. Her head sank to the table and she gripped her scalp, tugging at her hair.

* * *

Fiona Epsom had emigrated to Ottawa, where she was now a hairdresser. Records showed that she hadn't been back in the UK since departing for Canada eighteen months ago. When Ali phoned her father, he gleaned some interesting information.

'She never got over that awful accident, couldn't forgive herself, and she never attempted to drive again,' Mr Epsom informed him. 'She's got cousins in Ottawa. She needed a fresh start. We miss her, but we're glad for her sake. And it meant she got away from those awful letters from Mr Garman.'

'What letters?' Ali asked.

'He sent one every year, on the anniversary of his son's death. Fiona kept it to herself, didn't tell us until a while before she emigrated. I was appalled when I heard. I wanted Fiona to go to the police, but she wouldn't, she was so sorry for Mr Garman. Guilty too, even though it was an appalling misfortune for everyone concerned. But she'd dreaded the letters arriving, and it meant she could never put it behind her.'

'Were they threatening? Do you still have them?'

'Fiona threw them away. They didn't threaten, exactly, but they were horrible, saying things like, *I hope you can't sleep at night after what you did.* She showed me the last one she received: *Maybe one day you'll lose a child and then you'll know how it feels.* I was minded to go and have it out with him, but Fiona stopped me. She sent Garman a note before she left, telling him that she was emigrating. No more letters have come here since. When I found out about what had been going on, I rang Lu Forbes to ask her if she'd had any letters. She said no. Did Garman murder her? When I read about what happened, I pointed out to my wife that it was the anniversary of the accident.'

Ali relayed this to Siv as they drove to see Isaac's father, Aran Garman.

'Nasty,' she said, 'but why would he wait so long to kill?'

'There might not be any logic to it. Fiona Epsom's out of reach. Maybe he saw Lu, or something reminded him and he reacted.'

Mr Garman still lived at the same address, just off the Brighton Road. His wife had died two years ago, he told them. They sat in the living room in the late afternoon. He was a thin, spindly man with a dull complexion, bruised eyes and cropped hair in a widow's peak. A pile of glossy property brochures stood on the coffee table beside him, next to a bowl of apples.

'Are you an estate agent?' Siv asked.

'I run a house-sitting agency, so I do work with property.' He looked from Siv to Ali, shrewd and assertive. 'What is this about? I doubt that a detective inspector and sergeant are here concerning my complaints about the noisy parties at number sixty-five!'

'No, we haven't come about that,' Siv replied. 'I realise that this will be difficult for you, but we need to discuss your son's accident, Mr Garman.'

'Isaac? Why on earth do you want to ask about him?'

'We're investigating the murder of Luanna Forbes.'

'I saw that she'd died.' Garman spoke in clipped tones. 'Isaac's been gone eight years. And I don't call what happened to him an accident. What's his murder got to do with hers?' Despite his unimpressive appearance, he had a strong presence.

'We have to investigate any incidents in Ms Forbes's life,' Siv explained.

'*Incident*! Is that what you call my son's murder? How insulting of you!'

Siv rebuked herself for that clumsiness and threw a glance at Ali: *help!*

'The last thing we want to do is cause any offence,' he said soothingly. 'Our job often means treading on people's toes. We're aware that Lu Forbes was the driving instructor in the car when your son died.'

'She was. And she was as guilty of murder as Fiona Epsom was, but she got off scot-free, as did Epsom, more or less — all she had to do was pick up some litter and help old ladies across the road. That's all Isaac's life was worth.' Garman snatched up a pen and clicked the nib in and out. 'Epsom's lawyer told a sob story about how sorry she was and it had been a terrible mistake, and the court bought it. The judge even went on about what a great instructor Lu Forbes was! I was disgusted by the verdict. I wrote to my MP and tried everything I could. Isaac was our only son. We waited years to have him and then he was gone, and apparently no one was responsible.'

'Aye, it's hard,' Ali agreed, 'but the court will have weighed up all the factors in the case.'

'You weren't there, but thank you for your opinion,' Garman retorted with heavy sarcasm. 'That judge was a disgrace. He went on about Isaac's earbuds, commented that he was possibly distracted by his music and not paying attention to the road. Talk about victim blaming!'

Garman's anguish was still raw and there was no point in debating the results of the trial with him. His beliefs were unshakeable. He had a motive for murder, and Siv had spotted something familiar on a bookshelf. She regrouped.

'Have you been in touch with Fiona Epsom or Lu Forbes, or seen them since the court case?'

'No. Why would I want anything to do with *them*? Everything went through our legal team.'

'We've received information that you sent letters to Fiona Epsom.'

Garman flushed. 'She left the country. Ran away, like the coward she is. Isn't she lucky that she can turn her life around and enjoy new opportunities!'

'How would you know that, unless you've had contact with her?' Siv queried. 'Please, Mr Garman, be honest with us, however painful it is.'

His legs jerked and he started sobbing. Dry, painful gasps. He gripped his head with one hand and clicked the pen furiously with the other.

Siv mouthed, *Tea* to Ali. He left the room.

'My sergeant's making us a cuppa. Let's take a breather until you've had a drink.'

'No, because that will mean you're here for longer, picking at the scars, and I can't bear it.' Garman threw the pen down and pressed the palms of his hands to his chest. 'I wrote to Fiona Epsom.'

'Thank you. How many letters?'

'Half a dozen or so.'

'On the anniversaries of Isaac's death?'

'Yes. Gave her a piece of my mind. I could never forget what she'd done or find any solace, so why should she? It comforted me to remind her of what she'd taken from me. I realise that will sound skewed and vicious to you, but my spirits lifted each time I dropped the envelope in the post box. Well, for a couple of hours, anyway, and believe me, that was something.'

'I do understand, but it was unwise, and Ms Epsom could have reported you.'

'I wouldn't have cared. I've not cared about anything since Isaac died. Then she posted me a note saying that she was moving abroad. Running away. Fine for her. I kept that. Want to see it?'

When Siv assented, he rose and bent to open a long drawer beneath the bookshelf. Ali came back, holding three mugs of tea, stopping to level one that threatened to spill.

'Here we go, this should help.'

'This is it.' Garman handed Siv an envelope and sat back, taking a mug from Ali.

She slid out the plain cream card and read aloud.

Dear Mr Garman,

I am leaving the country and moving far away. Please don't send any more letters to my parents' house. What happened is nothing to do with them.

I'm so, so sorry. I realise you can't accept that, but I am. I hope you find some peace.

Yours,
Fiona Epsom

'Peace!' Garman gave another throaty sob and sipped his tea.

'What about Lu Forbes?' Siv asked. 'Did you contact her? You've spoken of her as a murderer as well.' She drank some tea and winced. Ali had loaded it with sugar. If he'd done the same to his, the monitor on his smartwatch would be going haywire.

'I didn't write to her, although she was responsible too. She was the instructor and she can't have been paying proper attention. But Fiona Epsom pressed the pedal, she was the killer.'

Siv got up and picked up an amber glass jar holding a scented candle from the bookcase. She checked the label underneath, showed it to Ali and then turned back to Garman.

'This candle is from Forbes Natural Skincare. Ms Forbes's sister makes them and they're sold in their shop at Lansdown Court. Were you at the shop? When did you buy this?'

'Last August. It was a birthday gift for my cousin, but then she didn't turn up when I was going to give it to her, and I couldn't be bothered posting it. I don't even like the thing.'

'You can buy scented candles in lots of places, or online.' Siv replaced it. 'Why Lansdown Court?'

'I'm not even sure why I went. Curiosity, I suppose. I'd read an article about Lansdown Court and the success of the Forbes shop. It seemed so unfair that someone like her was thriving when she helped put my son in the cemetery.' Garman got up and opened another window. A gentle breeze stirred the curtain. 'Lu Forbes didn't even recognise me. The place was busy and someone else served me — another woman, her sister maybe — but she was there, talking to customers. I didn't speak to her.' He resumed his seat, pressing his knuckles against his forehead. 'I can guess what you're thinking. I didn't kill her. I'm not a violent man. I just can't stop dwelling on what happened. I curse those women, I wish them ill, but I wouldn't actually harm them.'

'Where were you between seven and nine on Saturday morning?' Ali asked.

'Here, having breakfast, reading the paper and picking flowers in the garden to take to Isaac's grave. I went there mid-morning and spent an hour with him.'

'Can anyone vouch for you?'

'I wish there was someone who could, Sergeant.' Garman smiled sadly and made an open-handed gesture. 'I'm alone here, as you can see. Child gone, wife gone. And I'd like you to go now, if you've got what you came for.'

Ali lit a Gitane as soon as they'd stepped outside. 'Can't help pitying him. He could have done it, though.'

'Switched his focus to Lu once Fiona Epsom emigrated? Quite possibly. And realising that Lu was successful and thriving clearly angered him — he might have seen her again at the shop or somewhere else.' She leaned against the car and checked her phone. 'Garman's on Facebook. Get Patrick to show his photo around Lansdown Court, in case anyone saw him there, and ask him to get hold of Hendrix, in case he can tell us anything else about the accident.'

CHAPTER TWENTY

Siv bought an iced tea in Gusto and sat at a dark corner table near the back of the café. She closed her eyes and sniffed: rosemary, balsamic vinegar, rich olive oil and pesto. If there was a personal heaven, hers would smell like this. She'd arrived early, so that Tommy Castles would find her established at a table. He'd emailed her the previous day.

> *Hi Siv,*
>   *Can we please meet for a coffee soon? I'm not trying to hit on you. It's concerning a third party and a personal matter. I'd appreciate your time.*
>   *Cheers, Tommy C*

She didn't trust DI Castles. She'd come across him a couple of times and found him sarky and bumptious. He'd been Mortimer's protégé, and the DCI had wanted him for the job she'd been appointed to. When Castles had failed to get the promotion, he'd gone elsewhere. He was still friendly with Mortimer, went sailing with him regularly and had cosy meals with him and her mother. Mutsi, of course, had attempted to matchmake, taken with his rugged looks. Siv regarded him as Mortimer's snitch and had no idea what he wanted, but she was intrigued enough to give him half an hour.

He arrived on time and asked her if she'd like anything. When she declined he ordered a coffee.

'Thanks for agreeing to talk,' he said. 'You look well. Berminster must be agreeing with you.'

She was instantly suspicious. His tone was different, emollient. Placatory, even. 'It is, yes. How are you?'

'Fine. Never better. The move away was good for me in all kinds of ways.'

'That's good to hear.' This was a different tune to the resentful one he usually played. 'Isn't there enough to keep you busy with your new team?'

'Day off.' He smiled. 'Hence the casual wear.'

He was in jeans and a T-shirt. A handsome man, if you liked the square-set, musclebound, military type. Although his hair was longer than usual, softening his face.

'So, how are you? Busy? Enjoying life?' He fumbled with a tiny sachet of brown sugar, his blunt fingers failing to open it.

'I've plenty to do. Why did you want to see me?' *Goodness*, she thought, *he's actually making small talk and blushing!* She prayed that this wasn't in fact some cack-handed attempt to ask her out.

'It's a bit delicate actually, Siv.' He finally tore the thin brown paper and managed to spray most of the sugar on the table. 'Oh, bugger!'

Impatiently, she snicked open another sachet and handed it to him. 'Who's this third party? I hope you haven't got me here on false pretences.'

'Pretences? Oh . . . no, no. Just to put it out there, put your mind at rest, I've met a terrific woman, Tori. We're going to marry and have babies. Little Tommies and Toris.'

'Many congratulations. I do have to go soon.' Tommy and Tori. They sounded like characters in a children's story.

'Yeah. Look, I wasn't sure about this at all, but Will asked me to do him a favour.'

'DCI Mortimer?' Immediately, her guard was up.

'Yeah. Thing is . . .' He stirred his black coffee and licked the spoon. 'Thing is, he's really worried about your family stuff. Arguments and such.'

'My boss has been talking to you about my family?'

'As a friend. And not . . . not lots of details, honestly.' He widened his eyes. 'Just that you and your mum and sister have your differences.'

'What if we have? What's it to do with you?' If Mortimer had sent Tommy here on an information-gathering expedition, he'd be disappointed.

'Nothing. It's none of my business.'

'For once, we're in complete agreement. So, why are you here?'

He pulled at the sleeve of his T-shirt. 'God, I just knew this would be embarrassing. Tori advised me to stay out of it.'

Siv said nothing. Let him squirm. How nice that Tori was also in the loop. So many people chatting about her and her family.

'Thing is, Will wonders if the three of you might seek professional help. He's broached it with Crista. She's not that keen, but she's willing to consider it. Will hopes that you might talk to your sister and get her to agree.'

She was gobsmacked, uncertain if she was furious, insulted or amused. Undoubtedly a mix of all three. How fascinating that Mortimer had misjudged her so badly, sending Tommy Castles as his intermediary. Maybe the bad call pointed to his desperation. 'The DCI wants us to go to family therapy?'

'It can help people.'

'So I've heard. I resent this intrusion.'

'Yeah. That's no surprise.'

'I suppose that Will's life is uncomfortable at present, hence his proposal.'

'He doesn't like to see Crista so upset and he worries about the future if the difficulties continue.'

Mutsi must be making Mortimer's life hell with her dramatics. 'I'm sure he does. Still, when you make a commitment to living with someone, you take the rough with the smooth. You must be finding that with Tori.'

Tommy raised his hands. 'I get it, you're turning it back on me. Don't shoot the messenger.'

Siv picked up her bag. 'I don't have time for this. When you see Will, you can report that I declined.' She shoved her chair back. 'And tell him next time he wants to say something to me about family matters, not to use a go-between. Good luck with your babies.'

She stopped at the counter to buy lemonade for the team. When she glanced back, Tommy was busy texting. No doubt reporting that his peace mission had failed.

As she left the café, she felt oddly light-hearted.

* * *

They were all back at the station, drinking the refreshing lemonade.

'We've got nothing new from Hendrix regarding the accident,' Siv reported. 'Lu hadn't mentioned any recent contact with Mr Garman or referred to the accident since they got into recycling their relationship. I checked with Keira Durham too, but she knew nothing about it — it happened before she started at the driving school. We've established that Lu Forbes was terribly upset by Isaac Garman's death and it was one of her motivations for giving up being a driving instructor.'

'I phoned Yvonne Forbes,' Patrick reported. 'She remembered the accident, but Lu hadn't talked about it for ages. I've been checking Lu's phone and laptop. Nothing unusual to report. Quite a few calls and text messages to Hendrix since April. Lu had commented several times on Facebook about the Minster Beach development, including a post that she'd signed the petition.'

'Have we anything on Cherry Bolting?' Ali didn't sound hopeful.

'Sod all.' Patrick tapped his iPad. 'No sightings, nothing on CCTV from the station and her phone's been off. No activity on her bank account.'

Siv let out an exasperated groan and crossed to the incident board. 'Let's keep this murder as our main focus. People with possible motive and no alibi.' She asterisked names: 'Struan Hollis, Simon Terrance, Aran Garman. Maybe Hendrix, if the resurgence of romance was trickier than he's letting on. Hollis and Terrance would have been able to get hold of a key to Calloway's shop without too much trouble.'

'Now that we've tracked down Garman, it does seem a huge coincidence that Lu was murdered on the anniversary of his son's death.' Patrick glanced at Ali, who had a glum expression. 'Something up?'

'Pol's still stuck at her mum's.'

'Come round to mine for a bite,' Patrick said. 'Kitty and Noah are making curry.'

'Aye, I will, thanks. I could do with the company.'

'You coming, guv?' Patrick asked. 'We'll have loads.'

'Thanks, but I'm meeting Bartel for a drink.' She was staring at the board as if it might talk to her. This case was turning into a rich brew, with lots of possibilities. In many ways, that was stimulating, but it also opened up the chance of time-wasting with wrong turns.

Ali and Patrick exchanged glances. They had high hopes for the guv's friendship with the larger-than-life roofer. Ali reckoned that Bartel was just what she needed — someone gregarious and exuberant.

'I'll ask around Garman's neighbours tomorrow,' Patrick said, 'see if anyone noticed him out and about on Saturday morning.'

'Yes, good, and check his car on ANPR.' Siv emptied her tea. 'We need to scrutinise the objections to Terrance's development more closely. He's very smooth about his difference of opinion with Lu and I don't buy his composure.

It's worth talking to Cassia Wade, the woman who's at the forefront of the protest. You two head off now and we'll grab an early start tomorrow.'

* * *

Half an hour later, Siv was unlocking her car when she caught a glimpse of movement among the trees bordering that side of the car park. She peered, but couldn't see anyone. Maybe it had been a shadow cast by the evening sun, or branches shifting, heavy with leaves, or her eyes adjusting to the glare. She opened the door, but sensed a flicker.

'Hello. Is someone there?'

Cherry Bolting stepped out from behind a sturdy plane tree. She wore cut-off denim shorts, a patterned shirt and espadrilles. Her face was free of make-up, her hair flat and unkempt.

'Hello, Cherry. We've been worried about you.' Siv kept her tone neutral. The woman's expression was wary, as if she might take off.

'Yeah. I needed some time. To work things out.'

'And has that been helpful?'

'Hard to say.' Cherry half-jumped as a door banged at the side of the station. Someone chucking a rubbish bag in the bins. 'I want to talk to you.'

'Here? We could go to my office.'

'No! Can we just drive somewhere?'

'Sure. Get in.'

Siv started the engine and offered Cherry a bottle of water. She accepted, but didn't open it, holding it in her lap. She put her head back and closed her eyes. Siv drove to a quiet stretch of the Bere, a place where she sometimes met Bartel, and pulled off the road. The car faced the river, shielded by a canopy of alder and birch. She turned off the engine and opened the windows. Birds chattered, busy before sundown. Two swans idled on the water. Huge dragonflies flashed above them in a glittering dance.

Cherry opened her eyes. 'This is a lovely spot.'

'Isn't it? I have a friend who fishes here sometimes. I bring coffee and sandwiches for picnics with him. Cherry, do you mind if I call the station to say you're no longer missing? It will free up my colleagues to focus on other things.'

Cherry chewed her bottom lip and agreed. Siv made the call and texted Bartel to say that she'd be late. She switched her phone to silent and tucked it away.

'What fish does your friend catch?' Cherry asked.

'Pike and perch mainly. I just come for the chat and the peace.'

Cherry opened the water and drank, cleared her throat. 'Sorry for causing any worry.'

'You're here now. Where have you been?'

'Halse Woods, mainly.'

'You slept there?'

'Yeah. It was alright. Warm and dry. Quiet. I could breathe and work stuff out. Do I pong?'

'No. You're just a bit . . . musty.'

That raised a tiny smile.

'So, what did you want to talk about?' Siv watched a swan flexing its powerful wings and burrowing its beak in feathers to clean them.

'You won't like it when I tell you.'

Siv turned towards her. 'Do you want to confess to murder?'

'No!'

'Then anything else is down the scale, isn't it? Even if it's enough to make you run away.'

Cherry reached into her bag and pulled out a pack of wet wipes. She ran one across her forehead and down the back of her neck.

'Can I have one?' Siv asked. 'It's been a long day and that smells fresh.'

Cherry held out the pack. It promised the scent of garden blossoms. Siv took a sheet and rubbed it between her hands.

'I got scared,' Cherry said in a low voice. 'You were talking a lot to Struan and I worried that he'd tell you.'

'He's told us a few things.'

'About me?'

'No.'

'Oh. I wondered. He rang me yesterday lunchtime, after he'd been interviewed at the police station. He told me that he met Lu on the road the morning she died and that you'd got a witness. He'd made up a story for you about her being fed up with his music. In fact, she stopped him and laid into him, big time. She'd seen us together in the café, kissing. She threatened that she was going to tell Shona about what was going on. He promised me he hadn't revealed anything to you, but I wasn't sure whether he was telling me the truth. I could tell he was nervy, because you're persistent and you keep coming back to him. I had to get away from Lansdown and everyone to sort out my head.' She reached forward and pressed both hands against the dashboard, her head down. 'Me and Struan . . . we've been seeing each other for about six months.'

'Do you mean you've been having sex?'

Cherry stared out of the side window. 'Yes. It's disgusting, I know.'

'And illegal. Struan must still have been fourteen when it started.' It wasn't too surprising, given what she'd learned about him. 'Can you talk me through how it happened?'

'It just did, somehow. I didn't plan it, didn't see it coming at all. Struan's attractive, funny. He dropped by the café a lot and we'd chat. It got to be a regular thing after school. Sometimes, when it was quiet, I let Malcolm go early and I'd be there alone with Struan. One winter evening it was dark outside, we'd had hot chocolate and we started kissing. I could claim that I tried to stop it, but I didn't. He seemed much older than his years. It was exciting.'

'You had sex in the café?'

'A couple of times. Then . . . well, it wasn't very comfy in there, so we used to go to Jem's shop at night. Struan suggested it and got the key copied. He laughed that Jem was so disorganised, he'd never notice we'd been there.'

'Was this a regular event?'

'At least once a week. We had to be very discreet. Struan would unlock the shop when everyone had left for the evening, and he'd wait for me. We used a torch and made sure the blinds were down.'

'When was the last time you had sex?'

'The Wednesday before Lu died. We haven't since. I was too scared. I told Struan to stay away from the café.'

'Did Shona have any idea? Did she not notice that Struan was out in the evenings?'

'He said that she never disturbed him if he told her he was doing homework. Or he'd say he was just taking his skateboard out for a while, or practising with his football. We never had more than about half an hour together, so he wasn't gone long enough for his mum to start worrying.'

Siv was reflecting on the argument between Lu and Struan on the morning she died. 'Did Lu Forbes indicate to Struan that she'd told anyone else what she'd seen?'

'No. It sounded as if she hadn't. God, we were so careful. Neither of us wanted anyone to find out!'

Maybe Lu hadn't talked, Siv thought, but Struan might have boasted to someone. He had little to lose, and it might have suited him to puff himself up by talking about the older woman he'd pulled.

'I've been so stupid,' Cherry muttered. 'And I've been terrified since Lu died. I've risked everything, haven't I?'

'Yes.'

'What's going to happen now?'

'I'm going to arrest you and take you to the station to make a statement. You'd better phone your mum, she'll be worried. We had to contact her.' Siv cautioned her and started the engine. Cherry began to cry, her shoulders hunched. Siv drove, impatient and angry after what she'd heard. Cherry would lose everything — her reputation and her job. There'd be a prison sentence. And Struan? Siv had no doubt that he'd laugh and share his experiences on social media.

CHAPTER TWENTY-ONE

'I'm so sorry I was late, something cropped up as I was leaving the station.'

'No problem, Madame. Your job is unpredictable, unlike roof tiles. They sit there, year in, year out.'

Siv was sitting with Bartel in a bar in Polska, the Polish centre in town. They were drinking Ursa golden ale and sharing a platter of mushroom rolls, poppy-seed-and-onion flatbreads, pork-and-pickle crepes, and cabbage-and-mince pastries. Siv had left Cherry Bolting with the custody sergeant and messaged Ali and Patrick, informing them that the missing woman had surfaced and she'd update them in the morning. The issue of sexual assault would be dealt with by another team, but Siv had requested liaison and first dibs on talking to Struan.

'How's everything at home?' Siv was conscious of a low-level anxiety.

'All is well, no need to fret. Rik apologised to me, replaced the broken mug and bought me chocolates.'

'I'm glad. No further sign of Mutsi?'

'No.' Bartel licked foam from his top lip. 'I suggested to Rik that she should leave her mother alone and not tease her.'

'It's hard to break old habits, and Rik gets so much twisted pleasure from baiting Mutsi.'

'Neither of you like your mother, but you have such different ways of showing it.'

'How do you mean?' Siv didn't really want to enter a discussion about her family after a full-on day, but Bartel had earned a listening ear.

'You try to maintain a distance, keep Mutsi at arm's length. Mostly, you're diplomatic, or try to be, although there's always an edge in your voice when you see her.' Bartel ran his tongue across his teeth. 'Rik seeks her out, wants to annoy her, make her angry. Make her pay?'

Siv rested her head back against the padded cushion of the bench. 'You don't miss much.'

He shrugged. 'Up on roofs, I have plenty of time to think.'

Siv fortified herself with ale. 'Rik and I are different personalities. The way we are with Mutsi now is just how we were as kids. I was the quiet, nervy one, always trying to maintain a low profile and keep the peace. Rik was pugnacious, in your face, taking Mutsi to task. It's just as well I had Rik as my older sister. She fought my corner. But she was always a bit frightening too. Unpredictable.'

'People don't change much,' Bartel said.

'True. Rik still wants to make Mutsi pay, but it's pointless. Mutsi can't see she has anything to pay for.' She ran a hand through her hair. 'Are we all doomed to step around the floor in an endless, pointless dance?'

'As long as it's a fast polka . . .'

That made her smile. 'The thing is, Bartel, I just don't understand why Rik has come back here. She and Mutsi never could resist tormenting each other.' She started to relax, despite the topic of conversation. The ale was crisp and light and the food was replenishing her energy. 'Mortimer was bending my ear, saying that Mutsi was upset after the row. It was bad enough when there was just her to deal with, but now, with the two of them . . . contemplating it winds me up.' She was about to describe the meeting with Tommy Castles, but decided that he'd heard quite enough of her problems for one night.

Bartel gave his beard a tug. 'Another drink?'

'Better not, I have to drive home. I'll have a tonic water with ice.'

She finished her flatbread while he went to the bar. He towered over the other customers. While he was waiting for the drinks he folded his hands behind his neck and leaned back into them. It was a familiar gesture, easing the tension caused by his work.

When he came back, he fingered an earring. 'I realise that this situation is difficult for you, Madame.'

'Bit of an understatement, Bartel. Rik and Mutsi have gatecrashed my party.'

'Yes, yes. But Rik needed to come here. When you're wounded, it's natural to head for home, or the nearest thing to it.'

Siv looked at him. He held her gaze. His eyes were the same golden amber as the ale. 'So, Rik's told you why she's back here?'

'She has.'

'And are you allowed to tell me?'

'She hasn't instructed me not to.' He popped a last bite of mushroom roll in his mouth.

Siv flipped a coaster over. 'Rik hasn't said a word to me, but she's confided in you.'

'Are you hurt?'

'A bit, maybe.'

'D'you want me to tell you?'

Did she? It would just be more . . . stuff. Rik hadn't come near her after Ed died. There'd been the usual scant email. When she reflected on their childhood, it was true that Rik had often protected her, but she'd also been the source of plenty of trouble with her lying, stealing and drug use. Her sister's company had always been a mixed blessing.

'I don't have to say anything.' Bartel examined the cream head on his fresh ale, holding it up to the light. 'That's a thing of beauty. Heaven in a glass. Sometimes it's easier to tell people who aren't family your troubles. I expect that's the case with Rik.'

A nasty little stone was wedged in Siv's chest. *Yeah, maybe she's telling you a pack of lies because you're kind and she wants to draw you in.* Still, it was best to be in the loop and not be blindsided. 'Go on, then, spill the beans. What did Rik tell you?'

'Things got sticky in Auckland. Rik got involved with a guy who turned out to be involved in crime — mainly car theft, but drugs too. He was part of a syndicate.'

'Syndicate? Sounds like another name for a gang.'

'Undoubtedly. He was controlling too. Rik had moved in with him. He had a luxurious flat and she enjoyed the lifestyle until she discovered the truth about how it was funded. When she tried to get away from him, he turned nasty and hit her. In the end, he'd lock her in their flat when he went out. It sounds as if her life was hell. In the end, she managed to escape with her passport and a rucksack. She headed straight for the airport and got a flight to London. You could take it as a compliment that she turned up at your wagon.'

'Hm. She might have mentioned this to me, let me in on what had happened.'

'She must have had her reasons for keeping quiet. We can only tell a story when we're ready to.' He patted her hand. 'You should go home, get your head down. Remember, we live to fight another day.'

'Yes. That's what worries me.'

* * *

Shona Hollis was in a sniffy mood the next morning when she showed Siv and Ali into the living room.

'What's this about now? I've lost track of how many times you've spoken to Struan, grilling him over and over. He's missing vital school time and his exams are—'

'This can't wait.' Siv cut in. She'd had enough of Shona's maternal fussing. 'It concerns murder. If Struan hadn't lied to us on several occasions, he wouldn't have needed to miss lessons.'

'It's cool.' Struan smirked. His school uniform was spotless, his shirt a blinding white. 'It's history first two periods and I'm well up on all that fusty old crap.'

Ali tutted in irritation. Struan swigged a mouthful from a steaming mug of tea and rested it on the arm of the tartan sofa. His mother was sitting beside him and twitched, monitoring the mug.

'Cherry Bolting has turned up,' Siv announced. 'She's . She needed a break.'

'Thank heavens!' Shona clasped her hands. 'The café can operate properly again. Malcolm wouldn't have been able to run it on his own for long. Why on earth did Cherry go off like that, without a word to anyone? She's usually so reliable.'

'Try asking your son,' Ali snapped.

Siv shot him a warning glance. Whatever their opinion of Struan, he was a victim where Cherry was concerned.

'Struan?' Shona half-turned to her son. 'It's nothing to do with you, surely. Did Cherry tell you anything? You told me you'd no idea where she'd gone.'

'Unfortunately, it's everything to do with Struan,' Siv said. 'Do you want to tell us, Struan, or leave it to me?'

'Dunno what you're on about as usual,' he replied, but he wouldn't make eye contact.

'Right, if that's how you want to play it. This is going to be difficult for you to hear, Ms Hollis.' Siv drew her chair a little nearer. 'Cherry Bolting has been arrested. She confessed to numerous instances of sexual assault regarding Struan, and has been charged accordingly. Another detective will be in touch with you about that matter, and Struan will have to be interviewed by other colleagues. Counselling will be available if you want it. We're here in case Cherry's offences are in any way linked to Lu Forbes's murder.'

Struan had put his hand over his mouth. Siv wasn't sure, but suspected that he was grinning. His mother's face had fallen as if she'd been punched.

'I don't understand . . . sexual assault? What's it got to do with Struan? I just don't . . . what do you mean?'

'Oh, fuck's sake!' Struan bounced in his seat. 'Me and Cherry were shagging, Mother. That's what she means. Cherry was putting out and I was happy to assist. Always willing to help a lady! It was great, but Cherry got the wobbles after Lu died and the cops were sniffing around.'

Shona stared at her son, speechless.

'I'm sorry, Ms Hollis. What Struan says is true,' Siv told her. 'It had been happening for a while.'

'It's no biggie.' Struan finished his tea. 'We both wanted it and it was great. Why have you arrested Cherry? That's daft.'

'It's not about what you wanted or didn't want,' Ali said. 'Even if you were willing, you're under the age of sixteen, so in the eyes of the law you're unable to consent to sex and Cherry Bolting was committing a criminal offence.'

'That's crazy, that is. We were both up for it. Why did she have to spoil it? Stupid bitch.'

He wore a petulant frown. *Like a kid who's had his sweeties taken away*, Siv thought.

'Are you OK, Ms Hollis? Can we get you a drink?'

Shona was balancing on the edge of the sofa. 'When . . . when was this happening, Struan?'

'Whenever we could manage it. Regularly. Don't fret, Mother. I enjoyed myself. Learned a lot too. Cherry's fit.' He wriggled his hips and hummed 'Sex Bomb'.

'You used Jem Calloway's shop, when everyone had closed up for the day,' Siv told him. 'You had a key made.'

'Yeah. It was handy.'

'Where's that key now?'

'Dunno. I must have lost it. I searched for it, can't find it.'

'Oh, Struan!' Shona moaned.

'When was the last time you had the key?' Siv ignored her, pressing on.

'The week before Lu died — the Wednesday. I locked up, I remember doing that. Maybe I dropped the key in the yard. I was a bit hot and distracted.'

178

'Cherry has informed us that Lu Forbes had found out about your activities,' Siv said. 'That's what she was talking to you about when you met on the morning she died. Don't bother lying again.'

'Yeah, she was nagging on about it, saying it was disgusting and she was going to tell my mum. I told her to go ahead. I'd deny it and Mum would believe me.'

'That was a big risk, even for you,' Siv commented.

'You reckon?'

'Did you follow Lu back to Lansdown and attack her?' Siv challenged.

'As if! I wanted to get on and smash the footie training. I wasn't bothered about Lu and her rancid sermons.'

'You've proved yourself a terrible wee liar,' Ali growled. 'I don't believe a word that comes out of your mouth.'

'That's your problem.' Struan punched a cushion. 'I didn't touch Lu Forbes. She was annoying, but I was used to her ways and I let it all roll off me. Cherry — I definitely touched her, but from what you've said, that's no crime on *my* part.'

'All these lies, Struan.' His mother sighed. 'I brought you up to tell the truth and respect other people. Why have you been lying?'

'Oh, get a life, Mum. Haven't you ever told a porky? No need to get dramatic.'

Siv had had enough. 'We'd better leave you and Struan to talk now, Ms Hollis. Colleagues will be in touch.' She wasn't sure that Shona had heard. 'Make your mother a cuppa, Struan. She's had a shock. Best to skip school today.'

They saw themselves out. Ali noticed that Lu's shop door was open.

'Yvonne must be there,' Siv said. 'Let's get some drinks and grab the chance to ask her what she remembers about Lu's driving accident.'

They crossed to the Buttery and ordered takeaway coffees.

'Did you hear that boy?' Ali muttered. 'No shame on him at all, not a care in the world about any of it. That poor mother of his!'

'Nightmare for her. What do we make of him now? Is he a killer?'

'I'd believe it. An alley cat has more morals than him.'

'I can't work him out. He enjoys lying and playing games. His comment that Lu's scolding didn't bother him that much had the ring of truth.'

Malcolm Hayler brought their coffees. He was red in the face.

'Any news of Cherry? I'm run off my feet here.'

'Yes,' Siv said. 'She's contacted us and she's fine, but she won't be back here at present.'

'Oh, hell. I mean, I'm glad she's alright. Has she been ill?'

'In a way. You'll need to get some temporary help in.'

He wiped his brow. 'I'll consult Shona, see what she says.'

'Leave it for this morning,' Siv advised. 'She's already dealing with something.'

'Right.' He moved to the next customer, raising a cheerful smile.

Yvonne was rearranging shelves in the Forbes shop. Jem Calloway was there too, vacuuming without much oomph.

Siv handed Yvonne a coffee. 'Sorry, we didn't realise you were here,' she told Jem.

'No worries,' he replied morosely. He was sweating profusely, creating an alcoholic vapour like a force field.

'Hot work on a day like this.' Siv hoped that she never smelled like that after too many glasses of akvavit.

'Yvonne's a hard taskmaster.'

Yvonne flicked him with a duster. 'Take no notice of him,' she told Siv. 'He's down in the dumps because of Shona.'

'What's happened?' Siv asked him.

'She marched in on me and announced that if I don't pay all my rent by the end of next week, she'll give me notice to quit.'

'That should come as no surprise,' Ali remarked.

'I didn't think she'd actually do it. Can anyone lend me three grand?'

'Try a bank,' Siv suggested, turning to Yvonne. 'Have you got five minutes?'

'Sure. Have you any news for me about Lu?'

'Nothing as yet, but I do have a question.'

Yvonne sat on a pile of boxes. 'I remember reading somewhere that death is the big question mark.'

'Murder certainly is,' Ali said, 'but we'll get the answer.'

'That's good to hear.' Yvonne crossed her ankles, her pretty red sundress just skimming her calves.

'When Lu was a driving instructor, a young boy was accidentally killed by her pupil. Do you remember that time?' Siv inched as far away as she could from Calloway's odour.

'Oh, that was awful. Lu was married when it happened. She moaned that Bryan didn't support her as much as she needed. I remember how upset she was. She told me the kid ran out in front of the car and she didn't have time to react.'

'Sadly, the driver accelerated,' Siv prompted.

'That's right. It went to court. Lu was worried about the publicity and the effect it would have on the driving school. In the end, it was judged an accident and Lu's reputation was intact. It did stay with her, though, and she didn't enjoy instructing as much afterwards.'

'It was one of the reasons she chucked it in and started this business,' Jem added, twirling the vacuum nozzle. 'It got to her. It would, a kid dying like that. I mean, you'd never forget it.'

Ali found a press photo of Aran Garman on his phone and showed it to Yvonne. 'This is Mr Garman, the dead boy's father. Did he ever contact Lu, or come here?'

'Lu didn't say.' Yvonne rubbed her ankles together, the silvery glitter on her sandals winking in the light. 'Why would he do that?'

'Well, to be fair, Little Tree, he might not have been happy with the verdict,' Calloway said gently.

'Mr Garman was deeply unhappy with it,' Ali confirmed. 'Did you ever notice him around here, Mr Calloway? Take a look at the photo.'

'Me? No. I don't recognise him.'

'What's happened with Cherry? Any news?' Yvonne stood, dusting the skirt of her dress.

'She's safe,' Siv said.

'What was up with her?' Jem asked.

'I can't say any more for now.'

'Too many mysteries around here.' Jem gestured to Ali. 'You might have a customer, Yvonne.'

Ali was sniffing a moisturiser. 'I'll take one of these for my wife. A tenner, yes?'

He paid and they headed back to the car.

'*Little Tree*? Have those two got something going?' Siv turned the ignition.

'Could have, I suppose. They've been friends a long time, so they might have pet names for each other.' Ali undid the moisturiser, releasing a light fragrance and holding it under Siv's nose.

'Nice. You aiming to get in Polly's good books when she returns?'

'She deserves it. She's a living saint, the way she puts up with her cranky mum and never says a bad word to her.'

Siv gave a horse and its rider a wide berth, reflecting that such an accolade would never be extended to her.

*   *   *

When the police had gone, Yvonne grasped Jem's hands. 'I've told you not to worry about the rent. You can't blame Shona for doing her job. She has to run this place and balance the books for Angus. Anyway, if you're going to help me run this shop, it's not so important anymore, is it? We could change the name of the business to Forbes-Calloway. Sounds quite distinguished.'

'What, close my place down?'

'Maybe, eventually — or run the two in tandem.' She cupped his hands against her chest.

Jem rested his forehead against hers. 'I like my own place too, though. Whatever people say about me, I've put a lot of work into it. I really hate the idea of losing it. I'll try the bank, but I'm not hopeful.'

She slipped her arms around his waist. 'What if I contact the solicitor and ask if I can have an advance from Lu's estate? I inherit everything anyway, so I don't see why I can't have say, five thousand. That would sort out your rent and pay some in advance too.'

He smoothed her hair back and clasped her chin in his hands. 'You'd do that for me?'

'Sure I would. You're helping me, aren't you? I'm your Little Tree. We've been mates for ever and we're going to be a team, after all.'

He picked her up, swung her round. She threw her head back and then fixed her mouth on his, kissing him deeply.

CHAPTER TWENTY-TWO

Siv arrived in Hove early for her appointment with Zara Lennard. Patrick had queried why she was bothering and she'd reminded him sternly that in a murder investigation, you chased everything down, nailed everything tight. She parked near the seafront and found a wholefood shop with a café attached. While she waited in the queue, she saw that she'd had a text from Rik.

> *I apologised to Bart and ate humble pie. Sorry — although Mutsi started it, came round keen for a fight, so I gave her what she wanted. We still friends? I'm at the harbour tonight with Stellar. Drop by and I'll chuck you a gratis burger with fancy trimmings. x*

Bart? When did that happen? Siv had never heard him called that. She composed a reply.

> *Glad you made it up to him. I'll call by for a burger if I can. Not seen Mutsi since, although she complained to Mortimer. Make sure you stay away from her for a while. x*

Finger poised, she added:

Did you really write to Dad complaining about Mutsi?

She pressed the arrow, ordered a pot of tea and a cream cheese bagel and carried her tray through the busy café, hoping to find a space. She rounded a corner, watching her step because the tables were close together, and narrowly avoided tripping over the strap of a bag lying under a chair.

'Not like you to be clumsy.' A familiar voice sounded and her eyes met Mutsi's.

'Oh. Hello, Mum.'

'Here, sit, sit.' Mutsi pulled out a chair at her table for two. 'This is lovely, an unexpected meeting!'

Siv plonked her tray down. She really didn't want to have to do this. 'You shouldn't leave your bag on the floor, it's too easy to steal.'

Mutsi picked up the embroidered raffia tote and tucked it between her feet. 'Always the detective, Sivvi.'

'It's a habit. I wouldn't have expected to find you in a place like this. It's a bit . . . ordinary.'

The clientele were mainly parents with babies, hipsters and students. Mutsi stood out in her belted crepe-de-Chine midi-dress and silver waterfall necklace. She'd changed her hairstyle to platinum blonde in a feathered cut.

'The salads here are excellent, always fresh and zingy.' The oval dish in front of her was a colourful mix of pulses, grains and radicchio lettuce. 'I was just about to take a photo for my blog as an example of the kind of lunch I recommend.' She raised her phone and clicked several times. Then she tapped the edge of Siv's plate with a dark red nail. 'You should be having something green with that for vitamins.'

This from the woman who'd frequently failed to provide her children with basic meals. Siv bit into the bagel and poured tea. 'What brings you to Hove?'

'Wallpaper. There's a wonderful little shop here that does the most exquisite ranges. I chose two. One for the guest bedroom and one for the hall.'

'Have you almost finished the refurbishments now?'

'Yes, as you'd realise if you ever visited. You should see the house, Sivvi! You'd hardly recognise it. The kitchen's been refitted in white . . .'

Siv tuned her out. The danger time was approaching. Once she'd finished spending Mortimer's money and reshaping his house, Mutsi would get bored. If she stayed true to form, she'd leg it within the next six months. The possibility both thrilled and concerned Siv. The inevitable fallout with Mortimer was her main concern. If she found herself in that position, she'd probably have to apply for another job, which would mean uprooting to another area.

'. . . and slate-grey ceramic splashback.' Mutsi clicked her fingers. 'Are you listening?'

'Sounds amazing. What will you do with your time once you've completed the house?'

'I'm not sure.' Mutsi raised a small forkful of food to her lips. '*Quicksilver* would benefit from some attention, in my opinion, but Will rather likes it as it is.'

He'd have noticed his bank balance dwindling. Siv almost choked on her bagel at Mutsi's next airy remark.

'Will has talked about you, me and Rik seeking family therapy. I've been reading up on it, and I've come round to the idea. We could get everything out in the open, thrash out our problems. What's your opinion? I've not broached it with Rik, I wondered if you—'

'No. No way.' Was Mutsi aware of Tommy's intervention, or had Mortimer kept that move to himself?

'But Sivvi, it might well help us. Surely there'd be no harm in trying?'

She entertained a mental image of the three of them in a therapist's room, herself acting as piggy in the middle while her sister and mother went for each other. 'No. You and Rik can go if you want that kind of forum. I don't feel the need.'

'But we all have issues . . .'

'Yes. And I'll deal with my own. Just drop it.'

'So stubborn, as always.' Mutsi wore a wounded expression.

'That's me.'

Mutsi regrouped into an alternative universe, the one where she was a mother who got along well with her daughters. 'I might see if I can help Rik out, get her somewhere decent to live and encourage her to find a better job. She'll hardly want to stay renting from that lump of a roofer for too long. And serving burgers! Honestly, I nearly died of shame when I heard. At least you have a decent career, Sivvi.'

Siv finished her tea. 'Sounds like a plan.' It would go down like a lead balloon with Rik.

Mutsi ran a finger through her necklace, separating the strands and segueing into self-justification. 'I didn't start anything with Rik, I never do. She likes to irritate. Quick to anger, and then she moves on. She's always been the same. She reminds me of my grandmother. There was a saying in the family about her: "demon at breakfast, angel at supper". You were always more like your father. Anything for peace and quiet. He was so dull.'

Siv supressed a giggle. 'I've never heard you say anything good about him. What attracted you to him?'

'He wore tweed and black spectacles and he had misty eyes. He was academic in a sexy way. He used to read poetry to me.' Mutsi picked up a lettuce leaf in her fingers and popped it in her mouth. 'But, oh dear, he was so dreary once we married. Always had his nose in a book.' She dusted her hands together, scrutinised Siv. 'Are you still seeing Fabian? He's such a hunk and a great conversationalist. And really keen on you. Those amazing flowers he bought you!'

There'd been flowers, chocolates, gifts left at her door and far too many text messages. 'Yes, he was too keen. He had stalking tendencies. I finished it. Not that much had started.'

'Oh.' Mutsi sank back. 'I had high hopes. What do you mean, was he—'

'I've got to go, sorry. This was just a quick break. I have an appointment, work to do.'

'Well . . . I've enjoyed our little mother–daughter chat. Let's do this again soon. We get on, don't we? You were always easier company than Rik.'

'Bye for now. Do watch out for your bag. It signals designer, very attractive, and this is a higher-risk crime area than Berminster. It'd be better on your lap.'

Siv left the café and walked towards the public relations firm where Zara Lennard was a communications officer. She had to hand it to Mutsi, her company was never lacklustre. She paused by the impressive stone portico of a bank and laughed until her eyes moistened. She wasn't sure if she was weeping from mirth or misery. She ran a finger under her eyes and moved on.

At the offices of the PR company, she sat in a small beige-and-white room off reception and waited for no more than a couple of minutes before Ms Lennard arrived, bringing a surge of energy with her.

'Hello, Inspector Drummond. Can we get you a tea or coffee? Water?'

'No, thanks.'

'Please, do say if you change your mind. I've never actually talked to the police before. Bryan said you'd been in touch, naturally. It was so awful to hear about his ex-wife's death. He hasn't been himself since. I've been trying to console him. How can I help you today?'

She had long hair the colour of demerara sugar, swept across from a side parting. Her short-sleeved dress was a watery blue, her eye shadow and nails a matching pearly grey. A cool, elegant style. Her smile was eager, with lots of shining teeth. Siv found her a tad too enthusiastic and suspected the smile was professional. She pictured Zara putting it on in the mirror with her eyeliner and lip gloss.

'I'm not sure if you can help. What do you know about Lu Forbes?'

She crossed her bare, silky-skinned legs. 'Bryan was married to her. They divorced sometime back and went their separate ways, as happens.'

'Did Mr Hendrix comment much about the divorce?'

'Not a great deal. He told me that he and Lu were on friendly terms.' She flashed her smile.

Siv wondered if it was about to fade. 'Did he mention that he saw Lu around Easter?'

The question didn't disturb her. 'He did, yes. It was in the shopping centre in Berminster. They bumped into each other and went for a coffee. Bryan was glad that Lu was doing so well with her cosmetics and that they could be civil.' Zara beamed. 'That's for the best with divorce and people don't always manage it. I congratulated him on staying reasonable and not harbouring resentment.'

She doesn't know, Siv thought. Hendrix had cleverly recounted the meeting, in case anyone else had spotted him and Lu in public. 'You never met Lu, I take it?'

'Well . . . not as such.' Zara touched her mouth and giggled.

'What does that mean?'

'Oh dear. I was hoping you wouldn't ask that question.'

'I have, so could you answer it?'

Zara tweaked a little bow at the neck of her dress. 'You're a girl, so I hope you'll understand. I wanted to get a look at Lu, see what Bryan's ex was like.'

'Was this because you had suspicions about him?'

'No, no!' She gave a loud laugh. 'It wasn't that at all! It's hard to explain. Nosiness, that's all it was, just needing an idea of Lu. Have you ever gone out with a divorced man?'

'Not seriously.'

'Well . . . when a guy's got that kind of baggage, it's a bit of a mystery. You wonder what the ex is like — is she pretty, how does she sound, what does she wear? I just wanted an impression of her.' She flicked her hair back. 'You must be thinking that I'm off the wall, but I talked to my best friend about it. She'd hung around the office where her partner's ex works and it reassured her. She said the ex was wearing velour joggers! O-M-G!'

'How awful. So, how did you get this "look" at Lu Forbes?'

'Oh God, I'm going to sound like some weird kind of stalker. I went to the shop at Lansdown Court. I did buy some liquid soap. The stuff was lovely and beautifully presented. Lu was behind the little counter. I was glad to see that she was fairly ordinary. I reckoned that Bryan had done much better for himself with me.' She put a hand to her mouth. 'Does that sound horribly bitchy?'

'A bit.' Siv was finding the whole episode bizarre, but people were baffling. 'Did you speak to Lu?'

'Barely. There was a middle-aged guy there when I arrived and I got the impression they'd been arguing. I could sense an atmosphere. Are you sure I can't offer you anything? We've got iced coffee today, it's delish.'

'No thanks, let's stay focused on the shop. What was the argument about?'

'Oh gosh, it's hard to say, because they stopped as soon as I arrived. I started examining the testers. I did hear Lu tell him not to bother her again, or she'd make a complaint. He stomped out then and banged the door.'

Siv found the photo of Aran Garman on her phone. 'Was this the man?'

Zara *ummed* and *ahhed*, working her lips. 'Maybe. I saw his back. The hair's right. But I only glanced at him. I didn't like to stare.'

'It was Lu you wanted to stare at.'

'You've got me there!' She blushed. 'But I was subtle, I did little glances.'

'And when the man had gone, you bought soap?'

'Yes. I said something about how impressive the shop was. Lu thanked me, but she did seem a bit preoccupied. I didn't linger. I'd satisfied my curiosity.'

'When was this visit?'

'Late last October.'

So it appeared that Garman might have lied about only seeing Lu once, in August. 'You've been helpful, Ms Lennard. Thanks.'

'Is that man a suspect or something?'

'I can't comment.'

'Is that it, then? I um . . . *obvs*, I haven't told Bryan about that time I snooped on Lu. It might seem a bit icky, after what's happened.'

'I won't mention it to him.'

'Great!'

Despite her shallowness, Siv couldn't help having sympathy for Zara. Would Hendrix stay with her now? How would she react if she found out that she hadn't been an upgrade from Lu after all? She wrapped things up and called Ali on her way back to the car, telling him to get Garman to the station for another interview.

* * *

Patrick had a grizzling two-year-old clinging to his knee, which was now decorated with a sticky deposit. The little girl gazed up at him with dopey eyes and swayed.

'Are you sleepy or very drunk?' he teased.

Her answer was to open her mouth and bawl. He patted her hot little hand in alarm.

Cassia Wade took pity on him and swept the child up. 'Do you have children?'

'No.'

'I can tell. You look as if you've had enough sleep.' The girl had settled in a droning moan. Ms Wade rocked her back and forth. 'Come on you, you're overtired.'

'Sorry, I must have alarmed her.'

'No, it's not you. She needs a nap. I'll just settle her down. Do make a cuppa. I wouldn't mind one.'

'What about the other children?' he asked nervously.

'They're fine for now, playing in the garden. It's enclosed — they can't escape.'

Patrick had dropped in on Ms Wade, following the guv's admonition to follow up everything. Her home teemed with children's paraphernalia, the tools of her trade as a child-minder. Her two were at school and the three in the house belonged to other people. Patrick picked his way through trikes, building blocks, picture books and a wooden railway track to the kitchen, which smelled of tomato soup. He'd arrived as the kids were finishing lunch. The table was strewn with bowls, half-eaten slices of bread, empty yogurt pots and a mangled banana. He peeped through the window and saw two boys sitting on the lawn, fiddling with bendy animals. Not wanting to cause any further disruption, he ducked back before either of them noticed him, then found a tea towel and did his best to remove the crust of dried gunge from his suit.

He'd made two cups of tea when Ms Wade came back, knotting her hair in a grip. She was a tall, lean woman with a bony face and a no-nonsense, combative manner. Her wide linen trousers billowed as she walked.

'Oh, that tea's just what I need! Let's sit outside the back door. We'll be in the shade and I can keep an eye on the kids.'

They sat on two worn green plastic chairs. Three tall sun-flowers were staked in separate tubs just along from the window.

'Those are the children's,' Ms Wade told him. 'We measure them every day.'

'It must be hard work, entertaining them.'

'Yes, but it's worthwhile and it suits me.'

Patrick reckoned he'd better crack on and make the most of the lull. 'We're investigating the murder of Luanna Forbes.'

'Poor Lu! What happened to her was awful. She was so lively and talented.'

'It's very sad. I'm interested in her involvement with your protest about the Minster Beach development. I've read your Facebook posts.'

'Simon Terrance's vanity project? It's appalling.' Her eyes gleamed. 'We're holding another demonstration on the beach this weekend, with hundreds coming.'

'Did Ms Forbes take part in those?'

'She attended one last month. I met her through the Facebook page and she popped in here for a cuppa after the last demo. Lu's view was that Terrance was greedy.'

'In what way?'

'She reckoned that he's already wealthy, with thriving business interests. She had no objection to him starting up a new restaurant on the beach — the Tide certainly needs TLC — but she agreed that chucking out the kiosk owners was nasty and unnecessary . . .' She broke off, noticing that one of the boys was rubbing a toy tiger in the other one's face. 'Frankie, don't do that!'

'Ms Forbes worked alongside Mr Terrance at Lansdown Court. Did that cause tensions?'

'She did say they'd had words. He didn't like the fact that she was publicising the petition in her shop. I told her to stand her ground, but she removed it. Decided it was best to keep her workplace out of it in the end. Simon Terrance can play dirty.' She clapped her hands. 'Frankie! I'll take the tiger away if you don't stop!' She lowered her voice. 'Frankie can be a bit like Terrance. Charming but intimidating.'

'Sounds as if you have a personal gripe against Terrance.'

'Why shouldn't I? He made comments about me to councillors to undermine the support I've been gathering. Said I was a career protestor, a troublemaker. He cited my support for green causes. I glued myself to the tarmac in a motorway protest last year and I helped block oil deliveries at a garage recently. I make no apology for wanting to protect our environment, but Terrance has been trying to use it against me and suggest I'm some unreliable, crazed tree hugger.' She glowered at Patrick. 'I'll bet he's been terribly reasonable and polite with the police, but he can be nasty too. I went to Lansdown Court to have it out with him when I found out he'd been slandering me, but his shop was closed that day. I spoke to the woman who runs the place. She wasn't helpful at all, treated me as if I was a huge inconvenience.'

'Did you tell Ms Forbes about that visit?'

'I certainly did. She advised me to let it go. I got the impression she wanted to keep her head down at that point. She was sort of pensive, on reflection, as if her mind was on something else.'

No doubt fretting about how she was going to tell her sister that she was moving on. 'Thanks for your time, Ms Wade. You have a busy life, with your job and your protest activities.'

There was an enraged wail from upstairs. She rose, putting her mug on her chair.

'My alarm call! Can you see yourself out? And do come to the protest on Saturday, if you're so minded.'

'My brother, Noah, will certainly be there.'

She stopped in her tracks, pointed a commanding finger. 'Oh, you're Noah Hill's brother! I hadn't made the connection. You're not alike. Noah's been a terrific asset to us.'

The wail from above moved up a gear into a full-throated roar and she vanished.

CHAPTER TWENTY-THREE

Aran Garman was a sickly white. He gripped the water he'd been given so hard that it slopped on the interview room table.

Siv went straight in. 'Mr Garman, we've been informed that you visited Ms Forbes more than once in her shop. It's no good denying it, we have a witness.' That was stretching a point, but Garman wasn't to know.

'I didn't hurt her, Inspector. I just . . . let off steam.'

'Did you make two visits? More than that?'

'Twice. Last year, in August and October.'

'Why go back a second time?' Ali demanded.

'On that first visit, I didn't get a chance to speak to her. I told you that. It was frustrating, so I tried again.' Garman twisted his wedding ring. 'I wanted to show her a photo of Isaac and ask if she had guilty dreams. That's all I did and that's the last time I saw her.'

'How did she react?'

'She was shocked. Apologetic, to start with. She had the cheek to say she could imagine my pain! I started to get angry with her then. I told her she should have been jailed along with Epsom and there'd been no justice. Then a customer arrived and she told me to go, started to get annoyed. I left.

That was it. I didn't murder her. A life had already been eliminated. I wanted her to be alive and suffering unending guilt.'

'So why lie to us and say you'd only seen Ms Forbes once?' Ali said.

Garman lowered his head. 'I didn't want you to think badly of me, see me as some deranged, unpredictable lunatic.'

'Your behaviour is cause for concern,' Siv remarked.

'I accept that now. What can I say? Grief makes you mad. It's no excuse, but it does.'

Siv was debating whether or not to arrest him when the door opened and Patrick's head appeared.

'Word, guv?'

She stepped into the corridor. 'I hope you've something useful.'

'Two things. Garman's in the clear. A neighbour saw him in his back garden at eight a.m. last Saturday. He was in his pyjamas, cutting roses.'

'Thanks, Patrick, good work. The second thing?'

'Results came back on Struan's tracksuit. His mum had washed it. There were no traces of blood. Forensics said that despite the washing, they'd have expected to detect some given the amount of blood at the scene.'

'Right. I'd better put Garman out of his misery.'

She was relieved about Garman, even though he'd been such a likely suspect. He was a shell of a man, eaten away by grief, and she was glad that she wouldn't have to add to his torments. She went back into the room and wrote *ALIBI* on Ali's notepad. Garman sat with his head hanging.

'Good news, Mr Garman,' Siv reported. 'One of your neighbours has confirmed that you were in your garden on Saturday morning.'

He raised his head slowly. 'Does that mean I can go? I'm in the clear?'

'Yes, you can go home. I hope that you've learned a lesson. I must warn you not to attempt to contact Ms Epsom again.'

'I won't. I give you my word.'

Siv reckoned he'd had such a fright he'd give Fiona Epsom a wide berth. 'Please make sure you stick to that promise, Mr Garman. Talk to somebody, get some help to deal with what's happened.'

He fumbled with his jacket, dazed. She walked him to the station entrance and watched him stumble to his car. Ali came up behind her.

'He was shaping up nicely too, guv.'

'Back to the drawing board.'

'I'd believe that wee scrote Struan did it. He'd sell his granny for buttons if it suited him. And he had motive, means and opportunity.'

'You're in for a disappointment. There's the small but crucial matter of complete lack of evidence.' She gave him the update on Struan's tracksuit.

'That's a bummer.'

'Exactly. I'm not enjoying today.'

* * *

Siv leaned against the harbour railings and studied the sun setting as she waited for the queue at Stellar to clear. The moon was a pale silhouette in the sky, waiting its turn. Rik was on her own, wearing a silver apron and a chef's hat sprinkled with silver stars. When there was a lull, Siv crossed to the stall.

'You made it!' Rik tipped her hat.

'And I'm ravenous.'

'I can recommend the Dandy — beef patty, lettuce, gherkins, tomato, red onion and barbecue sauce in a sesame seed bun.'

'Please!'

Rik moved deftly in the small space, flipping, spooning and tucking layers in a huge bun.

'Been busy?' Siv propped herself against the counter.

'It gets full on, and then completely quiet. I like the unpredictability. Want me to add some capers as well?'

'Go on. How's Bartel?'

'He's good.' She threw Siv a glance over her shoulder. 'You didn't need to get so strung out about Mutsi. I told Bart, we've had much worse rows than that.'

'Yeah.' She was about to mention her chance meeting with Mutsi in Hove, but then decided not to. She might inadvertently report something that would give Rik ammunition. And it looked as if Mutsi hadn't yet broached family therapy with her sister. *Don't stir the pot.*

Rik was laughing. 'D'you remember that time Mutsi said I'd nicked twenty quid from her purse and her Chanel atomiser and I locked her out of the flat? She was on the landing for ages, hammering on the door!'

'I'd rather not remember, thanks. And she was right — you had.' Siv recalled that night and begging Rik to open the door, hating the storm of anarchy in the air, desperate for peace to be restored.

'Whatever. Here, with the chef's compliments.' She handed Siv a massive burger wrapped in paper napkins. 'Come round the back with it. I'll open the door and you can sit on the step. Can of Coke?'

Siv sat on the van step. The burger was amazing, like an explosion in her mouth. The free food reminded her of all the times Rik had foraged for her in childhood, making sure she didn't go to bed hungry. Rik stood, one eye on the counter, drinking a lemonade.

'Bartel told me why you left Auckland.' Siv caught a stray slice of gherkin.

'Some story, eh? Still, I got away.'

'Must have been scary, being with a violent man.'

'Yep. Bad call on my part. My danger scanner failed miserably. Lesson learned.' She giggled. 'I found where he kept his money stashed, though. I helped myself on my way out.'

Siv swallowed, had a swig of Coke. 'Oh, God. How much?'

'Never you mind. Enough to pay me back for the misery he'd given me. The look on your face! You're such a worrier.

Just enjoy your freebie. I'm really liking this mobile food gig. I wouldn't mind getting my own van eventually.'

'Would that cost a lot, getting set up?'

'No idea. I haven't gone into details yet.' She started slicing a huge beef tomato.

Siv watched her cutting thin rings, all the same size. 'Rik, did you write to Dad about Mutsi?'

She finished the tomato and wiped the knife on a sheet of kitchen roll. 'You still harping on about that? I might have. I can't remember now, too long ago. I might have imagined it.' She snapped the strap of her apron. 'Uh, oh! Mutsi alert! She and Will are coming this way. Out for a romantic evening stroll. Love's middle-aged dream. I wonder if he has any notion of how many men she's promenaded with like that?'

Siv crouched and gobbled the last chunk of burger, wondering if she might get away without being spotted. She hadn't seen Mortimer since the Tommy Castles episode, and she wanted to keep it that way for as long as possible. But she was too late.

'Good evening, Rik!' These were Mortimer's reedy tones. 'Isn't it a beautiful sunset?'

'Gorgeous.' Rik leaned out through the hatch. 'Can I interest you in a burger or two? I do a slimline version for the figure-conscious.'

'We've eaten, thank you.'

'We went to Amalfi.' Mutsi was using her best standing-on-my-dignity voice and point scoring; Amalfi was the most highly rated restaurant in town. It was hard to get a table there without booking. 'The lobster was heavenly.'

'I don't stretch to lobster,' Rik replied. 'Siv's here. Say hello, sis, don't be shy.'

Siv stood, brushing herself down and cursing Rik for her mischief. Mutsi and Mortimer were dressed smartly. She was in a cream shift with black piping and gold jewellery, a pashmina draped across her shoulders. 'Evening. I can recommend the Dandy burger, should you ever fancy one.'

'Slumming it, Siv?' Mutsi pulled a face. 'I never had you down as a fast-food person.'

'Rik's always been a reliable source of sustenance,' Siv said with meaning.

'I'm sure we'll try your fare one evening, perhaps when we're on *Quicksilver*.' Mortimer laughed nervously, avoiding Siv's eye.

Siv wanted to warn him not to attempt conciliation. He was straying into hazardous terrain.

'What made you decide to sell junk food, Rik? Couldn't you aim a little higher in life than a mobile stall?' Mutsi wrinkled her nose and adjusted her pashmina.

'I seem to have a talent for it and, sadly, I haven't been able to find any spare minor aristocracy or rich guys to leech from.' Rik's smile was frosty.

Mutsi flicked a glance at Mortimer and went for mock reproof. 'Rik, you are *terribly* naughty and always so tart. Now, I've just had a brilliant idea! While we're here, could I *please* have a photo taken with my two daughters? I haven't got one of us all together since the dark ages and this is too good an opportunity to miss. Will, can you do the honours?'

Rik started to protest. 'I'm not going—'

Siv grabbed her arm and hissed, 'Just do it. Then she'll go away.'

'But—'

'It's a photo.'

'She's manipulating us and—'

'Who cares?'

'I don't want to play happy families.'

'Oh, suck it up and just pretend you're Ms Bun the Burger Queen. You *owe* me.'

Rik huffed but followed Siv through the door. Mortimer was holding Mutsi's phone as if it might explode in his hands.

'Let's have the beautiful harbour as a backdrop, rather than a burger van,' Mutsi bossed. 'Rik, can you not take off the ugly apron?'

'No.'

'Very well, if it's too much to ask.' Mutsi beckoned Siv and Rik to her, positioning herself between them. She draped an arm around their necks and tilted a hip with one foot forward, model fashion. 'Now, are we ready? Take a couple, Will.'

'Say cheese,' Mortimer called.

The soft weave of Mutsi's pashmina brushed against Siv's arm. This was so bizarre, she might as well throw herself into it. She beamed, sure that Rik would be scowling.

Mortimer clicked away, until Rik slid from Mutsi's arm and marched back to the van.

'That was the highlight of my day, folks, but I must ask you to move along if you're not buying.' She gestured across the road. 'I spy customers approaching and I've targets to meet.'

A large group of young men were on their way, shoving and mock-punching one another, their shouts carrying over the harbour.

'Gladly.' Mutsi sniffed. 'Come along, Will, the lowlifes are approaching.' She hooked her arm through his and they departed.

'I'll head off too,' Siv said. 'Thanks for the burger.'

'Any time. The family dynamics were a surprise side order. Hope they don't give you indigestion.'

* * *

When she reached home, Siv saw that she had emails from Patrick and the station. She read a roundup of Patrick's activities, including his visit to Cassia Wade, and a message saying that a Fiona Epsom had called, wanting to speak to her. Siv changed into a sleeveless T-shirt dress and hovered by the fridge. She decided that she deserved a glass of akvavit after the emotional overload of two sightings of Mutsi in the same day, and that impromptu family gathering. She poured it and went with the drink and her phone to the river. She sat with her back to a willow, sipped the spirit and called the number in Ottawa, which was answered almost immediately.

'Hello, is that Fiona Epsom? This is DI Siv Drummond, returning your call. Is this a good time?'

'Hi, yes, I'm just finishing work. Hold on a minute and I'll go to the staff room.'

Siv had another drink. It glided down, easing her muscles. She missed Ed after scenes like that at the harbour. He'd always been so good at watching her back and containing her mother. She gazed up at the clear, dark heavens. Jupiter was stunningly bright tonight. She indulged the daft but consoling hope that there might be cycling lanes around the stars.

'Thanks for waiting, Inspector Drummond. I can speak in private now.'

'How can I help?'

'My dad called me. He told me about Lu Forbes and he said the police had been in touch, asking about Mr Garman and the accident with Isaac.'

'We need to ask lots of questions about Ms Forbes's past. Your dad gave us details of the letters Mr Garman sent you.'

'I liked Lu a lot. I'm so sorry about the way she died. Have you seen Mr Garman?' Fiona spoke fast, tripping over her words.

'Yes. He's admitted writing to you.'

'That was awful. Really scary.'

'You should have talked to someone.'

'That's what my parents said when I finally told them. I kept hoping each letter would be the last. Maybe I convinced myself that I deserved to be hounded by Mr Garman after what had happened. Is it him? Is he the murderer?'

'Mr Garman is no longer a focus in our enquiries.'

'Oh. That's a relief, to be honest. I didn't want his life to have got even more messed up. That man's been through enough.'

'Is that what you wanted? That reassurance?'

'No — I mean, it is good to hear. There's something I wanted to pass on to you. I'm not sure if it's significant, but it is about Lu Forbes, so I suppose it could be.'

'Can you talk a little bit slower? I'm missing some of your words.'

'Sorry. I've no halfway mode — I either talk too fast or too slowly.' Fiona paused, adjusted her pace. 'That accident, when Isaac was killed, was totally my fault. It was a split-second decision and I panicked and made the wrong one by slamming my foot on the accelerator. But Lu . . . Lu was distracted at that moment when Isaac ran in front of me.'

'Go on.'

'Her phone rang, and she'd reached into her pocket to silence it just as Isaac appeared. She always turned it off or put it in airplane mode before a lesson, but she'd forgotten that day.'

'This wasn't mentioned in court. Why not?'

'I never included it in my statement, and neither did Lu. We didn't refer to it afterwards. I decided not to, because I do genuinely believe that what happened was my fault and I liked and respected Lu. I didn't see any point in damaging her reputation and livelihood. Even now, I'm pretty sure that she couldn't have made any difference.'

'It was generous of you to stay silent about that. Your sentence might have been more lenient if the blame had been shared.'

'But she wasn't to blame, not really. Why get Lu into trouble? I held myself responsible and I was right to, end of.'

'So why tell me now?'

'Because I did mention Lu's phone ringing that day to someone years later. I was at a function in a hotel in town, the Dovecote. I'd had a few drinks and I started chatting and letting my hair down. It came back to me. This was shortly before I emigrated. I guess I was so happy to be getting away and leaving it all behind, I threw caution to the wind. And Lu had given up instructing and was running a business of her own, so whatever I said wasn't going to affect her.'

Fiona talked on, describing the social evening at the hotel and her father's wide networks and charity work. 'He meets loads of people and he's dead friendly. Always the last guest to leave a party! Oddly enough, he knows someone else who's connected with Lansdown Court. We chat every week, so I keep up with all the goss from back home.' She divulged another piece of information her father had passed on a couple of months back.

Siv listened avidly, hunching over the phone, the kick of the akvavit blending with an adrenalin rush. This must be the break they'd needed. She reassured Fiona that she'd been right to make contact and wished her well.

She finished her drink and lay flat on the ground, the knot of tree roots against her back. Jupiter blazed down at her. She threaded the nuggets she'd been given into other remarks, little snippets and reactions. She forced herself to be calm and not jump to conclusions. This was a step forward, no doubt, albeit tentative. It led in a certain direction, but that was all. Now it was a question of teasing out a confession, which was always a risky strategy. A few ideas were forming and she assessed them until she was satisfied.

She rang Ali, telling him about Fiona's call.

'Lu Forbes was a dark horse in more ways than one,' he commented. 'She looked out for number one, all right. It was rotten of her not to own up about that accident and leave Ms Epsom with all the guilt.'

'She was certainly complicated enough — and caused enough difficulties for others — to have aggravated someone.' Siv explained her strategy and told him to pick her up at eight in the morning. Ali agreed to update Patrick.

Siv closed her eyes and listened to the river's babble. She woke just after midnight, her back protesting from the hard earth, her mind clear and sharp. In the wagon, she brewed tea, fully awake now and realising that she wouldn't find sleep again easily. She switched on a lamp and sat at her small, fold-down table, where she creased and pleated paper for several hours, lost in creating shapes.

CHAPTER TWENTY-FOUR

In the car the next morning, Siv turned to Ali. 'I've been meaning to tell you, I searched for the Drummond clan motto. It's "Gang warily". That applies to today.'

'Ha!' He tapped the wheel. 'A good motto for the police.'

'For life in general. We go cautiously. We've no hard evidence, only hearsay via the Epsom family. You're clear on what I want you to do when we arrive?'

'Aye. I talk to Struan on his own, take him back over his story, and you speak to his mum. What if she won't play by our rules?'

'We have to keep our fingers crossed.'

'You reckon we'll get a result?'

Siv made a 'who knows' gesture. 'Worth a shot.'

'If we do, we'll have sorted this within a week. Mortimer will be chuffed.'

'Keeping Mortimer happy is all I live for. You're in a better mood, despite this heat.'

'Aye, true enough. Pol will be back next week, a bit early.'

'That explains it.'

At the Old Dairy, Shona was spruce in a green shirt-waister, although her expression was none too cordial when she saw them on the doorstep. There was a rich aroma of bacon and fresh coffee wafting from the house.

'Good morning.' Siv greeted her. 'We have a few more questions we need to ask.'

'More? Surely not! We're exhausted by it all. And we've had the juvenile people here too, quizzing Struan and noting down everything he says. It's starting to feel like torture. I was hoping for a peaceful weekend.'

'I can imagine it's a strain, but we have to do our job.'

'Well, you'd better come in. I can hardly turn you away, can I?'

Siv had had a few grudging invitations during her career, but that ranked quite high. In the living room, she stood by the fireplace and Ali stayed by the door.

'Is Struan in?' she asked.

'He's upstairs. He has football training this afternoon.'

'Would it be acceptable if Sergeant Carlin talks to him while I speak to you? It's going over the same ground with Struan about the murder, nothing new. Nothing to do with the matter regarding Cherry Bolting. Fact-checking, basically. It would save us time and be quicker for you.'

'I suppose . . . if you have to.'

'Thanks,' Ali said. 'I'll pop up to his bedroom, shall I?'

'Second door on the right.'

'Shall we sit down?' Siv moved to an armchair, taking control. She noted the flash of annoyance in Shona's eyes.

'D'you want coffee?' Shona reasserted herself. 'It's just freshly made.'

'No, thanks. How are you doing, after what's happened with Struan?'

'How would you expect me to be? I'm trying to keep things together, but it's hard. Struan's barely talking to me after I gave him a piece of my mind. Angus came round and tore a strip off him last night and he hasn't come out of his room since. I keep going over what that dreadful woman has been up to. Disgusting! How could Cherry behave in such a way? Surely there are enough men of her own age for her. It's beyond me. I did wonder about her sometimes, the way she wears those tight clothes, as if she's been poured into them. Drawing attention to herself.' Shona added bitterly, 'She'd better not show her face around here again. I can't imagine she will, but she's so brazen, it's hard to tell what she'd get up to. There'll be more bad publicity for Lansdown too, when the court case comes up. I could see that Angus was really fed up about the whole business.'

The strain was evident on Shona's face. Siv was happy to let her vent, but she hadn't come here to offer reassurance. Quite the opposite.

'I need to talk to you some more about Lu Forbes.'

'Yes, get on with it, then.'

'You'd known Lu for quite some time?'

'Yes. I met Yvonne first, then Lu.'

'And you always got on well with Lu?'

'Yes. There was nothing to fall out about. For goodness' sake, I've told you all this!'

'You have, but it's hard to swallow the version you've given. You claim that you had no issues with Lu, even though she was less than generous about your produce and made remarks about it to other people. She told Struan off too, for sleeping with Cherry. Most parents don't take kindly to other people criticising their children. So your attitude is remarkably generous.'

'We're all entitled to our opinions and I'm aware that Struan can be boisterous sometimes. I didn't hold any of that against her.' Shona dug a hand into her dress pocket.

'That all sounds very even-handed and diplomatic, but I've been getting the impression that, in fact, you weren't that keen on Lu. There are some issues that you haven't touched on during our interviews. It must have annoyed you that Lu was active in the protest about Simon Terrance's proposed beach development. The woman who's heading the protest — Cassia Wade — came here and spoke to you. You weren't keen on her calling on you. I can see why. Lansdown Court isn't just your job. Your home comes with it. You don't like to rock the boat, and you wouldn't want to attract bad publicity.'

'That Wade woman didn't stay long. I gave her short shrift. It was Simon she was after, so I sent her on her way.'

'But you can't have approved of Lu encouraging customers to sign the petition in her shop. You were aware of that?'

'Yes,' Shona muttered. 'Simon asked her to stop and she did.'

'You didn't mention that, yet it impacted on relationships here. Why didn't you tell us?'

Shona glanced up at the ceiling, tilted her head as if listening. 'It didn't seem that important.'

'Oh.' Siv raised her voice. 'Did it seem important to you that Lu was back with her ex-husband?'

Shona froze. 'Wh . . . what?'

'Lu and Bryan. You saw them together at Curlew, a boutique hotel along the coast. You were delivering homemade goods.'

'I can't . . . Who told you that?'

'It's true, yes? You realised that they were an item again.'

There was a sound from above, like chairs shifting. Shona turned towards the door.

'They'll be a while yet, no need to worry about what's happening upstairs,' Siv reassured her. 'You're friends with a Mr Epsom and you revealed your worries about Lu and Bryan to him when you saw him not long ago, after a football match. You have so many responsibilities. It must all get a bit much at times. Sometimes, you just need to unload, and I hear that Mr Epsom's a kindly man.'

'He is a good man. Sincere and a listener.' Shona blinked and rubbed the corner of an eye. 'He advised me to stay quiet about what I saw, in case it came to nothing.'

'"Least said, soonest mended"?'

'If only it had worked out like that. I spotted Lu and Bryan at that hotel. They were coming out as I drove away after the delivery. Arms around each other and kissing as if they'd never been apart.'

'What did you make of that?'

'I wasn't sure. I was stunned. It just didn't seem possible. They'd divorced, and Yvonne told me that Lu couldn't wait to see the back of him when the marriage ended.'

'But you must have dwelt on it — it would be tough on Yvonne if her sister and Bryan were going to make another go of things. You're so fond of Yvonne. Protective too. She's almost like a daughter to you, and you'd not seen so much of her since she and Lu bought a home together. No more cosy nights in, no more sleepovers. All in all, Lu was an irritation for you, a spoke in your wheel.'

Shona's eyes travelled upwards again.

Good. Time to crank up the pressure. 'I understand that you're worried about Struan and you're right to be, but please try to focus.'

'Have you got a teenager?'

'No.'

'Then don't lecture me about my son. You've no idea what this has been like.' She straightened, clasped a hand on one arm. 'He's been corrupted by that woman leading him astray. I hope she's thoroughly ashamed of herself. She should be jailed for what she did.' She added with less certainty, 'I've done my best by him.'

'No doubt, but he's got himself in quite a situation.' Siv needed to keep her distracted and off balance. 'Tell me about an evening you spent at the Dovecote Hotel a couple of years back. It was a fundraiser for inner-city kids' football clubs. Mr Epsom was one of the organisers. He's a referee, lives and breathes footie.'

Shona was poised forwards, as if she might bolt. 'That's ages ago, I can barely remember it.'

'Let me jog your memory. You met Fiona Epsom, Mr Epsom's daughter, and she told you something about Lu, from her driving instructor days.'

'Will this take much longer? I have a batch of preserves to make.'

'Never mind those. Tell me about Fiona.'

'Yes, yes! Her dad introduced us. She was pretty drunk. When I told her I worked at Lansdown Court and mentioned Lu, she started describing the accident and the little boy. Lu's phone rang as he ran into the road, so she wasn't paying full attention. It was appalling that Lu didn't own up about that and left all the responsibility with Fiona. I didn't think much of her for it, but it was years ago.'

There was thudding on the stairs and a door slammed. Shona half-stood, hand on the back of the sofa. Ali came in.

'All good. Struan's just popped out for a while on his skateboard.'

'Is he alright?' Shona turned to the window and stretched on tiptoe.

'He's fine, we had a nice chat. What have I missed?' Ali sat next to Siv.

'Quite a bit. Shall I summarise, Ms Hollis?'

'What?' She picked at the arm of the sofa.

'I'll take that as a yes. It turns out that there's plenty you've failed to tell us about the state of play at Lansdown Court and your relationship with Lu Forbes. You were annoyed with her for joining in the protest about the beach development and stirring up trouble here. You found out that she'd played a greater part in the accident that killed Isaac Garman, and that she'd resumed a relationship with Bryan Hendrix. That threatened the status quo with Yvonne. Perhaps you'd also discovered that Lu was planning to give up the shop and move away, which would make her sister's position even worse. Then there was the fact that she sometimes reprimanded Struan, ridiculed your homely produce and liked to blow her own trumpet. Lu must have seemed like a trouble magnet, and you have so much vested in running this outfit. There's quite a lot there to stoke antagonism.'

'Oh, very well! I didn't like her much. So what?'

'Ms Hollis, did you work up such a dislike of Lu Forbes, was she such a threat, that you murdered her?'

'Me?' She rocked back. 'Of course not! It never occurred . . . Yes, I see how you've come at it, how you've pieced together . . . Oh, that's rich!' She sagged against the cushion, staring at the window.

'Struan's got a lot to deal with,' Ali said. 'Stressful times ahead for him, no matter how much he plays the big man. This stuff with Ms Bolting might well impact on his school work and his football ambitions. Hard to say, but just putting that out there. We'll keep digging now, we'll be all over your life, and if you did kill Lu Forbes, we'll nail you. You've been finding it hard going so far? We haven't started. If you cooperate, it will be a lot easier on Struan. And on you too. It sits well with the justice system. If you don't, life here is going to be horrible and an awful strain on your son. Is it worth it?'

Shona roused herself. She walked to the window, scanned the court. There was the rumble of a skateboard and she smiled in relief, pressing a hand to the glass. 'You believe that *I* killed Lu? You're on the wrong track.' Her voice was tight.

'That suggests that you can tell us who did.' Siv's neck tingled.

Shona tapped a foot on the skirting board and faced them. 'I'm afraid I can't. Do you really think that I'd have kept something like that to myself?' She drew her hands across her forehead, pressing her fingers into her temples. 'I resent you coming here and making these allegations, using what's happened with Struan to try and coerce me. It seems to me that you're putting together stories and jumping to conclusions. If you want to talk to me with a solicitor present, I'll happily come to the station. Otherwise, I've nothing more to say.' She turned and tapped on the window, beckoning Struan. 'Now, I need to see to my son, make sure he's got his things ready for this afternoon. It's an important coaching session.'

Shona was maintaining great control, but Siv could detect the effort it was costing. Tension radiated from her. Siv had to accept that they were stymied for now. 'We will want to interview you formally, Ms Hollis, so do please contact your solicitor.'

She and Ali walked to the car under the beating sun, unspoken disappointment hanging between them. Ali started the engine and headed for Goose Lane.

'Sorry, guv. She's a tough nut, is our Shona. You reckon she did it?'

'Possibly, but if not, she definitely knows something.'

'Aye, but it won't be easy to winkle it out of her.'

Siv's frustration simmered. She was convinced that the resolution of this case was within reach, like a tantalising apple hanging just too high on a tree. Shona must be conflicted and wondering what to do. Maybe she'd be driven to consult someone other than a solicitor. She tapped on the dashboard and pointed to a farm track coming up on their left.

'Pull up and reverse in here!'

Ali reversed into the turning. 'We waiting to see if Shona makes a move?'

'Exactly. She'll be alarmed now and it might make her act on impulse.'

'Right. I hope it won't take her too long, or we'll bake like cakes in her oven.'

Siv handed him a bottle of water. 'Here. I predict movement in the near future.'

* * *

Yvonne was sitting with her father in the care home. He wore a shirt that was several sizes too big with mismatched buttons, and an unfamiliar pendant around his neck. She often found him wearing other men's clothes and he was infamous in the home for wandering into other residents' rooms and pinching jewellery. Every so often, the staff turned his room out, collected his misappropriated hoard and returned items to their rightful owners.

He was attempting a jigsaw of vibrantly coloured birds. The now empty box declared that it was specially formulated to delight people with dementia, stimulate conversation and prompt joyful memories. These promises were lost on her morose father, who was ignoring her attempts to chat and growing increasingly frustrated with the pieces. When she offered to help, he slapped her hand away so sharply that it hurt. Finally, he upended the puzzle, sending it flying to the far corners of the lounge.

'Here, you could have had my eye out!' a woman shouted from her chair in front of the TV.

'Sorry,' Yvonne called. 'It was an accident.'

'*He's* an accident,' the woman yelled. '*And* a tea leaf! Ted the tea leaf!'

'Shut your bloody mouth or I'll shut it for you,' her father muttered. His speech was indistinct because his dentures couldn't be found.

Yvonne got up to collect the jigsaw pieces, but a carer signalled to her that she'd do it. Yvonne sank back down. Her father had closed his eyes and was humming to himself. He'd no idea who she was today. She'd finally plucked up courage to come and tell him about Lu, but what was the point? He'd probably ask who Lu was and he'd have forgotten by the time she left. All she was achieving was causing herself pain.

'Dad?' She touched his hand tentatively.

He opened one eye. 'Who are you? Stop bothering me. Is there any tea on the way?' He fingered his mouth. 'Where're my teeth?'

'The carers couldn't find them. Maybe you've put them somewhere.'

'Where?'

'I've no idea. I expect they'll turn up.'

'I want my tea.'

'It'll be here soon.'

'I want some of those things with it.' He fidgeted fingers in front of his face. 'Sweet.'

'Biscuits?'

'That's it. Who've you come to see, then? Where's the tea?'

She gave up. How she hated this place, with its warm fug of decay and futility. It was almost noon and Jem had said that he could get home for a picnic lunch in bed today. She longed to be with him and share her news. It was pointless sitting here, having endlessly looping fragments of conversation with this man who regarded her as a stranger and would wipe her from his memory as soon as she left the room. She kissed a finger and laid it on her father's cheek. He flinched, as if she'd burned him, and rolled his head away.

She escaped and drove to Jem's, her hand still stinging but her heart lifting. Half an hour later, they were ensconced in his bed. The sun peeped through the curtains, bathing them in pools of creamy, fuzzy light. The tray propped between them held coffee and toast slathered with thick honey that she'd brought with her. Jem never had much in his kitchen, but he always bought great coffee.

She'd told him briefly about the care home visit. Jem didn't like hearing such grim stuff because it gave him nightmares. 'It's awful, seeing my dad like that. He used to be so witty and capable.'

'Terrible. Forget about it now, Little Tree. It's horrible, and what can you do? Let's enjoy the now.'

She reached up and ran a hand through his hair. 'I've got news, good news.'

'I always like good news.'

'I talked to our solicitor and she agreed she could release some money to me. I'll have it in my account next week.'

'Little Tree, that's wonderful, best news ever!' He kissed her with sticky lips.

'You'll be able to pay Shona.'

'Her face will be a picture! Thanks, you're a life-saver.' He ran a hand down his chest. 'It seems awful, in a way, to benefit like this from Lu's death. You're handling it all so well.'

'Am I? It's like I'm on auto. Being here with you helps me cope. You're my safe haven.'

'Sweetheart,' he murmured vaguely.

Yvonne snuggled back against the pillow. 'Jem, could you run the shop for me a couple of days a week? I've been getting my head round it. I reckon if I closed it one day a week for now, and if I worked flat out, I could make the produce during the days you're there, and then I'd manage it the rest of the time.'

'What about my shop? I don't want to neglect that.'

'You could put a sign up on yours, saying that you're next door and to come and fetch you. It's a bit patchy, but it's just a stopgap, a way of keeping it ticking until we can work out something more long term.' She leaned into him. 'You did say you'd help me out.'

'Well . . . I'm not sure . . . It'd be a big responsibility.'

'Please, Jem? I need your support if I'm going to get through this and I have sorted your back rent.'

He plucked at his bottom lip. 'We can give it a try, I suppose, see how it goes.'

'We'll make a good team. We always have. We could be so successful.' She put her thumbs on his eyebrows, smoothed them. 'You'd have to be reliable, though, and stick to the agreement. No turning up late or slacking.'

'Demands, demands!' He stretched and yawned. 'Do my best. Whatever you say. Are you finishing that toast, or can I have it? I'd better get back to the shop soon and open up for the afternoon. I can devote another fifteen minutes to you, so make the most of me!'

They were linking fingers and gazing into each other's eyes when the doorbell rang.

'Are you expecting someone?' *If it's one of his other women, I'll scream.*

'No. Ignore it, they'll go away.'

But the visitor was persistent. The bell rang again.

'I suppose I'd better see who it is.' Jem unfolded from the bed and drew on shorts and a T-shirt.

'Don't be long,' Yvonne called softly.

'Back in a tick, keep everything warm!'

Yvonne lay, her tongue sweet with honey, picturing a fruitful partnership with Jem where the two shops did a roaring trade. She was confident now that, with time, he'd come round to her plans for a joint future. Eventually, they'd marry and buy a place together. Maybe a sweet little cottage in one of the villages that they could decorate with his work. They'd be celebrated as one of those couples who had everything, the kind who featured in the colour supplements that Jem used in his art. *Meet Yvonne and Jem Forbes-Calloway, Berminster's golden creative partners.* She curled her toes in anticipation.

Jem reappeared. 'Little Tree, it's Shona, asking for you.'

'What does she want?'

'Didn't say, but she's got a serious face on.' He grimaced. 'On her high horse, as per. She barged in as if she owned the place.'

'Is it about Lu?'

'No idea.'

Yvonne slipped on her dress and sandals and followed him to the living room. Shona was sitting near the window, gripping a tissue.

'Hello. How did you know I was here?' Yvonne went to her and bent to kiss her cheek. She was rigid, her skin fiery.

'Oh, I just took a *wild guess* — if you weren't on the boat you were bound to be *here*. It's important that I speak to you.'

Shona's narrowed eyes flicked between her and Jem. It must have been obvious that they'd just got out of bed. Yvonne blushed and sat next to her.

'Why aren't you answering your phone?' Shona asked.

'I've got it on silent.'

'I can imagine. I don't think much of your choice in men, Yvonne. So disappointing.'

'OK, Shona, we're not interested in your opinion and we don't need any sermonising.' Jem flopped into a chair. 'What's so important?'

'I need to speak to Yvonne on her own,' Shona replied. '*Urgently.*'

'Could you make us a cuppa?' Yvonne asked him, mouthing, *Please*.

'Yeah, right. Whatever. But I have to get back to work soon.'

'I wouldn't worry, there'll hardly be queues of customers,' Shona snapped.

Jem laughed. 'Once you've finished your urgent chat, Shona, I'll give you the "good news".'

When he'd closed the door, Yvonne said, 'I know you don't much like him, Shona, but I love him. I've loved him for years. I was going to tell you as soon as—'

'I don't give a fig about Jem Calloway after what's happened.'

'Please, don't be cross about him. He means well, even if he doesn't always strike the right note, and I'm sure I'm going to have a future with him.'

'Listen to yourself, Yvonne, will you! You're living in cloud cuckoo land! What future?'

'What do you mean? I know you've been fed up with Jem because of the rent, but there's no need to—'

Shona gripped her wrists tight and leaned so close, Yvonne could see the saliva on her teeth. 'Never mind that. You need to listen to me very carefully. I'm at the end of my tether.'

'What is it? What's wrong?' But she could guess what was coming. A chill gripped her heart.

CHAPTER TWENTY-FIVE

Siv and Ali had waited for barely thirty minutes when they saw Shona drive past on Goose Lane. She was hunched over the steering wheel, a woman on a mission. They followed her, at a discreet distance, to the harbour, watching as she parked and then walked fast to the *Scarlett O'Hara*. Her white trainers flashed in the sun.

'It involves Yvonne, then,' Siv said.

'Those two are close. An unburdening?'

'But by whom? We'll let them start talking.'

'I wouldn't fancy living on a boat. I like solid ground below me. I'd be awake at night, worrying about a tsunami.'

'In *Berminster*?'

'Well, you never know, what with global warming and all. Coastal areas are going to see big changes and I can't swim.'

'Best to move into a high-rise flat, then. That way, you'll be sure of keeping your feet dry . . . Look!' Siv tapped his arm. 'She's coming back.'

Shona had reappeared, speaking on her phone as she retraced her steps and got back in her car. Her body language spoke of irritation. Ali hung behind her into town.

'Hang on, I'd say she's heading to Jem Calloway's, he lives along here,' he said.

'Curiouser and curiouser.'

They parked and waited while Shona descended the basement steps.

'We'll give them a couple of minutes.'

'Who's your money on?' Ali asked.

'At this point, I'll admit that I'm not at all sure.'

'Maybe I've been right about Calloway all along.'

'Let's knock on his door and see if we can justify your suspicions.'

When they reached the door, they could hear raised voices, including Jem Calloway's, but couldn't make out what was being said. Ali kept his finger on the bell and the flat fell silent. Finally, Calloway opened the door. He had his usual slept-in look, but alarm crossed his face when he saw who was at his door.

'Sorry, it's not a good time. I've got visitors.'

'Aye, and you have two more now,' Ali told him. 'We'll come in, thanks.'

As they approached the living-room door, a panicked voice — unmistakably Shona's — punctured the silence: '. . . can't cope. You have to go to the police, Yvonne.' Glancing at Ali, Siv pushed it open.

Shona and Yvonne sat side by side. Both had tears in their eyes. Heat lay heavy in the room and there was a heightened atmosphere. Jem's sweat mingled with a floral scent. He leaned against a bookcase, his shoulders slumping.

'We seem to have interrupted something.' Ali moved to stand beside Calloway.

'I dunno what's going on, but something's rocking off, that's for sure,' Jem said to no one in particular. 'I'm totally confused.'

'That's your usual state of mind,' Shona said.

'Oh, do stop!' Yvonne held up a hand and addressed Siv. 'Why are you here? Have you got news about Lu?'

Siv was studying one of Jem's abstracts. She turned, her expression blank. 'I'm expecting the news to come from someone in this flat, Ms Forbes.'

'Sorry?' Yvonne shrank back.

'I'd like you to tell me why Ms Hollis has come to see you in such a hurry after we met with her this morning.'

Yvonne glanced down and pulled at a thread on the hem of her dress.

'It's about Struan,' Shona cut in. 'I'm so worried, I wanted to talk to Yvonne.'

Siv took a seat. 'I don't believe you.'

'That comes as no surprise,' Shona responded robustly.

'Hang on, Shona, why were you telling Yvonne she had to go to the police?' Jem asked. 'Why have you come here upsetting her and what's it got to do with Struan?'

'Stay out of this,' Shona told him.

'This is my flat, thanks very much. I didn't invite you here. We were having a quiet lunch until you turned up.'

'Lunch!' Shona sniffed.

'Why does Shona want you to talk to us, Yvonne?' Siv spoke quietly.

'I . . .' Yvonne pressed a hand to her mouth.

'What is it, Little Tree?' Jem asked. 'Why are you letting Shona get to you? You don't have to put up with her bossiness.'

'Mr Calloway, would you please be quiet,' Siv warned him. 'I'd like to hear the truth.'

'It's like Shona said, she needed to discuss the situation with Struan.' Yvonne's voice was very small.

'The truth,' Siv repeated.

There was a silence. Yvonne wiped her brow. Shona gasped, leaned forward and clenched her hands together.

'It's no good, Yvonne. I can't keep doing this.'

'Shona . . .' Yvonne put a hand out towards her, but she pushed it away.

'I'm sorry, but too much has happened now, things I couldn't have foreseen. This business with Cherry — how will we live that down? God knows how Angus will react, he's already threatening to evict us.' Shona's face wrinkled with regret. 'I wanted to help, but everything's got far too complicated. I'm having to juggle too many problems. I did try, did my best, and in the end, that's all anyone can do. The strain's getting too much and the police won't leave me alone. I dread finding them at the door.'

Shona stood and rested against the wall, arms down, palms flat against it. Her complexion reminded Siv of the ashy grey of Ali's cigarette smoke. He stirred, moved forward a little. Siv put a finger to her lips.

Shona smiled with regret. 'I can't keep this up now, Yvonne. You have to tell them the truth about what happened with Lu. It's only fair on me and Struan.'

Yvonne gave a sudden high-pitched laugh and clamped her hand over her mouth.

'Ms Forbes, do you have something you'd like to tell us?' Siv asked.

Yvonne nodded and looked pleadingly at Jem Calloway. He was staring at her with incomprehension.

'What are you on about? Yvonne? What's happening?' Jem took a step towards her.

'I didn't plan it. It just happened,' Yvonne whispered.

Siv got up. 'Yvonne Forbes, I'm arresting you for the murder of Ms Luanna Forbes . . .' Her voice carried on, quiet and without emphasis. She then cautioned Shona, who closed her eyes.

'Lu came out with awful stuff, tormenting things. I snapped . . .' Yvonne continued.

'You can tell us all about it at the station,' Ali said.

Yvonne turned to Shona. 'Thanks for sticking by me. When you told me what had happened with Cherry and Struan, I realised it might all get too much. I know you've been out of your mind with worry. It was too much for you, I see that now. I don't blame you. It's all on me.'

'I don't get it, this is all too weird.' Jem shifted from one foot to the other. 'What's going on, Little Tree?'

'Sorry, Jem. It's a terrible mess. Everything's gone so wrong. Sorry. All my fault. It wasn't supposed to be this way.'

'You killed her? You killed Lu and let me walk in and find her like that? I almost had a breakdown!' He collapsed into the rocking chair that used to be his mum's.

'I didn't mean for you to find her. I panicked.' Yvonne cringed at the clunk and wheeze of the chair as it shunted back and forth.

Jem rubbed a foot along the floor. 'How could you do that? I might have got the blame!'

'I'd never have let that happen, honest.'

He stopped the chair, sitting bolt upright. 'What about my rent, though? I need that, sweetie. You'll make sure I get that, won't you?'

She made to reply, but then huddled into herself.

'Ms Forbes and Ms Hollis, we should go now,' Siv told them.

'I need to dress properly and rinse my hands. I've honey on my fingers,' Yvonne said.

* * *

Late on Saturday, Siv went through the two statements that had been taken. Turning first to Shona Hollis's, she read the core sections.

Yvonne rang me late on Friday 8 July, after Struan had gone to bed. She was terribly upset because she'd had a huge row with Lu. She told me that she and Lu had shared a bottle of wine and Lu suddenly announced that she was back with Bryan Hendrix, and they wanted to move away and buy a place together. It meant that she'd need to leave the business and take her share from the boat, although she wouldn't want the money from their home immediately. Yvonne was stunned and panicky. She'd begged Lu not to leave and tried to persuade her that even if she wanted to be with Bryan, they could live together in Berminster and Lu could stay in the business. But Lu said her mind was made up. She was tired of Lansdown Court, she'd outgrown it. She suggested

222

that they might sell the company, or if Yvonne was up to running it, she'd give advice and she'd help find someone else to front the shop. It was a thriving concern and she was sure that they'd have no trouble getting a replacement for her. They argued for a while and then Lu went to bed. I advised Yvonne that it was late and there was nothing she could do, although I understood why she was hysterical. I told her she'd need to talk to Lu again over the weekend, when they'd both calmed down. I reassured her that together they should be able to find a way forward.

I hardly slept that night. I'd suspected that Lu and Bryan were together again, because I'd seen them at a hotel. I hadn't told Yvonne, not wanting to upset her. I was hoping that I'd got the wrong impression, or that even if those two were seeing each other, it would blow over. I was cross with myself then for not telling Yvonne. It would have given her some warning and a chance to tackle Lu about it. I remembered how I'd kept that other business about Lu to myself as well, the awful stuff Fiona Epsom had told me concerning the child who was killed. Again, I'd been protecting Yvonne. Lu just kept getting away with things. Her behaviour was appalling, and I wasn't sure how Yvonne would handle it if she went ahead and bailed out. There was one problem after another at Lansdown Court.

The next morning, Saturday 9 July, Yvonne rang me at about 7.50 a.m. She was screaming at me to come to Jem's shop. I ran over there. Lu was dead and Yvonne was standing behind the door, shaking and spattered with blood. She was shouting that she and Lu had rowed again, that Lu had mocked me and Jem and said awful things about Struan. Something about him being a deviant. Of course, I realise now what that meant. Yvonne had got into a rage and killed her. She begged me to help. My first instinct was to protect her. I had a poor opinion of Lu, but Yvonne was like one of my own and twice the person her sister was. I told Yvonne not to tell me any more. The less I knew the better, and other shop owners might be arriving soon. We had to act

223

fast. I told her to go straight home, get rid of the clothes she was wearing and shower. When she'd gone, I wiped the handle of the knife in Lu's neck, the desk and the doorknobs. I closed the door and went home. Then Jem Calloway arrived and we called the police.

When Struan came home and learned about the murder, he commented that he'd seen Yvonne's car parked in the yard when he left in the morning. I told him that Yvonne had needed to see to something in the shop, but that he shouldn't mention seeing her car to the police or anyone else, as it would only complicate matters. He didn't question me and, for once, he did as he was told. I kept Yvonne's secret because she's dear to me and her sister had treated her so badly. We didn't speak much about the murder afterwards. I advised her to carry on as usual and I did what I could to watch out for her. Yvonne always stood by me and supported my work at Lansdown. She was one of the family. I don't suppose she'll forgive me for giving her up, but in the end, too much had gone wrong recently and I had to put my son first.

Yvonne's statement continued the story.

Lu and I had enjoyed a lovely meal that Friday evening on deck. We were both a bit tipsy. When we went inside to wash up, Lu suddenly went wobbly and started to tell me all about how she'd met up again with Bryan and they'd fallen back in love. I laughed at first, I couldn't believe it. She didn't have a good word to say about Bryan when they divorced. She made me sit down and explained that they were planning to move away and start afresh, leave behind all the old memories. That meant she'd need her equity in the boat and she'd be quitting the company. I was crying by then and she started too, but she was adamant that it was what she wanted. She said she was sorry, she'd never expected this to happen, it was astonishing, but her future was with Bryan. We argued for ages. I yelled that she was dumping me, and I'd never be able to run the business without her. I'd put my heart and soul into it, it meant everything to me. I pleaded with her, but she wouldn't budge. In the end, she went to bed, leaving me in a state of shock.

I tried calling Jem, but he wasn't answering, so I rang Shona. I could tell she was knocked for six, but she calmed me down. She was hopeful that me and Lu could talk things through and find a way to sort the situation, and she'd help in any way she could. I sat on the deck for ages and when I went to bed I lay awake. I was so angry. I'd been seeing Jem and keeping it a secret from Lu, because she wouldn't approve and I didn't want to upset her. She'd been pulling the wool over my eyes on a much bigger scale and she was willing to up sticks and leave me high and dry. I cared about her feelings, but she didn't give a fig for mine.

I only slept for a couple of hours. I was up at six on the Saturday morning. I'd lost a bracelet my mum had bought me. I'd been hunting around for it and I suddenly remembered that I might have left it on a shelf at Jem's shop, when I'd helped him tidy up the previous week. I decided to drive to Lansdown Court and search for it. Jem had given me a key to his shop at one time when he was going on holiday. I was restless and I thought I might as well be doing something and see if it was there.

I was so tired when I got to Lansdown, I fell asleep in the car for half an hour. Then I unlocked Jem's shop. I didn't find the bracelet, but I heard Lu arrive and open up. She'd seen my car and she was calling my name. I yelled that I was in Jem's, trying to find my bracelet. She came in and sat in the chair, saying she didn't understand how Jem ever managed to sell anything because the place was so disorganised and he was such an oddball. She was always being snide about Jem, she'd talked him down ever since we were kids. I love him and plenty of people say he's really talented, but she never had a good word for him. I was so tired and angry. My head was hammering. I told her that she was behaving awfully to me, and that I'd spoken to Shona, who agreed.

We were yelling at each other by then. Lu started on about Shona, saying she wasn't fit for the responsibilities *of running Lansdown and Struan was a monster in the making. She claimed that she'd seen Struan and Cherry Bolting with their tongues down each other's throats in the café. She'd kept quiet about it for a while, but she'd just met Struan on the road and challenged him. He'd denied it and been rude to her, told her to mind her own business. That had riled her and she'd decided to have it out with Shona later that day. I stood, listening to her denounce the people who meant so much to me. Why did she assume she had the right to throw her weight around, causing all this trouble and poisoning my life when she was about to dump me from a great height? Suddenly, it came to me that if she died, I'd inherit everything and I could get Jem to join the business with me. Then we'd be even closer and he might make a commitment, see that we were always meant to be.*

Jem had left one of his craft knives on the side of the desk. He's so scatterbrained, he just puts things down and forgets them. Lu was going on, saying that the way things were with Lansdown, it might not survive if there wasn't a major shake-up and she had a good mind to say as much to Angus Fraser. It sounded as if just because she was leaving, she wanted to destroy everything — me, Jem, Shona and Struan. It was like my head exploded. I picked the knife up and stuck it in her neck.

I was shaking, in tears. I rang Shona. She came over straightaway. She took charge, told me to go home, chuck my clothes away and shower. I drove back, put what I was wearing in a bin bag and hid it under my bed. When it was dark, I added a couple of heavy stones and dropped it in the deep water at the harbour entrance.

I'm sorry that I've got Shona into all this trouble. She has so much to deal with and I've added to her burdens. I kept Lu's remarks about Struan and Cherry to myself. It was so awful, and it would have shattered Shona. But it's come out now anyway.

I loved Lu. She'd always been more ambitious and successful than me, but that didn't bother me. I appreciated the way her drive got our business to fly. She persuaded me to sink everything into a life with her and I did it willingly. I was happy to work my guts out late into the night, spending hours on my own, because it was an exciting and rewarding enterprise. Then it turned out that Lu was ready to throw it all away for a man she used to describe as the 'Birmingham Bore'. I didn't plan to kill her and I'm sorry. I miss her.

Siv could hear Ali and Patrick coming along the corridor. They were laughing, in high spirits after the day's results.

'That's Yvonne and Shona tidied for the night,' Ali said.

'What about Struan?' she asked.

'Fraser has taken him to his place.' Patrick pulled out a chair and slipped off his tie. 'I checked that Fraser was up to speed with the Cherry Bolting situation. He sounded grim, muttered that Struan was going downhill fast. I doubt that uncle and nephew are going to enjoy each other's company.'

'Cherry Bolting's been bailed, by the way.' Ali reached for a banana. 'She's not allowed to go anywhere near Lansdown Court.'

'Yvonne was a bit of a sleeper, wasn't she?' Patrick was skimming through her statement. 'She handled herself well in the aftermath, kept things tight. Shona too, until the pressure got too much.'

'Shona's a hardworking, obsessive, proud woman. Control's important to her,' Siv said. 'She was exactly the right person to turn to in an emergency. Yvonne exhibited all the signs of distress you'd expect after the murder and she wasn't faking them. What she'd done had shocked her to the core, but she was able to disguise it as a sister's grief. It's always worth bearing in mind that tears can spring for a number of reasons in a murder investigation.'

'When we first questioned people about Lansdown, it seemed the picture of harmony, a traditional kind of place.' Patrick drew a question mark in the air. 'Who'd have guessed it was pulsing with antagonism, deceit and resentment?'

'Not to mention sexual abuse,' Siv added.

'Yeah, and not speaking ill of the dead, but Lu Forbes turned out to be quite a player, manipulating and lying when it suited her,' Patrick said.

Siv tucked the statements away. 'We had several people shaping up as suspects, but after talking to Fiona Epsom, I went to Lansdown Court this morning convinced that Shona was our killer. She'd found out quite a few negative things about Lu Forbes, and one way or another, they impacted on her little empire. It seemed as if resentments had reached a flashpoint. They had, but for Yvonne, not Shona.'

'Yvonne's a foolish woman, getting stuck on that screwball Calloway. No way was he ever going to be a keeper. He's got *fly-by-night* written through him as if he were a stick of rock.' Ali aimed his banana skin at the bin. 'Giving him the money to pay his rent! One satisfaction is that without Yvonne he'll be out on his ear.' Ali bent to retrieve the banana skin and put it in his pocket, muttering about fruit flies.

'Yvonne was utterly deluded.' Siv sighed. 'But Lu had the true measure of him.'

Ali grinned at her. 'Sisters! Have you ever considered murdering yours?'

'That would be telling, and I don't want anything used in evidence against me. I wonder if Fraser will sell Lansdown Court now? The place might have brought him too much trouble. Maybe Simon Terrance will buy it if his Minster Beach proposal isn't successful.'

Patrick started tidying his desk. 'I'm starved. Anyone fancy going for fish and chips?'

Ali checked his watch for his blood sugar reading. Acceptable. 'I'm wild hungry too. A last blowout before Pol gets back. There's a new place opened on the harbour, and I've heard it's mustard. Guv?'

'I'm in,' Siv said. 'Give me five minutes to email Mortimer.'

She sent a brief update. He and Mutsi were sailing *Quicksilver* around the coast to Dorset for the weekend. She pictured him reading the email on deck, lying on one of the rattan recliners while Mutsi cooed in his ear. They might be researching therapists with the skills to deal with family tensions. Mutsi would go for the most expensive, especially if Mortimer had agreed to foot the bill.

In the loo, she splashed her face and ran a comb through her hair. Her phone buzzed with a text from Rik.

I did write to Dad. I've remembered now. It was when we were in that damp flat in Hornsey, above the crazy woman with the parrots. Mutsi stayed out all night and there was nothing for breakfast. I stole a stamp from her purse for the letter. He never replied. x

Siv smoothed moisturiser into her hands. Despondency murmured in her ear and dragged at her heart. *Why did you have to come here, Rik, undermining my memories, disturbing my peace, upping the ante with Mutsi?*

Ali called outside the door. 'You ready? My stomach's starting to think my throat's been cut! It's only me and Patrick, no need to doll yourself up. And anyway, why improve on perfection?'

She rallied and smiled. Blood feuds could wait until another day. Tonight, she'd kick back with her other family.

THE END

THE JOFFE BOOKS STORY

We began in 2014 when Jasper agreed to publish his mum's much-rejected romance novel and it became a bestseller.

Since then we've grown into the largest independent publisher in the UK. We're extremely proud to publish some of the very best writers in the world, including Joy Ellis, Faith Martin, Caro Ramsay, Helen Forrester, Simon Brett and Robert Goddard. Everyone at Joffe Books loves reading and we never forget that it all begins with the magic of an author telling a story.

We are proud to publish talented first-time authors, as well as established writers whose books we love introducing to a new generation of readers.

We have been shortlisted for Independent Publisher of the Year at the British Book Awards three times, in 2020, 2021 and 2022, and for the Diversity and Inclusivity Award at the Independent Publishing Awards in 2022.

We built this company with your help, and we love to hear from you, so please email us about absolutely anything bookish at feedback@joffebooks.com

If you want to receive free books every Friday and hear about all our new releases, join our mailing list: www.joffebooks.com/contact

And when you tell your friends about us, just remember: it's pronounced Joffe as in coffee or toffee!